THE SCARS
BENEATH
THE SOUL

DAVE SIVERS

First published as an eBook in 2013

Paperback edition first published in 2015

Copyright © Dave Sivers, 2013

Cover design by Jessica Bell

The Scars Beneath the Soul is a work of fiction. Names, characters, places and incidents are the product of the author's imagination or are used fictitiously. Any resemblance to actual events, locales or persons, living or dead, is purely coincidental.

ISBN: 978-1511849647

For Dave and Rob.

Friends for a lifetime

ACKNOWLEDGMENTS

I hope people who live in my part of the beautiful Chilterns will forgive me for taking some liberties in creating a slightly more shadowy version of their world. Some of the streets are fictitious, and you won't find the Northfields Estate in Aylesbury. Dan Baines' village, Little Aston, although it resembles many of the brilliant communities to be found in and around Aylesbury Vale, can only be visited on the page.

Some of the other detail in the book owes a big debt of gratitude to people who have kindly given their time to help me get my facts straight: SOCO Steve of Thames Valley Police for some valuable forensic details; Brian Morgan for his insights into facial scarring and plastic surgery; Sarah Richards and other social workers for helping me to understand their world; and Stephen Dawson for his advice on family law.

All mistakes are my own.

Thanks also to the real Karen Smart, whom I only met after inventing her namesake, for letting me keep her name.

And special thanks to Debbie Porteous, and my wife, Chris Sivers, for their patience in reading the manuscript and making invaluable suggestions; to Jessica Bell for her amazing cover design; and to Chris 'The Guru' Longmuir for her advice and assistance in helping me get this book into print.

Buckinghamshire, 2015

1

October 2010
Two years before.

Lizzie Archer dips slyly into Rob's crisp packet, comes out with half a handful, and crams them into her mouth.

He regards her with mock exasperation. "I thought you didn't want any?"

"I don't," she mumbles round the smoky bacon, "I'm just helping you with your career."

"How do you make that out?"

Archer swallows the crisps and washes them down with a slurp of her pint of bitter.

"Can't allow a hunky fireman like yourself to get fat, can we? You might find yourself falling off your pole, next time you slide down it."

It has become a Sunday morning ritual for them, when they are both off duty. Up late, breakfast with the papers, then down to the local for a couple of pints before a late lunch. Some might find it boring, doing the same thing all the time, but she finds it nice to have something predictable in her life when the job thrusts so much random horror and misery in her face.

She knows Rob has seen some pretty heartrending things in his own line of work and guesses he feels the same.

There is also a rule that on Sundays when they are together, neither of them talks about work. Ironic, when it was their respective jobs that brought them together. A suspected arson, Archer part of the investigation, Rob part of the team that attended the fire. She'd asked him some questions and handed him her card, urging him to call her if anything else occurred to him.

1

He called her an hour later and said it had occurred to him that they should have dinner together. And, giving him ten out of ten for cheek, she agreed. They've been an item for about eighteen months now, and he more or less moved into her flat a year ago, although he hasn't yet sold his own on account of the depressed state of the property market.

Rob smirks at her reference to sliding down his pole. It's a standard joke between them in bed. She sees a look in his eye that hints at some pole-sliding this afternoon, and she happily waves goodbye to her plans to visit the garden centre.

Her mum has asked her a couple of times whether she thinks Rob might make an honest woman of her any time soon. She'd quite like that, she thinks, but she isn't going to pressure him into a proposal. They are happy enough together as they are.

"By the way, I got a call from Charlie the other day," Rob says. Charlie is an old mate from school. "He and Olivia would like us to go over one evening, so we'll need to coordinate our diaries."

"Sounds good." She likes Charlie, although Olivia can be a bit of a pain - too glass half empty for Archer's liking.

"And I was thinking," he adds, "I might try and get some tickets for Muse at Wembley Stadium in September. What do you think?"

She shrugs. "I don't know. I'd like to, but you know how it is. We've had tickets before and then something comes up."

"I'll get them anyway," he decides. "I can always flog them on eBay. Or give them to Charlie."

Before she can respond, there are sounds of a scuffle behind her, the smashing of glass, a young woman's scream. Archer is already halfway out of her chair.

"Lizzie, no," Rob protests. "You're off duty..." But she is turning to see what the trouble is.

Later, when she plays it back in her mind, everything is in slow motion. She sees a young man with his back to the bar, looking like he is pinned there. A second young man, evidently the worse for wear, sways a foot or two away from him, brandishing a broken beer bottle. Shards rise above the surface of the spreading pool of beer on the bar top like small brown icebergs on a frothy sea.

A young woman looks on, hands to her mouth, her eyes wide. The whole pub has gone silent.

By the time Archer has reached them, she has already pulled her purse out of her bag and is holding up her warrant card.

"Police," she says. "Now let's all calm down."

She's on autopilot now. Back in her early days in uniform, she broke up many an ugly situation by sheer force of her own authority. Where reason failed, she was able to look after herself. So she's confident now. One half-drunk young twat, who most likely feels a bit of a tosser for breaking that bottle, and will doubtless be grateful for a way out. She can re-establish peace in a few moments and get back to her pint.

But, if the guy with the bottle is looking for someone to put a stop to this, he doesn't show it. He turns towards, her, pointing his makeshift weapon her way. His original target looks relieved that someone else is on the firing line.

"What's it to you, you nosy cow?"

She smiles, still certain she can deal with this. Top of her class in self-defence, disarming fitter and tougher opponents than this clown looks to be.

"I'd stop calling me names for a start, if I were you, sir," she says. "There's no need for it, and I'm sure you don't want to do anything silly. So what say you put the bottle down?"

He blinks. And then the way his eyes become shifty, the sloppy grin that smears itself across his face, in some way communicate what he is thinking. She sees it, but just a fraction too late.

"You want the fucking bottle? Here you are, then." And he thrusts the jagged glass at her.

Her self-defence training instinctively kicks in, and she tries to twist out of the line of danger whilst simultaneously grabbing his arm, but the jagged edges are close, so close. As she uses his momentum against him, as she sends him crashing into a table, the bottle spinning from his hand, she thinks for a moment that she has got away with it.

And then the pain begins, deep in her left cheek, first as cold as ice, then blooming into an explosion of searing fire. Yet even now, she is focused, ignoring it, going after him, planting a knee in his back and pinning his arm behind him.

"You're under arrest," she begins, and blood runs into her mouth. It is warm and tastes coppery. She glances to her left and can see it splashing onto the shoulder of the white jacket she is wearing. She looks around her. She is surrounded by a semi-circle of onlookers, their faces masks of horror.

One of them is Rob.

"Fuck's sake," she snarls through the blood, "don't just stand there. Call the police. An ambulance would be good, too."

2

May 2012

Last night, he had dreamed about Jack again.

In his dreams, he never saw his son as he had last seen him, eleven years ago. In his dreams, that three-year-old had grown into the teenager he would be by now, if he were still alive. Fourteen years old, but still indisputably Jack Baines, the same familiar blend of both his parents' features. The same cheeky grin.

Last night, Dan Baines had dreamt the two of them were playing football in the garden of the house they had lived in as a family before the Invisible Man came calling and destroyed everything. Jack was wearing a Queen's Park Rangers replica shirt and was a better player than his father, taunting him, nutmegging him, little step-overs à la Lionel Messi or Cristiano Ronaldo. He had been laughing with the sheer joy of life, and Baines had been laughing with him.

Baines had woken with tears on his pillow. Had traced the outline of his wife's face in the photograph beside his bed, wishing more than anything that she was still there for him to talk to.

A shower, two cups of black coffee and a slice of toast, and he was ready for work. But the dream and the emotions it had conjured stayed with him as he drove from his home in Little Aston to Aylesbury police station, a journey so familiar that he tended to do it on auto-pilot.

It was Monday. His first day back in the rank of Detective Sergeant, after being acting Inspector for just under six months. His old boss had finally succumbed to cancer eight weeks ago, and Baines would have been lying if he had denied that he'd been hoping to fill the dead man's shoes himself on a permanent basis. Instead, a new DI was starting this morning and Baines was going to have to work hard to put aside what he knew was an unreasonable resentment.

He didn't know much about the newcomer, who was currently ensconced with Detective Chief Inspector Paul Gillingham. She was transferring from the Met, by all accounts for personal reasons, and it seemed that not so long ago she had been quite badly hurt whilst making an arrest. Baines didn't know the details, which was typical Gillingham.

He supposed it was the DCI's same lack of people skills that had led him to inform Baines of this forthcoming change as though it was good news, and not the kick in the teeth it was.

He just hoped the new woman wasn't going to spell trouble for him.

He'd seen it before. Coppers from bigger forces who couldn't hack it any more, washing up in the comparative backwater of the Aylesbury Vale Division of Thames Valley Police, and looking for a cushier ride. Well, no one had gone easy on Dan Baines eleven years ago, and he wouldn't have stood for anyone trying. He'd found a way through it all on his own, rebuffed the offers of counselling, and simply got on with his job.

He realised his mind had wandered off, and tried again to focus on the report he was typing. A particularly bone-headed murder of one neighbour by another because the music at a party had got a little loud.

Baines thought the idiot who'd taken a kitchen knife and plunged it into his neighbour's chest ought to try working at Aylesbury nick, if he wanted to find out what real noise was like. The room he was trying to work in was open plan, with colleagues bantering, bawling into phones, or rattling keyboards. Phones rang and printers chattered.

The glorified coffin he'd shared with another DI until last Friday hadn't been much, especially when his room-mate had been in - which thankfully had been rare - but at least it had been relatively peaceful. Being reintroduced to this parrot house today had been something of a rude awakening.

He notched up another resentment against the new DI, and then laughed at himself. All this negative thinking was going to get him nowhere. No doubt the new woman was going to be easy enough to get along with, and keeping a positive attitude would do more for his promotion prospects than being surly and unhelpful.

He took a swig of cold coffee and got back to his report, tuning out as much background noise as he could, and consulting his notes as to what the suspect had said when apprehended:

"It was bloody rap! I can put up with most things, but bloody rap blaring out all afternoon... I asked him to turn it down and he told me to piss off, so I stabbed him."

Well, Baines thought soberly, who wouldn't? He hated bloody rap himself.

It dawned on him that the room had fallen silent. He glanced about him and then followed his colleagues' collective gaze to the doorway, where DCI Gillingham stood with an attractive-looking, blonde woman. She was tall - perhaps five eleven and, Baines judged, probably a tad younger than his own 38 years. Her hair was cut short with a centre parting and a bit of a fringe, and her grey suit looked expensive at first glance. She wore a skirt, rather than trousers, displaying a pair of shapely calves.

"Everyone, I'd like to introduce DI Lizzie Archer," Gillingham announced. "As most of you know, she's come to take over DI Britton's old post. I know you'll make her welcome."

There were ragged mutterings of "Yes, sir," and "Morning ma'am." Lizzie Archer smiled and nodded. Baines thought there was something slightly off about her smile.

"Thank you, sir," she said to Gillingham, and then she addressed the room. "I'm looking forward to working with you all. As you know, I've transferred in from the Met, so I'm going to have to build up my local knowledge pdq. I'm sure I can count on all of you to help me there."

Without further ado, Gillingham led Archer over to Baines' desk. As he stood up to meet them, he saw the whole of her face, not just the right profile she had presented when she first entered the room. The left side, from just below the eye, bore a white, crescent-shaped scar. Just below the scar line, her features sagged slightly, as if they were starting to melt.

"Lizzie, this is DS Dan Baines," the DCI said. "He's been keeping your seat warm, so you'll need to get up to speed with him."

Archer held out a manicured hand. Baines noted the immaculate blood-red nail polish. "Pleased to meet you, Dan," she said.

"Ma'am." He shook her hand, which was cool and dry, her grip firm. The smile on one side of her face was friendly, and there was a twinkle in her blue eyes. On the left side, the smile was wrong. It slightly reminded him of the Joker in the 'Batman' movies.

He hadn't thought he was staring, but he thought she withdrew her hand just a little hastily, and she seemed to turn her face away. Some of the friendliness seemed to have gone out of her expression. The scarring was evidently something she was sensitive about, and he felt guilty that maybe his scrutiny had been a little unsubtle.

"DI Britton used to work quite closely with Dan," Gillingham was saying, "and I dare say you'll be doing the same. He's a great copper, and we're lucky to have him."

Baines couldn't help wondering if the flattery was a bit of a sop. A booby prize for being reduced in the ranks. Still, he knew he needed to get off on the right foot.

"You'll probably find the Vale a good deal different to what you were used to in the Met, ma'am," he told her. "Aylesbury's a decent-sized town, but otherwise it's small towns, villages and hamlets and an awful lot of fields. I don't suppose you met many farmers down in London?"

"Not so many, no." She still sounded a bit cold. "Well, Sergeant, you'll have to give me a guided tour some time soon." Sergeant. Two minutes ago, it had been Dan. It wasn't like he'd been actually gawping at her scar. Had he?

"It's a date," he said, trying to inject some warmth into his voice.

"Look," Gillingham said, "I reckon the best thing is to leave the two of you together. You'll have a lot to talk about, and Dan can show you around."

The DCI disappeared. There was a long, awkward silence between them.

"Why don't we go into my office for a chat?" she suggested finally. "DI Ashby's out this morning, so we'll have it to ourselves. It might be easier than trying to talk in here."

He wondered if the relative quiet was her true motivation, or whether she was putting him firmly in his place by showing him that it was her office now. Maybe the scar wasn't all she was sensitive about. Maybe she felt insecure about working with someone who knew her job a damn sight better than she did herself.

She was already striding away, and he had little choice but to follow her, feeling that somehow they had both got off to an inauspicious start.

* * *

Lizzie Archer cursed herself as she led the way back to her new office. Leaving the Met, leaving London, and coming out here to Buckinghamshire was supposed to be a new beginning. If that upheaval was going to be worthwhile, she needed to be a bit less precious when she caught anyone noticing the scar. Because they were going to notice, unless they were in possession of a white stick or a guide dog.

People who knew her said the scar was barely visible now, and that you soon forgot it was there. Rob had said it too, but he had also admitted that it was one of the reasons he'd put an end to their relationship. He said it reminded him of how he'd failed to protect her.

She'd never seen it that way, never blamed him for anything. They'd simply been in the wrong place at the wrong time. When things had kicked off, her policewoman's instincts had kicked in, but it hadn't been Rob's job to back her up. He was a fireman, not a copper, and the whole episode could have ended far worse than it had if he'd weighed in.

9

Unfortunately, his sense of machismo wouldn't let it go. Either that or it was just a good excuse for not looking at her ruined face any more. Hard to make love to someone who looked like the Bride of Frankenstein on one side.

The office she was to share with DI Steven Ashby, whom she hadn't yet met, was bijou to say the least. Two scuffed metal desks pushed together, a swivel chair that had seen better days behind each of them, and a shared filing cabinet with dents in the drawer fronts. The walls were decorated in the sort of beige her mother had once told her was fashionable in the Seventies, and she could well believe that it was thirty-odd years since they had last seen a lick of paint.

Despite the workplace smoking ban that had come into force in 2007, a musty, tobacco smell hung in the air, and Ashby's desk was a sea of clutter, spilling over onto hers. She wasn't sure she was going to enjoy her new room mate.

DS Baines followed her in and she gestured to Ashby's vacant chair. Common sense told her it would be well worth investing some time and effort in him. After all, five minutes ago this had been his office, and it was perfectly possible that her arrival had put his nose out of joint. She knew she needed his cooperation and support if she was going to make a flying start in this job.

And, God knows, she needed a flying start.

"Coffee?" she suggested, ferreting a jar out of her handbag. "I think I can do better than the stuff the machine makes, if you point me towards a kettle."

"It's muck, isn't it?" he agreed, lowering his wiry frame into the chair. "But no unofficial kettles allowed here. Health and safety and energy efficiency."

She stared at him, then shook her head. "We'll see about that." She returned the jar to her bag. "So. Muck or nothing?"

He grinned, a smile that touched his soft brown eyes. "Thanks all the same, ma'am, but I've already had a cup of muck this morning. I like to ration myself. There's only so much pleasure one man can take."

She giggled and sat down, feeling relieved that the ice had been broken a little.

"So. What cases do we have on the go at the moment?"

He stared at the ceiling, as if he was going to find the answer there, and then he evidently did, because he started reeling off information. A man knifed to death by his neighbour in a barbecue dispute. A botched petrol station holdup. An Asian family burned to death after someone firebombed their home: possibly a racially motivated crime, but more likely a matter of family honour. A local gang leader in hospital after a drive-by shooting.

"You actually have gangs out here in the sticks?"

"Oh, yes. And now some of them have actually progressed beyond flintlock pistols." He shrugged. "It's nothing like the scale you'd be familiar with from the Met. Basically, there's a few kids on the Northfields estate who see gang culture on telly and decide it's just what they need to brighten their dull existence. There's two real gangs: The Bloods and The Barracudas."

Archer raised a querulous eyebrow. "Very macho."

"It's been going on for about a year now. At the start it was all about tough talk, a few duels with handbags, and some low-level nuisance. But it's gradually got more serious."

"Such as?"

"We're pretty sure The Bloods are into drug dealing and the Barracudas would like to muscle in on that. And there's been some stabbings. Of course, no one's saying anything. The real trouble is, there's not enough going on around here to interest the less imaginative members of our local youth."

"I've always thought being bored was pretty lame excuse for breaking the law," she reflected.

"The lad in hospital - Brandon Clark - is the leader of The Barracudas, and a lot sharper than the others. He's critical but stable. We're guessing he knows more than he's saying."

"And presumably we've questioned members of The Bloods?"

"Sure. No way it was them. You ask them, they'll tell you."

"And no members of the public saw anything?"

"If they did, they're not answering our appeals to come forward. He was shot outside a newsagent's in the town, where he'd just been buying cigarettes. We questioned the newsagent and the customers who were inside at the time. They heard the shot, but saw nothing."

"So they say."

"So they say. My guess is The Barracudas are biding their time and planning on getting their own back."

She shook her head in wonder. "This doesn't sound at all like the Sleepy Hollow I thought I was coming to. Don't tell me there's a danger of a full-scale gang war on the streets of Aylesbury?"

"Hardly full-scale. As I say, they're small gangs. But it could get very messy if they start going in for tit for tat."

"Especially with guns involved."

Baines nodded soberly. "This is the first time it's escalated to firearms, so far as we're aware. It's a worrying development."

"Maybe I should have a go at this Brandon Clark. A different face?"

She thought she saw a reaction to her choice of words and kicked herself for laying herself open to it. But he nodded reflectively.

"Got to be worth a try."

"So what else are we working on?"

But Baines never got the chance to reply, because the door swung open and DCI Gillingham leaned in.

"Sorry to interrupt your briefing, Lizzie, but there's a new case for you to cut your teeth on. A body's been found in Wendover. Why don't you take Dan and head over there?"

Archer felt a surge of adrenalin. A mix of anticipation and nervousness. "Of course. Do we have any details?"

Gillingham took a couple of paces inside the tiny room and handed her a piece of paper. "That's the address. SOCOs and the pathologist are on their way." He frowned. "Be warned. It sounds like a nasty one."

3

37 Menzies Drive was a bog standard 1930s semi in a cul de sac composed almost entirely of similar houses. As they had driven up to the house in Baines' Ford Mondeo, he'd noted nice cars in some of the drives. Number 37 had roses in the front garden and the paintwork on the windows and the front door looked well maintained. The only thing that spoiled the image of the quiet, comfortable suburban life was the blue and white crime scene tape festooning the outside of the house and the posse of emergency vehicles scattered along the roadside.

It was a little after 10.30 in the morning. Baines guessed most of the neighbours were at work, but there were a few people around, on the pavement opposite, or standing on their drives, watching the activity. They were mostly elderly or mothers with small children.

Baines recognised the uniformed constable who was controlling access to the property and introduced Archer in answer to his quizzical look.

"What exactly have we got here, Constable?" she asked.

"Well, ma'am, the victim's a Stephanie Merritt. It seems her husband, Richard, commutes into London. He set off for work just after half seven, leaving his wife at home. She works locally and doesn't leave for work so early. He got to the station only to find that there was some sort of major signal failure disruption. He hung around for a while, but he decided he was going to be so late that he might as well work at home. He rang home to say he was on his way back, but got no reply. When he got home, he found his wife dead in the kitchen. Bludgeoned to death, by the look of it." He grimaced. "It's not pretty."

"You've been inside?" Baines asked.

"I was first on the scene. The SOCOs are in there now, and the pathologist has just arrived."

"And where's the husband now?"

"In the ambulance with the paramedics. He's in shock obviously, but I doubt if they'll take him to hospital."

"Any kids?"

"One of each, but they're grown up and fled the nest."

"Thanks," Archer said. "That gives us a good start." She turned to Baines. "Let's take a look at the scene. Then I think I'll have a chat with the husband and you can gather up a couple of uniforms and get some door to door going."

In many cases, the victim's nearest and dearest was often a prime suspect, as was the person who raised the alarm. When these were one and the same person, it was important to have a go at them early, before they had a chance to think too much, or get lawyered up.

Baines knew that, if this had happened a week ago, he would have been the one questioning the husband and dispatching someone else to handle the door to door grunt work. Archer's request was a perfectly reasonable one, but he thought she might have handled him a bit more delicately. Again it crossed his mind that maybe she was asserting her authority right from the start.

They went back to his car and donned white paper overalls and shoe covers, then he followed her into the house, where hooded Scenes of Crime Officers were taking photographs, dusting for prints and collecting evidence. One of them directed them to the kitchen, where the pathologist, Barbara Carlisle, was examining the body. She was petite and serious-looking, which belied her dry sense of humour, and Baines knew that her hood concealed a lush mane of auburn hair. She was in her fifties, but looked more like thirty.

"Morning, Dan," she greeted him. You've drawn the short straw, have you? Sorry it's a messy one."

That was an understatement. The woman lay sprawled on her back, her arms stretched out. Her face looked nothing like a face any more. In fact, the head looked nothing like a head.

The body looked like a torso with a mass of bloody pulp attached to the shoulders.

The tiled floor was swamped with blood, and there was splatter everywhere - on the walls, on the pristine kitchen units, even on the ceiling. Baines and Archer took in the whole grisly scene. Outside it was a brisk May morning, but it felt warm in the house. The reek of blood assailed his nostrils.

"Doesn't take a genius to work out that cause of death was probably blunt force trauma to the head," Archer observed. "Looks like a pretty frenzied attack, too. I'd imagine the killer must have kept on hitting her long after she was dead."

Carlisle nodded. "That seems a fair summary, Sergeant..?"

"Sorry," Archer said. "I should have introduced myself. It's Inspector actually. I'm DI Lizzie Archer."

"Barbara Carlisle. Pleased to meet you. New to the Vale?"

"Yes, first day today. DS Baines was just bringing me up to speed when we got the call."

There she goes again, Baines thought. DS Baines. Making absolutely sure everyone knew who was boss and that he was just a sergeant again. The rational side of him knew he was just being childish, but that didn't make him any the less touchy.

"So, what can you tell us?" asked Archer, all business now the introductions had been made. "Any feel for time of death?"

"Body's still quite warm, no rigor mortis. Taking all the other factors into account, she died some time after half past five. My best estimate at the moment is within the last two or three hours."

"That seems to chime with the husband's statement," Baines said.

Carlisle stood up. "As for your frenzied blunt force trauma theory, Inspector, I'll be able to say for sure after the post mortem, but in reality I'll just be looking to see which blow actually killed her. This is about as savage and brutal as anything I've ever seen."

"You think it could have been personal?"

"You're the detective, but I'd say there had to be a lot of rage behind the attack. It would take a lot of physical effort to keep on bludgeoning someone with such force so many times."

Baines was reminded of two young boys up north who'd administered a sustained beating to another kid a few years back. In court, they'd said the only thing that had stopped them from actually killing their victim was that their arms got tired. He wondered how exhausted this killer might have been by the time he'd finished.

"We need the SOCOs to look for sweat," he suggested. "It's warm in here, and we're talking about a lot of exertion. Maybe the killer sweated. Maybe some of it dripped."

At least one of the SOCOs had been eavesdropping. "Good point," he agreed. "We'll make sure we swab the floor for that. The bastard may have left us some DNA. Although, with all this blood, I really wouldn't hold my breath."

"Any skin under her fingernails?" Archer asked.

Carlisle gently lifted one of the dead woman's arms. It was a mess. "Lots of defensive injuries to the arms and hands. I'd say she was much too busy trying to protect her head and face to grapple with him. Meanwhile he kept on swinging."

"Any sign of a murder weapon?" asked Archer.

"No, and I won't commit myself to what it was until I've done a thorough examination back at the mortuary."

"But if you were to hazard a guess..?"

The pathologist sighed and rolled her eyes at Baines. "She doesn't give up, does she?" She shrugged. "If I were to hazard a guess," she said to Archer, "and I would never do such a thing, you understand. But my guess would be something heavy and brutal, like a hammer."

Baines had a vivid mental image of a hulking male figure swinging a lump hammer, over and over again, blood spraying off the head with each swing, his victim putting her arms in the way only for the weapon to shatter them. There would have been some screaming, he supposed. But not for long. Maybe not long enough to attract attention.

He noted that the kitchen window was open. "Someone might have heard something."

"Time for that door to door," Archer agreed. She looked across at the SOCO. "Any idea how he got in?"

"No sign of forced entry. Our best guess is he rang the doorbell, she opened up, and the attack started. She couldn't get past him into the street, it was too late to try and shut the door, so she ran inside."

"Maybe she headed for the kitchen to try and grab a knife to defend herself," Baines suggested.

"Or to get out the back door." The SOCO indicated the glazed door that led to the garden. "Either way, she didn't make it."

Baines nodded, images filling his head again. They seemed to blur for a moment with pictures his imagination had conjured eleven years ago, and which he'd never been able to rid himself of.

But he knew this wasn't the Invisible Man returning. Eleven victims, Louise Baines the last one, and then neither the killer, nor three-year-old Jack Baines, had been seen or heard of again. Baines had always felt in his bones that he would resurface some day, but this wasn't that day. The MO was radically different. He shook his head to try and shake the images in there.

"Are you okay?" Archer asked him, and it sounded half-concern, half-challenge.

"Fine," he lied. "It's just..." He dragged himself back to the matter in hand. "Forcing his way in and starting hitting. Could it be random?"

"I see what you mean, but I doubt it. If it wasn't the husband - what was his name?"

"Richard," Baines supplied.

"Richard. If it wasn't him, then someone waited until he'd gone - knew he'd be going - before making his move. No, Dan, the attack may have been frenzied, but this was planned. There's a personal motive here. Either someone had something against Stephanie Merritt, or she fits in with some whackjob's mad fantasies."

"Let's hope it's the former," Baines said.

"Quite. Well, lots to do," Archer said to Baines. "I want to find out if Stephanie had any enemies, who her friends were, what dirty little secrets she was keeping. I suggest you start with the rubberneckers across the road. What did they see, what did they hear? Did they notice anyone hanging around, acting suspiciously? A strange car out of place?"

Baines, who actually did know how to conduct a door to door and knew what questions to ask, bristled once more.

"I think I can cope, ma'am."

She fingered her scarred cheek. "I'm sure you can, Sergeant."

He noted how she constantly shifted between using his first name and referring to him by his rank. He wasn't sure yet what that indicated. Mood swings, maybe. Just what he needed.

"One last thought," he said, pausing on route to the kitchen door. "We keep calling this killer a 'he'." He turned to Barbara Carlisle, who had hunkered down by the body again. "Any chance it could be a woman?"

She looked up at him, her green eyes glinting behind her silver-rimmed spectacles. "We may be the weaker sex, Dan, but I can think of a few women in my own social circle who could get enough force behind a hammer, or whatever did this, to inflict this kind of damage. So I wouldn't rule it out."

"Thanks," Archer said. "That's useful." She nodded to Baines. "Let's meet up by your car in, say half an hour and see where we've got to."

He took a last look at the scene. This had been a neat, orderly kitchen. Even the breakfast things were stacked tidily beside the sink waiting to be washed. The trappings of a normal home life that some bastard had come in and smashed to pieces. The feeling was so familiar that he felt his fists clenching in impotent rage.

* * *

Archer was irritated by Baines' visible response to being asked to organise the door-to-door. It was obvious to her that he felt that, having acted up as DI for a few weeks, this sort of thing was now beneath him. Well, the sooner he accepted he was a sergeant again, the better for both of them. She certainly wasn't prepared to put up with any moodiness.

She understood from DCI Gillingham that Baines had lost his wife and child in tragic circumstances. Gillingham thought it explained why Baines' dark hair was shot through with so much grey, but beyond that he would only say that Baines didn't like to talk about it and would tell her or not when he was ready.

It had clearly been traumatic, and she felt sorry for Baines. But it sounded as if it had all happened a long time ago. It didn't seem to justify sulking over being allocated duties that were entirely appropriate to his rank.

At least he hadn't shown too much sign of looking at her scar since their initial introduction. Maybe she'd overreacted to that. Perhaps their whole relationship was just off on a wrong footing.

She wondered about a drink after work. Get to know each other better. It was an undeniable fact that she was going to have to rely on him until she got her feet under the desk, and she could probably have done with a couple of days' breathing space before this murder enquiry came along.

Never mind. This was the sort of case that could get a DI noticed. And if there was one thing Lizzie Archer didn't used to lack, it was ambition. She was determined to get it back.

Even so, she was already having second thoughts about whether this transfer had been such a good way of achieving that. She was a London girl, born and bred, and some of her erstwhile colleagues had tried to wind her up, saying she was moving to Hicksville, where everyone chewed straw and wouldn't accept a townie like her for at least 30 years.

She hadn't taken much of it seriously. She had imagined that a patch that was only some 40 miles from central London would have a suburban feel to it. Maybe a bit like Hampstead or Richmond. Actually, it was nothing like either, but Aylesbury still had some similarities with parts of London, and the fine countryside she had already glimpsed promised to be a bonus. DCI Gillingham had assured her that the Chilterns had as much to offer as, say, the Lake District or the Yorkshire Dales.

Her real concern was that she was going to feel lost for quite a long time. She didn't know this patch. Didn't know the geography, nor the local politics. Didn't like narrow, winding country lanes that were unlit at night, where oncoming headlights seemed dazzling, even though they were dipped.

And, with the best will in the world, the rural side of the Vale was a closed book to her. She might have chosen to take Baines' remark about not seeing many farmers as a crack at the city girl, but it was also true. She had a lot to learn.

On the short journey from Aylesbury, Baines had given her the low-down on Wendover. She'd heard of it, of course, but never been there. He'd described it as a small, quiet market town that preferred to think of itself as a village, whatever that meant.

As Baines had steered through the centre of the town, she had glimpsed some old buildings, a couple of promising restaurants and a number of slightly quirky-looking one-off shops. Baines had drawn her attention to the clock tower. All in all, she liked the look of the place. She wondered about the real villages, though. The wags in the Met had insisted that villagers were interbred and had pale skin and high foreheads.

In all fairness, apparently Baines lived in a village, and he did look fairly normal. But maybe he was just an exception to the rule.

She found Richard Merritt in the back of the ambulance with a blanket wrapped around his shoulders. The recent weather had been unsettled, but at least it wasn't raining at the moment. There was a bit of a breeze though, and she knew how shock could make a person feel cold. Even if it turned out that Merritt was his wife's killer, he could still be affected.

She showed him her warrant card and introduced herself.

"Mr Merritt, I'm so sorry about what happened to your wife."

His face was wet, his eyes tear-stained and vacant. "Thank you." It was the voice of an automaton, as if all that made him human had been ripped out.

"Richard," she said, dropping into the use of his first name, "I know this is a terrible time for you, and I can't begin to imagine how you must be feeling. But we want to catch the person who did this as quickly as possible, before they hurt anyone else. Are you up to answering a few questions?"

"Of course." He swiped at his eyes with a sleeve. He was a little overweight, and balding, but generally in decent nick for a man who must be in his fifties.

"I gather you were off to London this morning?"

"Yes."

"What kind of work do you do?"

"I'm a civil servant. Food Standards Agency."

"I gather the trains were disrupted."

"They said major signal failure. Nothing moving for at least an hour. I waited a while, but it was obvious that it would probably take longer than that. Even then, the trains might run slowly because of congestion. It's happened before."

Archer knew this was easily checked. She supposed Merritt may have killed his wife before setting off for work and then used the train troubles as a good excuse for phoning in early and playing the grieving husband. His anguish looked genuine enough, but she had been taken in before.

"So you decided to go home and work from there?"

"I've got an official laptop. I can dial into my office - get at my documents, my e-mail... The connection can be a bit dodgy at times, but..." His face crumpled. "I'm waffling, aren't I?"

"That's okay. Tell me what time you got home."

"I walk to the station - as you know, it isn't far." She had no idea where the station was, but let him talk. "With the hanging around, I'd been gone... maybe an hour, so say half past eight. I'd rang from the station, but there was no answer, so I thought maybe Steph had already gone."

"But she hadn't?"

He shook his head. "When I got there, her car was still on the drive. At first I thought she was just running late. Hadn't heard the phone for some reason. I let myself in and shouted hello or something, but I knew straight away something was wrong."

He was staring earnestly at her, as if he was desperate to be a good witness. She wondered if he'd even noticed her scar. She fingered it unconsciously.

"Wrong in what way?"

He shrugged. "I don't know. Just wrong. It was like she ought to be there, but the house felt empty. I called out her name, but there was nothing. I thought maybe she was ill, or still in the shower, so I looked for her upstairs first."

"Not in the kitchen?"

"None of the downstairs rooms. I don't know why now. I just thought she must be upstairs. When she wasn't, I was really worried."

"You didn't think maybe she'd gone off to work after all?"

He looked bewildered. "Her car was in the drive," he repeated.

"But it could have broken down. She might have got a taxi."

"I suppose. She would have called me though. I do all the car stuff. She'd have expected me to sort it out."

"From London?"

"I could have tried to get someone to come out to it in the evening." A look of suspicion came into his eyes. "What's all this got to do with anything? The trains were in a mess, I came home, I found my wife dead. Why are you asking me all this about where I looked and what I thought? Do I need a solicitor?"

That was interesting.

"Why would you need a solicitor, sir?"

"I know how it works. Suspect the husband first."

He was in danger of becoming belligerent now. She knew not to read too much into that. Grief made people want to lash out.

"No one's suspecting you yet, Richard."

"Yet?"

"I just want to build up a picture. We'll need you to make a formal statement later, but I need to get as full an account as possible from you now, while it's fresh in your mind. Any little detail could be important."

He seemed to relax a little. "I'm sorry. It's just..." He shook his head ruefully and went on with his story. "I looked in the lounge, and then I looked in the kitchen, and there she was..."

He gave a little shrug and the blanket slipped from his shoulders. He wore a striped business shirt and a tie. Both were smeared with blood.

"How did you get the blood on your clothes, Richard?"

He looked down at himself. "I cradled her body. Thought about trying to revive her, but I wouldn't have known where to start. Besides, it was obvious... I mean, the state of her..."

He started to sob. She patted his shoulder and waited until he had subsided.

He rubbed his teary eyes with the heels of his hands. "What I said about not knowing what to do. It's not quite true. I did a course once, through work. But when it came to it..."

It sounded convincing enough, but obviously whoever killed Stephanie Merritt would have got a lot of blood on themselves. Then again, if Richard had done it, why not changed his clothes? He could have hidden or disposed of the bloody garments before dialling 999.

If he was thinking properly, that was. People who murder their wives in a fit of passion don't always think properly. He wouldn't be the first killer to be in a total daze once the enormity of what they had done hit home.

"Richard, I'm going to have to ask you some difficult questions now," Archer said. "How were things between you and Stephanie? Were you getting on all right? Any arguments?"

There was a spark of anger, quickly extinguished. "Nothing out of the ordinary. No real rows. She nags me about stuff like emptying the bins and I moan about her tidying up my stuff so I can't find it. Nothing major, just everyday niggles between married people. We were getting on great on the whole." He started to weep again, quietly this time. "We were happy."

Archer could have named several occasions when everyday niggles over emptying bins or over-zealous tidying up had led one partner to kill another, but she kept it to herself.

"And you had no reason to suspect that she might be having an affair, anything like that?"

His eyes widened. "What? No! Why would you say that? Are you saying you think she was having an affair?"

"Sorry Richard," she soothed. "I don't mean to upset you. I've no reason to think anything of the sort, but I have to ask, do you see? If you thought she had a lover, then you could be angry about it. Or, if there was a lover, then he could be angry about something. Like I say, I'm just getting as good a picture as I can, so we can catch the person who did this." Her scar itched, and she scratched her cheek. "Were you having an affair, by any chance?"

"No." Dully. A bit sulky.

"All right," she said. "One last question for now. Can you think of any enemies Stephanie might have had? Anyone who might have wanted to hurt her?"

"Well, she's a social worker. She deals with a lot of people in difficult circumstances, and a lot of them get angry with her because they don't get what they want, or they think she's interfering. Do you think it was one of them?"

"It's really too early to form any theories, sir," she said. "But did she happen to mention any cases recently where she was frightened a client -" Was that what you called them? Or customers? Patients? "- might become violent towards her?"

"A few. She did get assaulted a couple of times."

"Recently?"

His forehead creased. "I don't know. Maybe three months ago?"

"Did she happen to mention the name?"

He looked cagey. "She isn't supposed to, of course, but she does bring her work troubles home to me sometimes. The name though... I can't remember. How stupid. Maybe it's the shock."

"That's all right," she said patiently. "Can you have a think, though? Make us a list of clients you think she might have had trouble with?"

"I'll try."

"Thanks. Now, apart from the people she came in contact with though work, was there anyone else she might have had problems with?"

"No. Everyone likes Steph. She makes friends easily..." He covered his face with his hands. "Oh, Christ. I keep talking about her as if she's still here. But she isn't, is she?"

Archer felt desperately sorry for him. She wondered who was contacting the kids with the bad news. They would also have to be interviewed.

"That'll be all for now, Richard. The Scenes of Crime Officers will need your clothes, I'm afraid."

"My clothes? But why?"

"It's just routine. We need to eliminate you and it's also possible some evidence has transferred to you." She didn't mention that they would also be looking to see if the bloodstains formed spatter patterns consistent with conducting a frenzied attack on another human being.

Merritt simply nodded, his attention already sliding away.

"Once again, I'm so sorry this has happened," said Archer. "We'll arrange for you to come to the station and make a formal statement later today. It'll mean going through all this again, but we might think of some more questions, and you might remember something." She held out a card to him. "If anything occurs to you, however small, please give me a ring."

She walked away, not much the wiser. Barbara Carlisle's estimated time of death could easily have included the time just before Merritt left for work.

She supposed he could have set off to catch the train, and then, when there were problems, decided to use it to his advantage. But that would have required a degree of deviousness inconsistent with the idea of a man so dazed that he goes calmly off to catch his train with blood all over his shirt. Still, she decided, it would be unwise to dismiss Richard Merritt as a suspect at this early stage.

She glanced at her watch. It was time to catch up with Baines.

4

Dan Baines was finding questioning the good people of Menzies Drive about as profitable as trying to get anything out of any of the Northfields estate gang members. It seemed no one had seen or heard anything of any real help to the investigation, with the exception of Mr Harry Falconer, who lived next door to the Merritts at number 39, the other semi in the pair.

Harry Falconer was a sprightly man in his seventies. He admitted to hearing a few screams through the wall just before eight am, but said he had assumed his neighbours had their TV on loud.

"Was that like them? Loud TV at that time in the morning?" Baines had asked.

"No, not at all. They're a lovely couple, very quiet and polite. If they made a habit of it, I'd have been round there complaining." He shot a rueful glance at number 37. "I wish I had now. Maybe..."

"I don't think it would have helped, sir."

Harry Falconer could add little more, but at least he had helped to narrow down the probable time of death. Just before eight. Perhaps twenty minutes after Stephanie's husband had set off on his abortive journey to work. To Baines, it suggested a killer who had it all planned. Who had waited until the coast was clear, maybe given it a bit longer, on the off-chance that Richard Merritt got halfway down the road and then realised he'd left his wallet or whatever at home.

A killer who'd struck when he was sure he would not be disturbed.

Baines had continued to ask questions, in tandem with some uniformed officers, taking a special interest in those gawping at the proceedings from the other side of the road. If just one of them had paid as much attention earlier on to events at number 37 as they were doing now, maybe one of them had seen something significant. But it seemed that, at the time in question, all of them were either having breakfast, or having their ablutions, or watching the news on TV.

All except one. Mrs Shirley Hathaway, smack opposite the murder house, admitted that she had happened to be opening her bedroom curtains at around 8.15 am when she noticed a figure walking briskly along the pavement on the other side of the road.

"I suppose he could have been coming from number 37," she said, fiddling with a silver locket on a chain around her neck. "He disappeared down the alley."

"Alley?"

She gestured up the road to her right. "You see the house about eight or nine along from number 37? The one with the hideous purple garage door? Well, between that one and the next house, there's a little footpath you can use to cut through to the High Street."

Interest stirred in Baines. "And you say this was about 8.15?"

"I couldn't swear, but it would have been around that time, yes. I'm a creature of habit."

And a curtain-twitcher, Baines very much suspected. But such nosy parkers often came in handy to the police.

"And it was no one you recognised?"

"I don't think so, not that I saw his face."

"Can you describe him at all?"

"Pretty average all round is my impression. Average height and build. Dark hair, cut very short, I'd say. He was wearing some sort of dark anorak, which I remember thinking a bit excessive, even on a day like today. Dark blue, I'd say. Hood down, of course. Blue jeans and... let me think... dark shoes."

Not bad, considering she had just happened to notice him.

"Definitely a man?"

"That was the impression I got. Something about the walk. Oh, yes, by the way, he walked a bit hunched over."

Baines thanked Mrs Hathaway and said he'd like her to make a formal statement later. Then, his curiosity piqued, he crossed the road and walked down towards the violent purple door she had pointed out. Sure enough, a tarmac footpath ran alongside the house. Baines stood looking down it, imagining a cool killer who had parked his car in the High Street, or even in the car park next to the library.

The killer would have carried a dark anorak or parka over his arm, perhaps concealing the murder weapon. He'd have walked through the alley and emerged into Menzies Drive. Maybe he waited on the corner, from where there was a clear view of number 37. He'd have seen Richard Merritt coming out and setting off for work.

Baines thought the killer would have been patient. He wouldn't have gone straight to the Merritt house as soon as Richard was out of sight. He might have waited fifteen or twenty minutes, just to be sure he was unobserved, before going and knocking on the door. Stephanie Merritt opened up, not suspecting that a brisk May morning was about to become the worst of her life.

Afterwards, the killer would have slipped on the anorak to hide what must have been copious bloodstains on his clothes. Maybe he had also brought a change of shoes with him, perhaps in a pocket of the anorak, knowing he'd get blood on the ones he wore during the attack. Baines imagined him opening the front door a crack, seeing no one about, and letting himself out, walking quickly back towards the alley, just as Mrs Hathaway was opening her curtains.

Baines checked the second hand of his watch and began walking briskly down the alley, checking his watch occasionally on the way. In precisely 73 seconds, he was standing in the High Street. He could see the 16th Century façade of the Red Lion Hotel and, nearby, the traffic lights by the library. If the killer's vehicle was in the car park, it wouldn't be much of a walk. Better still, from Baines' point of view, there were CCTV cameras in the car park. If a figure in a dark anorak could be spotted getting into a car at the time in question, they would have a make and model. With luck, even a registration number.

Something wasn't right, though. He thrust his hands in his trousers pockets and began walking slowly back up the alley. If the killer had entered Menzies Drive on foot, he would have had to loiter around there for up to half an hour before being sure the time was right. It would have looked suspicious, and several people were likely to have noticed him.

Unless somewhere in Menzies Drive offered a place of concealment from where he could see the rest of the road, observe his victim's husband departing, and judge when the time was right to make his move.

Back at the top of the footpath, he turned again to look back down towards the High Street end.

And froze.

Standing there, at the far end of the alley was a slim figure in jeans and a blue and white hooped football shirt. Queen's Park Rangers colours. It looked so much like Jack in his dream last night that Baines almost called out his name.

Half-wondering if it was some sort of mirage, or perhaps his dream had somehow come to life, he rubbed his eyes. When he looked again, the figure had gone.

He stood there, heart pounding, his tongue stuck to the roof of his mouth. There had to be an explanation. Shaking off his torpor, he sprinted back to the High Street and stood looking up and down. For a moment he was convinced that it had all been his imagination, then he caught a flash of blue and white across the road, disappearing around the corner towards the car park.

Heedless of traffic, he hurtled across the road, incurring the blare of a horn. People were out and about, shopping, but the street was not exactly crowded. He plunged into the car park access, staring wildly about him. A few cars were coming out, and he peered inside. No QPR shirt. A passer by was coming away from the ticket machine and Baines blocked his path.

"Excuse me, have you seen a teenager in a QPR shirt?"

The man, probably in his late sixties, blinked at the wild-eyed stranger confronting him. "QPR?"

"A football shirt. Blue and white hoops."

"Hoops?"

29

"Like stripes, only..." Baines inscribed vertical patterns with his fingers.

"Can't say I've noticed. Sorry."

The public toilets? The library? He charged over to the gents and peered inside. No sign of the youth. He ran to the library, bursting in, breathing hard. The two women behind the counter regarded him curiously. Impulsively, he produced his warrant card and told them who he was looking for. Both shook their heads. He conducted a search anyway, without results.

Fearing a little for his sanity, he headed back to the alley leading to Menzies Drive, telling himself to get a grip. Maybe it hadn't been a QPR shirt at all. Reading also played in blue and white hoops. Or maybe Baines had seen a tee-shirt that somehow gave him the impression of a hooped football shirt. As for the kid's sudden disappearance, maybe his dad was waiting for him in the car, just around the corner. By the time Baines got to the end of the alley, they were already away.

Baines liked this explanation. It made sense. What were the alternatives? He was being haunted by the fourteen-year-old son of his dreams? Or he really was having hallucinations? Either way, those explanations meant he was going mad. The idea terrified him.

It was strange that in the dreams he'd been having, and in the vision - if that was what it had been - Jack was wearing a QPR shirt. When Baines was told that his new baby was a boy, he'd immediately imagined a time when the pair of them would be going to Shepherd's Bush to watch the club Baines had supported since childhood.

Baines' father, and his grandfather before, had been ardent R's fans. Even though he was Buckinghamshire born and bred, his parents having moved there when his dad's job relocated in 1972, there had been no question of which team he would support from the moment he was conceived. Dan Baines had hoped he could pass on the QPR gene to Jack, too, although he'd never had the chance to put it to the test. He wondered if the shirt in his dream simply represented a lost opportunity for some serious father-son bonding.

Even as he dwelt on the significance of a football shirt, he knew that it was a convenient way of evading a third explanation for what he had just thought he had seen. That Jack was somehow, impossibly, alive and living right here in the Chilterns. It was a possibility that Baines tried ruthlessly - and not always successfully - to deny himself.

Because the thought of Jack alive was somehow even more painful than the thought of him dead.

* * *

Archer experienced a twinge of annoyance when she spotted Baines emerging from what appeared to be an alley a few doors down from where she leaned against his car. She wondered where he'd been sloping off to, when he should have been questioning neighbours and making sure the constables were keeping their noses to the grindstone.

She saw him looking her way and waved him over.

"Where have you been?"

He looked vague for a moment.

"Uh," he mumbled. "That alley leads back to the High Street."

There was something a bit off about his look.

"Are you okay?" she asked. "You look like you've seen a ghost."

He went a shade paler and laughed nervously. "No. No, I'm fine."

"Well, you don't look it." She looked at him suspiciously. "The High Street? Where that pub was, that we passed? The Red Lion?"

"It's actually a hotel..."

"Please tell me you didn't slip in there to sample their wares."

He looked affronted. "What are you saying? That I slipped off for a sly one while on duty?"

"I don't know."

He stared at her, pale and angry-looking. "For Christ's sake. I doubt they're open yet, but even if they were..."

She wasn't sure whether she altogether bought the injured innocence, but she shrugged the whole thing off, wondering if he protested too much. "All right. So what's so interesting about that alley?"

Still looking annoyed, he told her what had come from his questioning of neighbours so far.

"I was just about to see what the constables have got," he said.

"Okay, do that in a moment." Archer reflected on what he had told her. "I agree that this figure in the anorak sounds promising, but I also agree that the notion of him hanging around in Menzies Drive for half an hour or so doesn't ring true. He'd have looked too suspicious and people would have spotted him. Ask the uniforms whether they've had any other such reports, but I'd be surprised. Too risky. No, you're right. It only works if he could have concealed himself somewhere."

She looked up and down the road. A few doors down from Mrs Hathaway's property stood a 'For Sale' sign. Without a word to Baines, she headed that way.

"That one's empty," Baines informed her as he brought up the rear. "I'm told the owners have moved abroad and are trying to sell it. The front garden's quite overgrown."

But by now Archer could see that. The shrubs at the front of the property had got quite tall.

"You're thinking he was lurking behind the bushes?" Baines prompted.

"Maybe. Maybe not." She pushed open the front gate. It resisted a little, mainly because a number of weeds had sprung up behind it, pushing through cracks in the concrete path to the front door and forming a barrier. She shoved harder, got it open and advanced up the path.

"The bushes aren't bad," she said, "but there's still a risk of being spotted. And they're not the best of vantage points." She climbed the two steps to the door and investigated its lock. The wood next to it was cracked and splintered, the door barely fitting. She turned the handle and pushed, and was rewarded by the door swinging inwards.

"Bloody hell." She was gratified to detect a note of admiration in Baines' voice. "He forced the lock. He was probably watching from behind the curtains upstairs."

"I'd guess he'd been planning this for some time. He saw the possibilities of this place and broke in - probably in the early hours of this morning when all the neighbours would have been in their beds." She glanced across at number 37. "I suggest you go back to the Merritt house and tell the SOCOs that, when they've finished there, they need to check out this one - number 30."

"I'm on it." But he hesitated. "What you said about him having planned all this. I agree with you. It reinforces our theory that Mrs Merritt was deliberately targeted."

She started to move back towards the gate. "The husband said an interesting thing. He said, as a social worker, Stephanie upset her fair share of people. It must go with the territory sometimes. I think we need to find out more about her current and recent caseload. See who she might have been pissing off."

5

There had been no need to put Richard Merritt through the anguish of formally identifying his wife's body. Her skull had been battered so badly out of shape that she was frankly unidentifiable anyway. Fortunately, despite the brutality to her entire face, Barbara Carlisle was confident that the teeth would provide enough for Stephanie's dentist to go on.

It was mid-afternoon when Archer and Baines joined Carlisle in the post-mortem room at Stoke Mandeville Hospital. What was left of Stephanie Merritt had already been washed and stripped. The face had been cleansed of dried blood, but didn't look very much better for it. In some ways, Baines thought it looked worse.

He could not imagine what the poor woman had gone through, and could only hope that she had died, or at least lost consciousness, early in the attack. Hopefully, Barbara Carlisle should soon be able to give them some idea about that.

No matter how many post-mortems he attended, Baines thought he would never be able to be dispassionate about them the way many of his colleagues were. The smells, the noises the tools made, and the sight of a human being undergoing this final desecration always both sickened and saddened him, even though he'd long since managed to keep his stomach under control.

Carlisle worked as she always did, her movements neat and efficient, whilst she gave a commentary for the benefit of the recording that would later form the basis of her report. Baines was the note taker, a job he would have delegated to another sergeant a few days ago.

He was particularly careful to note what she said about the damage to the skull.

"There are numerous cracks and indentations. They appear roughly uniform in size and shape. It appears highly likely that the murder weapon would be a hammer, or something similar."

When the pathologist's work was done and Stephanie Merritt's organs had been removed and weighed, fluids collected, Archer began to recap on the main findings.

"So time of death is confirmed as between eight and eight-thirty?"

"The closest I can get."

"And C.O.D. was as we thought?"

"Massive haemorrhaging of the brain due to blunt force trauma to the head. As I said, any one of at least six blows would have been the fatal one. For what it's worth, I doubt she would have remained conscious for long. I suppose that would be some comfort to the family."

"I suppose." Archer sounded as doubtful as Baines felt. "Now, what about the murder weapon? You're sure it's a hammer?"

A wintry smile flickered across Carlisle's lips. "Dan will tell you I'm rarely absolutely sure about anything, especially at this stage. But that's my best assessment."

"If we got hold of the hammer, could we match it up with the indentations in the skull?"

"I'll talk to the forensics guys," Baines said. "They might know some sort of hammer expert who can tell us the make and model. I wouldn't hold my breath though."

"It was so much easier before the government, in their infinite wisdom, shut down the Forensic Science Service. You knew who to go to back then." Archer shook her head. "The real trick, though, is to get hold of it. Either he's tossed it somewhere and we have to hope it turns up, or he's holding onto it and we have to hope we get a suspect soon."

"I've asked Joan Collins to get hold of the CCTV camera from the car park in Wendover."

Archer shot him a suspicious look. "Joan Collins?"

He felt himself colouring. "Sorry, ma'am. Not the actress, obviously. Detective Constable Collins. You might not have met her yet. Her name's Joanne, but everyone calls her Joan because -"

"I see." She cut his gabbling explanation mercifully short. "Well, good. If our killer had his car waiting there, we ought to be able to pick out someone in a dark, hooded anorak."

"And, if we can get a number plate, we're halfway there."

"Then let's hope our killer did keep his hammer." She turned to Carlisle again. "You said there was no evidence of sexual assault?"

"That's right."

"Did you have any more observations?"

"I think I've covered everything. You'll get my report tomorrow morning, but it won't contain any surprises. What I will try to do is produce a scale sketch of the shape of the hammerhead. It might not be much use..."

"Thanks," Archer said. "It'll be useful to have a better idea of what we're looking for." She took a last glance at the cadaver on the table. "I can't shake the idea that whoever did this must have really hated her."

Baines pocketed his notebook. "They say there's a thin line between love and hate. What do you think about the husband?"

"I don't know. He's coming in later to make a statement, but his grief seemed genuine enough. Besides, the timing doesn't quite fit with him leaving the house when he did, going to the station, hanging about and deciding to go home."

"If he was telling the truth about any of that. He could have left ostensibly for work and loitered somewhere quiet." He pondered for a moment. "He could have had the anorak with him, slipped it on, and retraced his steps. Maybe even part-changed in the public loos. As for his grief, just because he killed her, it needn't mean he isn't grieving for her."

"I don't know." She rubbed her scar. "What about the broken lock on the house opposite?"

He shrugged, seeing an opportunity to dent her ego. He thought she might have been a bit too pleased with herself over what was admittedly a very smart piece of detection. "Maybe just coincidence. Could have been kids, spotting an empty house and deciding to break in out of devilment."

She was silent for a moment, then nodded. "I don't think so, but I see your point. The SOCOs are already going over his clothes and car, and he's coming in later today. I'd like you to sit in on the interview with me."

"Sure." She hadn't taken the bait, and Baines knew better than to push his luck. "When's he expected?"

"About half four."

"Just give me a shout when you need me."

* * *

Richard Merritt wore a sweatshirt, even though the day had warmed up. He looked gaunt and older than his years, and he said he hadn't been able to get warm all day.

His married daughter had driven him to the station to make his statement, and she was waiting in reception. Archer had decided to continue treating him like a victim and not a suspect for now.

Merritt had a cup of coffee in front of him. She'd toyed with dispatching someone to get him a decent cup, but had been told that the nearest Starbucks was a ten minute walk away. By the time it arrived and he started to drink it, the coffee would have started to go cold.

They ran through his story again. Archer had decided to allow Baines to lead the questioning, to increase the possibility of inconsistency creeping in, but he more or less stuck to what he had told her at the scene.

"And you're absolutely sure you went straight to the station?" Baines pressed. "You didn't stop off anywhere on the way?"

Merritt blinked. Up to now he had been the grieving husband, helping the police with their enquiries. But something different came into his eyes no, something more guarded. "Stop somewhere? Why would I do that? I had a train to catch." He looked imploringly at Archer. "Stop where? Jesus, you said the clothes were just for elimination, but I'm a suspect, aren't I?" He began breathing hard. "I don't believe this. You should be out there catching Steph's killer, and instead you're asking me stupid questions, treating me like a suspect."

He was flapping his hands about in agitation. His right hand caught the coffee cup and sent it flying across the table, its contents cascading into Archer's lap. She leapt up, suppressing curses and holding the skirt away from her to avoid scalding.

Baines was up as well, a snotty handkerchief in his hand. He reached towards Archer's groin with it, thought twice, and offered it to her. She declined, searching his face suspiciously for any sign of a smirk.

"Don't worry about it, Mr Merritt," she said, not even looking at the man, who had offered no apology or any other comment. "I'll just pop into the ladies' and try to clean this up," she said, heading for the door.

"Ma'am," Baines said as she opened it, "I think we've got a problem."

She turned to see Richard Merritt clutching his chest, his mouth open in what looked like a silent scream.

She thrust her fingers into her hair, her sodden skirt forgotten. "I think he's having a heart attack. Call an ambulance, and then see if anyone's got some aspirin." He dithered. "Do it now," she said firmly, resisting the temptation to shout and agitate Merritt still further.

As Baines fled, pulling out his mobile as he went, Archer took a couple of deep breaths to calm herself and then walked over to the stricken Merritt.

"Try and keep calm, sir," she said soothingly, taking his hand in hers. "You'll feel better if you calm down." There was terror in his eyes. "The thing to do is not to panic, and you'll be just fine. We're calling an ambulance for you, and we're trying to find some aspirin to take while you're waiting."

He was still fighting to breathe, his face pale and waxy. "You... think..."

"Don't try to talk."

"... think... I... killed... Steph..."

"We don't think anything yet, sir. Don't worry about that. Just you keep calm."

A couple of minutes later, Baines hurried back in, brandishing a strip of tablets. He held a glass of water in his other hand. "Aspirins. Ambulance on its way."

Merritt's daughter, Andrea was right behind him.

"Oh, my God," she wailed, eyes wide. "Oh, dad!" She went to him, hugging him a bit too roughly for Archer's liking in the circumstances. Her eyes flashed Archer's way. "What have you done to him?"

"I think the important thing is we keep calm"

"Keep calm?" Andrea shrilled. "Mum was murdered this morning. You come round demanding his clothes and now you've got him in here, giving him the third degree. If he dies..."

"Nobody is going to die," Archer told her firmly.

"Actually, ma'am," Baines said, "I think he's stopped breathing."

* * *

It was a nightmare end to one hell of a first day. Richard Merritt had indeed suffered a cardiac arrest, and Archer had performed CPR on him whilst Baines tried to control a hysterical Andrea. By the time the ambulance arrived, he was unconscious but stable. Andrea went to the hospital with him, still muttering darkly about suing the police as the ambulance doors closed.

Paul Gillingham was a long way from chuffed about a grieving husband collapsing under questioning on the day of his wife's murder. The DCI seemed more concerned about how it would play in the local press than whether the investigation was making any progress.

She tried to stand up for herself. "With respect, sir, we had to make sure Mr Merritt's story was sound. So many murders are committed by people known to the victim, often loved ones, and the person who calls in the murder is often the culprit."

"Don't teach granny to suck eggs, Inspector," he growled. "What did you and Baines do to him? Shine lights in his eyes and play good cop, bad cop?"

"It really wasn't like that, sir. All Baines asked was -"

"Not interested. This is a serious PR cock-up, and your first day's not even over yet. And don't try to blame Dan Baines."

"I wasn't..." His accusation stung her.

He sighed. "I gather you at least did all the right things to help him. Possibly saved his life. I suppose that's something," he added grudgingly.

When she emerged from Gillingham's office, Baines was hanging about outside. She glared at him. He was probably trying to gauge whether she would last out the week. No doubt he expected to be back in her chair by Friday.

"What do you want?" she demanded.

"I just wondered if you were okay. A bit of a tough baptism today, one way or another."

"You think? Well, don't you worry about me, Dan. Touching as your concern is, I'll be fine."

There was no way he could miss the sarcasm in her voice, and he visibly stiffened. "Suit yourself."

He started to stalk away, and she realised that she really didn't want to end her day at odds with her boss and her sergeant.

"Dan," she called.

He stopped walking, turned to face her, arms folded.

"We seem to be getting off a bit on the wrong foot. I don't quite know why, but it's not good if we're going to work together. We need to reach an understanding."

"Yeah?"

"Yes. Look, I'm staying at the Holiday Inn until I sort something out. Why don't you come over for a drink this evening? We can have a proper chat, away from the office. Get to know each other..."

His expression might have softened a little, and he even unfolded his arms, but he gave his head a shake.

"Sorry, ma'am. Not tonight. I've already got an appointment. Maybe another time, yes?"

She searched his face, not entirely sure whether she believed him. Was he blowing her off because he'd already decided to undermine her as much as possible? Or... God, she'd invited him to meet her at her hotel. Alone. Had he got the wrong idea?

"Sure, Dan," she said hurriedly. "Another time. No problem."

"I've got a ton of things to do before I call it a day," he said. "If you'll excuse me, ma'am."

She watched his upright, retreating back with mingled resentment and embarrassment. She'd left behind the Met, and London, to start with a clean slate, and in a single day she seemed to have blotted her copybook with just about everyone, one way or another. And now she had an evening at a plastic hotel to look forward to, with only her thoughts for company.

She drooped back to her office. As she walked in, a balding, moustachioed man at the desk opposite hers hastily opened a draw and fiddled inside it. Even without the distinct sound of a cigarette being stubbed out, the pall of smoke in the room and the stink of tobacco would have been something of a give-away.

He sprang up with guilty eyes, holding a hand out. "You must be Lizzie. We meet at last. I'm Steve Ashby. I gather we'll be co-habiting."

The smoke made her eyes sting, and she made a decision. She'd fallen out with everyone else. Why should she make an exception here?

"Nice to meet you, Steve," she said, shaking the proffered hand and noting the nicotine stains on his fingers and his moustache. "But before we go any further, there's something we need to get straight."

6

October 2001.

When Dan Baines pulls up outside his house, the place is in darkness. It's not yet midnight. Later, he will wonder why it didn't occur to him right then that something was wrong.

But it's Friday night and he's absolutely knackered. He knows what a toll this case is taking on him. Even as a lowly Detective Constable, a mere foot soldier in the scheme of things, he feels keenly the burden of responsibility for catching the killer known as the Invisible Man.

Five women and four small children dead. A fifth child missing. And still no breaks. Every family in the Chilterns has been living in terror since the police acknowledged there was a serial killer on the prowl, but he has continued to kill and to abduct, as regular as clockwork.

Every Friday.

A mother dead in her home. Her child abducted. The child taken last time brought to the new murder scene and also killed. And an agonising seven day wait for another family, grieving over one loss and living in the inevitable shadow of a second.

Always one-child families targeted. And the short gap between killings indicating meticulous forward planning.

The Invisible Man. So called because of his ability to get into people's houses, kill them, and get away, taking a child with him and leaving no trace. There has never been a witness who saw him coming or going, nothing on any CCTV camera to help the police. An idiot in uniform had said something about they were almost looking for the invisible man in earshot of a tabloid journalist, and the nickname had stuck.

Not only stuck, but massaged the killer's ego. Afterwards, he started leaving a calling card at each crime scene. He'd find a scrap of paper and a pen at the latest victims' home and draw a disembodied pair of dark glasses with a smoking cigar underneath.

Baines knows that, if the established pattern continues, there are two more bodies waiting to be found. The only surprise is that they haven't already had the call. The knowledge that another Friday has come and gone without a break feels like a failure. He wonders why the expected bodies have not been found. He cannot imagine the agony of the Richardson family, who have been holding their breath for a week, knowing that the next time they saw Jessica she would almost certainly be at the mortuary.

He locks the car and walks towards the silent house, fumbling in his jacket pocket for his door keys. It's not like Louise not to wait up for him, but there have been several nights in the past few weeks when he's arrived home just after midnight. Maybe she was tired, poor love, and decided on an early night.

He lets himself into the silent house, debating whether to have a shower before bed, even though it is late. There is something about this case that makes him feel filthy.

He goes into the kitchen, pours himself a glass of milk, and looks in the fridge for something to eat. He's not been eating properly for weeks, mostly just grabbing fast food when the need to refuel is urgent. Sometimes Louise will leave him a sandwich, but not tonight. He finds a block of cheddar, takes it out, deciding to cut himself a chunk of cheese and eat that. He can't be bothered to get bread out.

As he closes the fridge door, he pauses to admire Louise's beloved collection of fridge magnets. There is something different today. Maybe she has spotted a new one that has taken her fancy. A wave of love for her washes over him.

And then he freezes, the hairs on his neck rising.

There is no new magnet. It is the scrap of paper, held in place by a magnet in the shape of an ice-cream cone, that has caught his eye, and the first wave of dread twists in his stomach.

He looks at the closed door that separates the kitchen from the lounge diner, and a hideous knowledge - a hideous certainty - settles upon him.

And, suddenly, he is on the verge of vomiting, puking his guts up like a drunk teenager for the first time since his first post mortem.

He waits until the urge has passed. Only then does he approach the door, a clammy hand held out towards the handle, but at the last minute he funks it. Instead, he charges out into the hall, takes the stairs two at a time, and bursts into Jack's bedroom, first on the right after the bathroom, frantically switching on the light.

Jack is curled up in his bed, wearing that familiar expression of fierce concentration as he sleeps.

For a moment, Baines thinks he actually sees that. But then reality crashes in. The bed is empty.

He rushes out onto the landing.

"Lou? Jack?" But he knows even as he bawls their names that he has already made enough noise to awaken...

(The dead).

He goes back downstairs, his feet feeling like blocks of lead, knowing what he has to do. Part of him wants to call it in now, let someone else make the grim discovery, but he knows he can't do that. He's a cop.

He opens the living room door, and he staggers as in the darkness he makes out two lumps in the middle of the carpet. His mouth is dry. He reaches for the light switch, nearly funks again, then swallows, steels himself, and flicks it on.

At that moment, he feels as if his heart is being torn out of his chest. The heads, swathed in the cling film that has suffocated them. A woman and a small child, side by side.

He knows there's no hope, but he has to see if he can help them anyway. He stirs himself and goes to the bodies. He looks at the child and is ashamed of his relief that it is a girl, almost certainly Jessica Richardson, and not Jack. He mentally discards the child then and moves to his wife, dropping to his knees and feeling for a pulse. There is none, and she is cold to the touch. She has been dead for hours.

Only then does he check on Jessica, although he knows it is pointless. He knows how the Invisible Man works. Louise and the child would have been killed within minutes of one another, if not simultaneously. No one knows for sure in what order he does his work.

He feels a roiling blur of emotions. A huge hole has been punched out of him by loss, a hole he knows nothing will ever fill. He feels the grief of Mark Richardson, who has now lost a daughter as well as a wife. And there is a rage there, too, an overwhelming desire to tear apart the monster who has done this.

Above all, though, clawing at his raw heart, is the terror of what next Friday will bring.

7

"Do you think Jack could still be alive?" Baines said suddenly.

Karen Smart looked at him, a forkful of smoked salmon and salad paused halfway to her mouth. She sighed, and when she spoke there was sadness in her voice.

"What's brought that on? You haven't mentioned Jack for... well, quite a few years."

He didn't answer.

Karen laid down her fork. They were in a The Marchmont Arms, a smart pub restaurant on the outskirts of Hemel Hempstead.

"You know what I think, Dan. Jack must be dead. It's just that no one has found his body yet."

"But the Invisible Man stopped after Louise. We waited a week, trying to find him. Knowing we wouldn't. Expecting to find Jack lying next to some other poor woman, on the following Friday, anticipating another abduction. But nothing. Why did he stop?"

"We've been over this. You might as well ask why he started."

He treated it as a new question, instead of the much chewed-over old chestnut it had become. "We had this profile. The psychologist who compiled it thought it had something to do with the killer's own mother."

"Oedipus complex. I know."

"Except there was never any evidence of anything sexual about the killings. And it was never clear where the kids fitted in. The best the shrink could manage was that the children were some sort of surrogate representation of the killer himself. Even that didn't make a whole lot of sense. Three dead girls. Two dead boys. And Jack, gone without a trace."

Karen tilted her head slightly to one side, the gesture so reminiscent of her twin sister that, even after all this time, it squeezed Baines' heart.

"I'll ask you again," she said gently. "What brings this up now?"

He sighed. "I've been dreaming about him lately. It's weird. I don't see him as he was when he was taken, but as he would be now. Might be now, I suppose is more accurate. And today I thought I actually saw him. At a crime scene. I tried to get to him, but I lost him."

He couldn't imagine talking about this to anyone else. Had not talked about Louise to anyone but Karen for years. Of Jack, he had spoken to nobody at all in almost a decade.

He knew some people thought it was unhealthy for him to spend time with the double of his dead wife, but that was their problem. Karen was his best friend and she understood him like no one else.

Now she regarded him keenly. "That first year, after Jack disappeared, and Louise died, you used to think you saw one or both of them all the time. At the bus stop, in the street, at the supermarket. Why do you suppose it's started again?"

"I have no idea. And why have I conjured up this fourteen-year-old version of him?"

Both of them had forgotten their food now.

"Why do you think it is?" Karen asked. This was what she did - turn a question back on him when deep down he already had an answer.

He took a deep breath. "I can't help thinking maybe he's still alive and trying to send me a message."

"What sort of message?"

"I don't know. I keep running through the options." This was something else they used to do a lot in those early days. "He's dead. Or he somehow got away and got taken in by people who raised him as their own. Or the Invisible Man still has him."

He took a large gulp of his white wine. "If he'd followed his usual pattern, he would have killed a seventh woman exactly seven days after Lou. He'd have also killed Jack at the scene and taken his new victim's child. But he didn't. He stopped. For all we know, he kept Jack, for some reason. For all we know, that has something to do with why he targeted me."

And that was another mystery. The Invisible Man's last victim had been the wife of a detective working on his own case. Although it could have been mere coincidence, Baines had always assumed it was a deliberate choice, because the Invisible Man had already been taunting the police with his calling cards. At the time, Baines had been the most junior member of the investigation team, but he was also the only one with just the one young child. The only one whose family fitted the killer's pattern.

What both Baines and Karen had tried not to confront was what might have been happening to Jack for all this time in the unlikely event that he was still alive. No one knew what had happened to the other children between their abduction and their death. They were well-nourished and showed no sign of physical or sexual assault. But the killer had only had them for a week.

Eleven years, though. The possibilities were endless, and Baines had tortured himself with them in his darkest hours. In the end, he had simply closed a door in his mind, doing his best to seal off such thoughts - and with them, all other thoughts of his son - and to move on with his life. Until now.

Karen reached across the table and took both his hands in hers.

"Dan," she said, very softly, "I'm going to say something, and you're not going to like it. I think you need help. You've never really had it. You took a few days off, and then you went straight back to work. You refused everything the force offered you - proper compassionate leave, counselling..."

He grinned crookedly. "I didn't need all that. I've had you."

"Not for the best part of two years you didn't."

That was true. For the first 19 months, each of them had carried their grief alone. His for a soulmate who had looked far too much like her, and for a lost child. Hers for a sister with whom her bond had bordered on the telepathic. The other half of herself.

Karen had told Baines, much later, that she thought she had known the moment of Louise's death. Had actually felt the connection between them sever, so profoundly that she had wanted to drive over to the Baines' home in Little Aston and make sure her sister was okay. Her husband, Nigel, had talked her out of it. Even when she had phoned instead and got no reply, he had rationalised it to her, insisting that Louise was probably just out for the day.

That had been the beginning of the end for Karen's marriage. It probably couldn't have survived her daily resentment that her husband hadn't taken her seriously that day. But coupled with that, Nigel was unable to withstand the level of grief that she displayed, day after day, with no sign of moving on. The day he left her, he said he no longer recognised the woman he had married.

That had been the day Karen had turned up on Baines' doorstep, unannounced and slightly drunk. For the first time since the murder, each of them felt able to pour out their feelings to somebody, aided by copious amounts of alcohol. Almost inevitably, they had ended up in bed, a desperate, cathartic coupling that brought them both a brief kind of relief, even though neither of them could be sure afterwards who Baines had really been making love to.

The sex had never happened again, nor been spoken of, as if the idea of a repeat performance was just too weird for both of them. But they had discovered a closeness that might always have been there on some level, but which now became an unbreakable bond. Barely a day went by without them speaking on the phone, and they met regularly, often after work like tonight. Baines knew he could tell her anything, and he also knew the feeling was mutual.

"Well?" Karen jerked him back to reality.

"What?"

"What about getting some real help? I don't like the sound of these dreams and visions, or the crazy idea that Jack is trying to make some sort of psychic contact with you."

He frowned. "You don't buy it?"

"I've always been honest with you, Dan, and that's not going to change now. I think something's going on with you, and I worry about you."

He found himself taking his hands back. "Enough to want me to see a bloody shrink, apparently."

People on neighbouring tables glanced his way, and he realised he had spoken too loudly.

"Take it easy," Karen soothed. "It was only a suggestion. Obviously a stupid one." She started pushing food around on her plate. Neither of them had eaten much. "So, why would Jack be trying to contact you now?"

He relaxed a little, swigged some more wine. For some reason, it was starting to go to his head.

"I've been asking myself the same. What if..." He hesitated, then plunged on. "What if the Invisible Man has been keeping him somewhere all these years? Like locked in a trunk under the bed, or chained up in a soundproof basement? I mean, you hear of these things."

Karen knew when to speak and when to say nothing, just let him keep talking. A waiter appeared at the table and asked if everything was all right, eyeing the almost untouched plates.

"We're fine," muttered Baines, irritated by the interruption. He looked at Karen again. "All right, here's the thing. What if Jack's somewhere he can't get away from and the Invisible Man has died? What if no one knows and Jack's starving to death somewhere?"

She shuddered. "You can't think like that. You'll go insane."

"But what if he is?"

"You've no way of knowing what these dreams are all about. Okay, you don't want professional help. So let's try and figure this out between us. What's changed in your life lately?"

He poured them both a top-up from the wine bottle, saw it was low and judiciously eked out the remains between them.

"Another?" he suggested.

"I think we've had enough, and I think you're evading the question."

"You'll think I'm pathetic."

"Never. Tell me."

"I've got a new boss. A new DI. Which means, of course, that I'm not acting DI any more, and they didn't offer me the job."

"And you resent that?"

"Actually, I do. I know it's stupid, but my career's been going nowhere fast since I made sergeant. I'm sure they must think I'm unstable because of what happened to my family."

"But you did make sergeant after that."

"And I started having the dreams well before the new boss was announced, so it's all a bit irrelevant anyway."

"Maybe. Maybe not. Perhaps worrying about whether you were going to revert, and then finding it was actually happening, has all fed your insecurities about everything else."

He was sceptical. "Now you're sounding like a shrink."

"But my rates are more reasonable. You say the new boss arrived today and then you thought you actually saw Jack?"

"Yes."

"Were you having these visions before you met the new governor?"

"No. Just the dreams."

"So his arrival could have increased your anxieties."

"It's a her. The boss, I mean."

Karen arched an eyebrow. "So you resent working for a woman?"

He bristled, genuinely irritated at the suggestion. "Don't be ridiculous. You know me better than that."

"Have you had a female boss before?"

"No, but..." Why was she pressing the point?

She tilted her head on one side again. The gesture, and the way her brow furrowed in thought, were both so Louise-like that it hurt.

"When did you last see anyone?" she asked suddenly.

He was momentarily confused, and a little angry. "You know I haven't seen a shrink, and I just said I had no intention of -"

"Whoa!" She held her hands up in surrender. "Who's talking about shrinks? I meant, when did you last date anyone?"

He found it didn't make him much less irritated. "What - you think I need the love of a good woman? That there's nothing wrong that a good shag wouldn't put right?"

She ignored the ire in his voice. "Well, maybe it would."

"Are you offering?"

The words were out almost before he'd realised he was uttering them. He saw her recoil and felt his face flame.

"Let's not go there," she said quietly. "In fact, I think we should call it a night."

He was mortified by the turn things had taken. "Don't be like that, Karen. I'm sorry, okay? It just slipped out. It was a joke, yeah?"

"So you say."

"So I say?" His temper quickened again. "You think I'd try it on? After all this time?"

She looked at him appraisingly. "Maybe, maybe not. You've been acting too normal for far too long, and now you're getting all weird for the first time in ages. I don't know what's going on with you, Dan, but it's clear I'm not the person to help you right now."

"But..." He felt the first pangs of desperation. "I haven't got anyone else. You're the only one I can talk to. The only one who understands." He knew he sounded pathetic. "Look, why don't we get out of here? Come back to my place for coffee, and -"

"Coffee? After what you just said? Just coffee?"

"Oh, come on. I told you, it was a bad joke."

"It's not a good idea, Dan."

And that was when his mouth really began to run away with his brain. "No? What about you? When's the last time you 'saw' someone, as you put it?"

"Get the bill, will you?"

"There's been no one for ages. Not for either of us. And who did we run to whenever another potential relationship turned into a train wreck? I always came to you. And you came to me."

"So what are you saying? That we should take our friendship to 'another level'?" She made parenthesis with her fingers, a gesture he knew she detested in others.

He opened his mouth, unsure of what reply he might make, but she spoke again, hastily, cutting him off.

"No," she said. "Best you don't answer that. Look, this is getting out of hand, and maybe I'm reading too much into what you say was a bad joke. That one time before - it felt right then. Because it was something we both needed, that time, that night. But I really don't know if our friendship could survive it happening again. All the time, I'd be asking myself if I was just a stand-in for Louise, and I'd end up hating you for it. Hating myself for allowing it."

"You're right," he said. "This has all got way too heavy. I'm sorry for what I said. Best we never speak of it again, yes?"

"I suppose."

"Just friends then?"

She shrugged, her eyes still guarded. "Just friends."

There was an awkward silence. Baines realised he had no idea what Karen was thinking, but he felt utterly bereft, without being altogether sure why. It had just been a throwaway remark that she had blown up out of all proportion.

Finally, Karen drained the last of her glass and blew out a long breath.

"Okay," she said. "So why don't you get the waiter to take all this cold food away, get us some coffee, and tell me all about this new boss of yours?"

Trying to shake off an unaccountable feeling of hurt and rejection, he looked around for a waiter.

"Not much to tell, really. I can't work her out at the moment. She's a good detective. I can't decide whether she likes me or not. She's got this nasty scar on her face, which she's clearly sensitive about."

"Did you stare at it?"

He spotted a waiter and waved at him. "I tried not to, but you know what it's like when you first see something like that.

She's transferred in from the Met. I know she got hurt making an arrest. Maybe this has something to do with it."

Karen shrugged. "If she's sensitive, maybe she should consider plastic surgery."

"I don't know why she hasn't. I suppose it's not for everyone."

"Even so..."

The waiter came, but Karen decided she'd changed her mind about coffee. They got the bill, halved it as they always did, and walked out to the car park.

"Think about some counselling, Dan," she told him by her car. "Those dreams mean something. Don't ignore them."

"We'll see," he said, not prepared to argue.

When he went to kiss her goodnight, as he always did, she didn't kiss him on the lips as usual, but offered her cheek. He watched her drive away with a hollow feeling in his stomach, fearing that a few stupid words after a couple of drinks had put a dent in their relationship.

He also wondered if there was any point in talking to her about Jack, if all she was going to do was nag him about counselling. He drove home feeling lonely, miserable and confused.

8

Archer arrived at the station tired and tetchy after a bad night's sleep. She'd tossed and turned, and when she awoke from the one little bit of sleep she managed, she was sweating after a fragmented dream in which at one point she had been trying to revive Stephanie Merritt.

The patient's face hadn't been the bloody lump she'd encountered yesterday morning, but the face of the pleasant-looking woman in her late forties who smiled out at the photograph on the major incident room wall. The harder she tried to resuscitate the woman, the worse the face became.

Baines was standing idly by, and every time she asked him for help, he said, "You're the DCI, not me."

She had awoken just as DI Steve Ashby had burst in, with a lighted fag in each hand, surrounded by a fug of cigarette smoke.

It didn't take a Freud to work out what had prompted the dream. Strangely, it was the Ashby image that stayed longest in her mind.

To say her room-mate had reacted badly to being reminded that the station was a non-smoking building was an understatement. He hadn't actually refused to stop smoking in the office, but he had muttered childishly about how no one else seemed to mind, and new bloody brooms, and what was she going to do - tell teacher? She was sure he had been staring hard at her scar all the while, and that it had been a pathetic attempt to intimidate her.

Now it was just after nine, later than she would have liked, but there was no sign of Baines. She was on her way to make a coffee when she passed a room where someone appeared to be watching TV. Curious, she looked in and saw that the viewer was a young, black woman, and that the film she was watching was all of one spot in a car park. The woman looked round at her.

"Can I help you?"

"Good morning," Archer said. "You must be DC Collins. I'm DI Archer."

Collins scrambled out of her seat. "Morning, ma'am. Yes, I'm Collins. Joanne, but everyone calls me -"

"Joan," Archer completed for her. "So I've been told. You look a little younger than the original though."

"And I hate shoulder pads."

Archer gestured to the screen. "Is that the footage from Wendover car park?"

"Yep, just got it. I'm looking for a window between eight and eight-thirty. A figure in a dark, hooded anorak."

"Mind if I look with you for five minutes?"

"Four eyes are better than two, ma'am."

Archer took a vacant seat and Joan Collins started fast-forwarding the film, stopping to check the time and date stamp, and fast-forwarding again.

"Here we go," she said finally. The time was 8.01 yesterday morning. Collins played the film and they watched cars turning up to park, people getting out, obtaining pay and display tickets, putting them on their car dashboards, and departing for whatever business they had in Wendover. It was a bit early in the morning, so the joint wasn't exactly jumping.

"There," Archer suddenly said, and Joan stopped the film. They could see the side view of a hooded figure walking through the car park. It was 8.17 am by the time stamp. Collins began to advance the film frame by frame.

"That's not Richard Merritt," she said after a few moments. The height and build were all wrong. But it might match the 'average height and build' that Baines' nosy witness, Mrs Hathaway, had described.

"Come on, sunshine," Collins urged. "Smile for the camera. Show us your face." But the figure refused to oblige. He opened the door of an old, dark Vauxhall Astra, apparently without unlocking it first, seemed to put something on the front passenger seat, and then got in. Moments later he was driving out of the car park. Collins stopped the tape as the front of the car was about to move outside the camera's range.

"I can't make out the plate," Archer said. "Is there any way you can enhance it?"

"Not me," Collins said. "But there's a civilian on the team - Ibrahim Iqbal - who's a whizz at this sort of thing."

"If you get anything, get someone to check it out. See who the registered owner is," Archer said. "And you'll need to go back to see when he arrived. Maybe you'll catch a glimpse of his face."

"Maybe." Collins sounded dubious. "I've done quite a bit of this, ma'am, and you get to know when they're aware of the cameras. I think this one will have avoided showing more of himself than he could help."

"Well, we may get lucky. Good work, Joan." Archer levered herself out of her seat. "By the way, any idea where DS Baines is this morning?"

"Dan? He's gone to the hospital. Did you know about the gang leader, Brandon Clark? The one who was shot? Well, he's been asking for DS Baines."

* * *

Baines had arrived home last night with his conversation with Karen replaying in his mind like a snuff movie on continuous feed. He'd felt childishly depressed and aggrieved, still without really knowing why. He had tried to make it go away with a few slugs of whisky. It hadn't worked, and this morning he had the beginnings of a headache. Being despatched, with DC Jason Bell in tow, to speak to Brandon Clark, was unlikely to make it go away.

Stoke Mandeville Hospital, best known these days as an international centre for paraplegia and spinal injuries, had actually started life as a cholera hospital in the early 1830s. An epidemic had swept across England, hitting the village of Stoke Mandeville hard, and the hospital was founded on its parish border with Aylesbury, to keep the infection away from both population centres.

The hospital continued treating infectious diseases until the turn of the Twentieth Century. The risk of spreading infection had increased to unacceptable levels by the inexorable expansion of Aylesbury, and so the treatment of such diseases moved elsewhere. But the hospital remained, and when the National Health Service was founded in 1948, Stoke Mandeville became Aylesbury's main hospital.

In the same year, on the opening day of the Olympic Games in London, the hospital held a sports competition for World War two veterans with spinal cord injuries. The event was repeated in 1952, with Dutch veterans taking part alongside the British, the first international event of its kind and a precursor to the first Paralympics, held in Rome in 1960. This summer the Paralympics was coming back to the UK and Stoke Mandeville stadium was preparing to play its part.

Baines had been told most of the historical stuff by a nurse he had dated a couple of times during a doomed attempt to move on from the loss of his family. Michelle Madison had been bookish but fun, but it had never been going to work with Louise's ghost still looking over his shoulder. At least she had given him an insight into why the less than impressive 'Nightingale' wards, constructed during World War Two, coexisted so uneasily with the more modern facilities that had been grafted on over the years, including an Accident and Emergency Unit.

Brandon Clark was being treated in what would normally have been a private room off one of these wards. Despite his lack of cooperation so far, there was concern that whoever had shot him might turn up at the hospital and try to finish the job. DCI Gillingham had reluctantly taken the decision to tie up a uniformed PC on protection duty round the clock. Baines wondered how an unarmed constable was supposed to stop a determined gunman, but it hadn't been his shout.

Clark was propped up in bed watching daytime TV. Anyone seeing him for the first time would have been surprised that a puny figure with bad skin and thick spectacles could command a teenage gang, even one as pathetic as The Barracudas. What it took a while to appreciate was that, underneath all the street talk and tough posturing there was a sharp brain that could have been much better employed gaining a good education and setting its owner up for a lucrative career.

As Baines approached the bed, he saw that Brandon Clark wasn't actually watching the TV at all. He tried to slip the book he had been reading under the covers, but his movements were still sluggish after his injury and the operation to remove the bullet. He finished up fumbling the paperback onto the floor.

"Let me get that for you," Baines said, bending down. He inspected the cover. "My word, Brandon. Dickens. And you act as if you can't read." He tossed the book to Bell. "What do you make of that? Required reading for a tough gang leader?"

Bell made a show of flicking through the pages. "Doesn't seem to be a comic hidden inside."

"Give me me book, man," Clark protested in the street accent that had become trendy with young people in recent years.

"Give the man his book, Constable," said Baines, helping himself to the chair by the bed. "So, Brandon. I gather you'd like to talk to me, so here I am, obeying your summons to audience."

Clark looked at him suspiciously. "What?"

He sighed. "What did you want to say to me, Brandon? Do you know who shot you?"

Brandon Clark found something interesting on the bedspread to look at as he mumbled something.

"I didn't catch that."

Clark still didn't meet his gaze. "It was Michael Sturridge, innit."

"Sturridge? The leader of The Bloods?"

"I don't know no other dude by that name."

Sturridge was as well known to the force as Clark himself was. His brother Ryan, 19 and a real hard case, had started the gang. Their father had long since buggered off, and their mother didn't give a toss about her boys, being more interested in working her way through all the lowlife males in Aylesbury and getting pissed every night.

As a result, neither of the boys was especially well-adjusted. Ryan was doing time for aggravated assault, and Michael was essentially keeping his seat warm until he was released.

Michael Sturridge was at the opposite end of the spectrum to Clark in appearance and personality type. Six foot two and built like a brick outhouse, he had a kind of low cunning, rather than the genuine intelligence his opposite number in The Barracudas tried to play down. He dominated his gang by the threat of - and sometimes the use of - violence, whilst Clark's leadership appeared to be more about his character.

Baines personally suspected that Michael was only able to keep control due to the threat of Ryan returning. It was like some low-grade version of The Godfather, only without the horse's head, and definitely without any of the charm or style.

Still, Baines was shocked at the notion of Sturridge getting hold of and using a gun. He had thought The Bloods' leader's fists were his weapons of choice, and he'd privately speculated that some newcomer to the gang might be trying to make a name for himself by escalating their rivalry with The Barracudas to a new level.

"So tell me what happened."

"Not much to tell. I went into the shop for some ciggies. I come out, went to light up, and this car drove by. I see Michael Sturridge in the passenger seat with a gun. He shot me."

"Who was at the wheel?"

"I dunno, man. All I see was Sturridge."

"What sort of car?"

"I dunno. It all happened so fast."

"Colour, then. You must remember the colour."

"I'm not sure. Blue, maybe. Maybe green."

"Was there anyone else around who could corroborate your story?"

"What?"

Baines was beginning to lose his patience. "Stop acting dumb, Brandon. I know you're smarter than you try to let on. You know what corroborate means. And do me a favour and get rid of the bad accent. You're rubbish at it."

Clark mumbled again.

"And, for Christ's sake, speak up," snarled Baines.

"I said I dunno if anyone saw it. I was dying, man. I'd been shot, innit."

Either he was ignoring Baines' comments about this phoney accent, or it was such a habit he didn't even know he was doing it.

"But you're sure it was Sturridge?"

"I don't think he's got a doppelganger."

"Doppelganger? Careful, Brandon, your intellect's showing. Fancy word, eh Constable?"

"Very fancy," Bell agreed.

"All right then," Baines said to Clark. "The other thing I want to know is this. Are The Barracudas going to take this lying down? Because if I hear that one of your lot has got hold of a gun..."

"I don't want no gun war," Clark said, meeting his eyes for the first time. "To be honest with you, I'm sick of the whole gang thing. I might break The Barracudas up when I get out of here in a couple of days."

"Break up your gang?"

"Yeah."

Instinct told Baines not to pursue it, even though he doubted that even Clark could break up the gang if they didn't want to break up. A new leader, with less brains and more brawn, would emerge - perhaps escalating the conflict to new levels of violence.

"So you're saying it was Michael Sturridge who shot you."

"Yeah."

"Well, we'll be looking into that. You take care." He pointed at the book on the bedside table. "You should stick to reading the classics, Brandon. No one ever got shot for reading a book."

"You think? There are countries all over the world that ban books, man. And they execute people caught reading them."

Baines suppressed a smile. "Not Dickens though, eh?"

As he and Bell walked back to their car, he decided that Clark really was wasted running a little gang on the Northfields estate.

He also thought about the teenager's account of what had happened to him. There was something way too glib about it, as if Clark had felt he had to give the police a name. Had he picked on Sturridge as the obvious candidate, or was he telling the truth?

Of one thing, Baines was certain. Brandon Clark was very frightened of something.

* * *

It had been a slow morning for Archer so far. She needed Joan Collins to come back to her with some more information about the figure on the CCTV tape before she could make much progress with that. And, after yesterday's fiasco, she wasn't going to attempt to question Richard Merritt any further for fear of finishing him off.

She also wanted to pay Buckinghamshire Social Services a visit to see what Stephanie Merritt had been working on in the recent past, but she had been holding off - hoping for some snippet of information that might point to something specific, rather than go in with a blunderbuss approach that would eat up time and probably shed little light on the case. In the event, nothing useful looked likely to materialise, and she had asked Collins to set up a meeting for first thing tomorrow morning.

Despite yesterday's drama, and the fact that the person on Collins' tape was so obviously not Richard Merritt, she hadn't taken the victim's husband out of the frame yet. It was just possible that old Mrs Hathaway had simply seen someone passing through, or visiting a neighbour, and that they had nothing to do with the murder. She had dispatched a couple of uniforms to ask if anyone else had seen the mysterious hoodie, or better still knew something about him.

At least Steve Ashby hadn't been in the office at all this morning. She wondered if he was off following leads, or whether he was a skiver. Either way, as far as she was concerned, the less she saw of him, the more she thought she might like it.

Baines had provided her with the files on all the cases he'd had on the go when she relieved him, and she was leafing through them when a call came through to her that they had Andrea Bowmaker, the Merritts' daughter, in reception asking to see her.

Andrea was shown into an interview room and sat opposite Archer, looking daggers at her.

"So how's your dad?" Archer ventured.

"They seem to think it was only a mild heart attack. No thanks to you."

"Andrea, I'm really sorry about what happened to your dad, but we were only asking him a few questions."

"He said you were practically accusing him."

"We need to know where everyone was when your mum was attacked. We'll need to know where you were."

"What? I'm a suspect now?"

Suddenly weary, Archer said, "I really am sorry your dad got ill, and I'm glad he's getting better. But if you want to make a complaint -"

"I do. But it's not what Dad wants. He asked me to give you these."

She opened her bag and produced a small plastic bag, which she handed over. Inside was a diary and piece of paper torn from a notebook with a list of four names. Alongside each name was some detail.

"He said you wanted the names, and he's added what he knows about how they got on with Mum. You'll find her appointments with them in the diary."

"That's really helpful," Archer said sincerely. It was more than she'd expected. She hesitated. "I don't suppose there are more diaries?"

"Sorry. Mum used to shred the old one as soon as she started a new one. Something about data protection. Dad used to nag her that she'd want to refer back to something, but she said she never had yet. Is it really useful?"

"It's really useful."

"And will it help you catch the bastard who killed Mum?"

"It will help us focus our investigations, Andrea, but it's early days. Do you know of anyone who might have wanted to hurt your mum?"

"Course not. Everyone loved her. This must have been some sick pervert. Some sort of psycho." She started to cry. "Poor Dad. He says every time he closes his eyes he can see her lying there." She swiped the tears away. "You catch him, Inspector. It's the least my mum deserves."

* * *

Archer had transferred the names and details from Richard Merritt's list to a table on her computer, and was going through dates in her diaries relating to the names when Baines tapped on her door frame and wished her a good morning.

"How was the Holiday Inn?"

She shrugged. "Comfy enough. How was the hospital?"

"Same old, same old." He glanced at the file open on her desk. "Have you read up on the Brandon Clark case yet?"

"Haven't got to it yet. Any progress?"

"He's changed his tune from, 'I didn't see nothing' to, 'It was Michael Sturridge'."

"Sturridge being?"

"Leader of The Bloods. A fathead. I can imagine him deciding to raise the ante with a gun, but..."

"But you're not convinced?"

"Brandon could have fingered him days ago. Why now? And he's talking about shutting The Barracudas down. His power base."

"Maybe being shot gave him some sort of epiphany. Maybe he re-evaluated his life and has decided he wants to devote it to world peace."

He looked sceptical.

"I take it you're going to talk to Sturridge?"

"That's why I dropped in. I wondered if you'd like to come."

It was tempting to get out of the office and do something. "No," she decided. "I'd like to, but I want to be here in the early stages of the Merritt case. Besides, I'd like you to keep running with the Clark case."

He stopped leaning on the doorpost and took a step towards her. "I hope I'm not being sidelined from Merritt."

She rubbed her tired eyes and fixed him with a steely stare. Why did he have to do this? Get the hump over everything?

"No, Sergeant, you're not being sidelined. I've got a feeling that this investigation is going to need every pair of hands I can get hold of, and that certainly includes yours. But we can't neglect other cases, and the Clark shooting is important. If we cock it up, we could see the Northfields estate going up in flames."

"I doubt it. Clark's bright enough, but the rest of them are wankers and wannabes."

"In my experience, they're the most dangerous kind. Some of them will be looking for their fifteen minutes of fame. I want to get a result sooner rather than later."

His demeanour changed as though she had flicked a switch. "You mean Gillingham's leaning on you and you want me to rush it? Get a name in the frame? Clark fingers Sturridge and that's good enough for you, is it?"

Her own anger flared.

"For Christ's sake, Dan, get over yourself. I was showing a bit of faith in you, that's all. Maybe it was misplaced. I thought you'd actually want to see the case through, seeing as you've been leading on it so far."

He was silent for a moment. When he spoke again he sounded a little remorseful. "Yeah, well, I do, but I want to do it properly."

"So do I. Let me give you a piece of advice, Dan."

He stood there stiffly, looking as if the last thing in the world he required was advice from Lizzie Archer. Tough. He was going to get it.

"It's pretty clear that you resent me coming in over your head and you being bumped back down to Sergeant. Maybe you thought the job was in the bag. Well, I'm here because I wanted a transfer, not because I wanted to kick DS Baines in the teeth. And, if you want your career to go anywhere, you'll do it by showing me how good you are. Not by sulking all the time, and not by vanishing from a crime scene with no real explanation."

"Finished?" He all but sneered. "Because I've got work to do."

"Don't take that tone with me, Sergeant."

"No, ma'am."

She sighed, not wanting to let it drop, yet too tired to keep it up either.

"So what's your next move?"

He shrugged, his point - whatever precisely it was - apparently made. "There's something about this shooting that we're just not seeing. I mean, I'll talk to Sturridge, but I reckon Brandon's just trying to deflect us from something he's scared of talking about. And Brandon Clark doesn't scare so easily."

"Do you think there's a new gang on the estate? Tougher, ready to resort to firearms?"

"I'd have thought I'd have heard, but I'll ask Sturridge, for what it's worth.

"Tell you what," she said. "I'll skim the file after work, see if anything jumps out at me. Give you my first impressions of Clark."

"That would be good."

He was about to leave when Joan Collins appeared in the doorway.

"Is this a bad time, ma'am?"

"No, Joan. DS Baines was just leaving, but he might like to wait and hear this, if it's an update on Merritt."

"It is. Ibrahim managed to enhance and enlarge the CCTV footage. The car was a '97 plate Vauxhall Astra. But here's the interesting thing. It was stolen the day before yesterday and found this morning on Aston Hill, burned out. It was assumed to be joy riders."

"And now it's more likely a killer, making sure any evidence he might have left on the car has been destroyed."

"I've contacted the SOCOs about seeing if they can salvage anything."

"Good. Thanks, Joan."

"By the way, we've had our first confession."

"Don't tell me," Baines said. "Kenny Vaughan."

"Got it in one. It seems that Stephanie Merritt was a filthy whore and he strangled her."

"He always strangled them," Baines grinned. "Good thing we're keeping the probable murder weapon away from the media, so we can filter out nutters like Kenny."

"Yes, well, he's having a cup of tea and a biscuit, and then we'll give him a nice ride home in a police car, as per usual."

Collins left them to it. Archer told Baines about Richard Merritt's list and Stephanie's diary.

"I'm going to make an appointment to see Social Services in the morning and I'd like you to come along. In the meantime, I'm going to get the team together in an hour or so to make sure we all know everything about the case. Will you be back from Sturridge by then?"

"Depends how long it takes to find him. Can you make it two hours?"

"Okay, sure. I'd like you there."

"How soon can you look at the Clark file?"

She gave him a rueful smile. "Life's such a giddy social whirl, I don't know. Probably over my room service dinner."

He hesitated and then said, "Suppose I swing round to your hotel around nine and meet you in the bar? We could have that drink and you could tell me what you think about the case. If you want, that is."

She regretted her sad remark about room service dinner. He probably felt sorry for her. Carrying her scar had made her hate pity even more than revulsion. But she did want to spend an hour with Baines off duty, away from the office. Try and get past the friction between them, if she could.

"Nine is good," she said. "You're buying."

9

Baines had heard of some housing estates that were so rough that even the police dogs went around mob-handed - and that was in broad daylight.

Aylesbury's Northfields estate wasn't quite that bad. Yet.

Built in the 1970s, with a mix of flats and family housing, it was occupied by an uneasy blend of what politicians call 'hardworking families' and some of the more disadvantaged members of the local society. It had never had an antisocial behaviour problem of any note until The Bloods and The Barracudas had sprung up about a year ago.

Even then, the two groups of school-age teenagers had at first been little more than background noise. A little bit of drug dealing was rumoured but never proven, there had been a couple of inter-gang fights, and some of the walls on the estate had been targeted by self-styled graffiti 'artists'. By far the biggest problem they had caused was the mess made by the cans and takeaway boxes they casually discarded on a daily basis.

But Ryan Sturridge in particular, the Bloods' original leader, had soon got bored with such small-time stuff. By the time he was sent away for beating up an Asian youth who had 'looked at him funny', his small gang were thought to be raising their game in the local drugs trade, and violence between the rival factions was on an upward spiral. Members on both sides had been stabbed, and a fatality was surely a matter of time.

Both the gangs claimed to 'own' Northfields. Ask the average resident and they would insist they didn't know what you were talking about. The last thing people wanted to do was make themselves a target.

By the time Baines caught up with Michael Sturridge around lunch time, doses of paracetamol had finally despatched his headache. The current boss of The Bloods was sitting on an old sofa outside the block of flats where he lived with his mother. He was barely sixteen and ought to have been at school, but he had been excluded so many times that he had effectively dropped out, despite the system's attempts to pretend that it was still educating him.

Sturridge had a couple of his mates - also probably truanting - with him, and they were all playing with hand held computer games. The chances were that these had been extracted with menaces from kids who could afford them. Sturridge held the lead of a large scruffy mongrel with lots of teeth that he doubtless imagined looked menacing and added to his hard image.

He wore a black tee-shirt with a white skull and crossbones emblazoned across it, underneath which 'Pure Poison' was inscribed in red letters.

"Well, well," he said as Baines and Bell approached, picking their way though litter. "Look what the cat sicked up."

"It's good to see you too, Michael."

"You been busted back to foot patrol, Mr Baines? Caught with your hand in the till?"

Sturridge sniggered and his sycophants followed suit. Baines thought too much of this humour might split his sides.

"I've come to talk some more about Brandon Clark," he said, cutting to the chase.

"Is he dead?"

"Why? Would that make you happy?"

Michael Sturridge shifted his muscled bulk. "It wouldn't break my heart. Pity the twat who did it was a lousy shot."

"Yes? What kind of shot are you, Michael?"

"I told you before - I don't do guns. None of my boys do. It don't mean that guy wouldn't have been doing me a favour. Pain in the arse, is Brandon."

"You know, it's funny. If the pair of you are to be believed, none of you shower has anything to do with guns. Yet here we are with Brandon lying in hospital with a gunshot wound. And you know what? A little bird said you were the guy who pulled the trigger."

Sturridge leapt from his seat, all belligerence and wounded feelings. His mongrel obviously thought a walk was in prospect. It bounded about, barking and wrapping the lead around its owner's legs.

"Shut it, Noddy," he snapped, yanking on the lead.

"Noddy?" Baines grinned widely.

"Where's Big Ears?" Bell wanted to know.

"Look, man," Sturridge growled as he untangled his legs, "I dunno who told you them lies." He drew himself up to his full height, dwarfing the two officers. "I was nowhere near that shop when the Barracuda Boy got what was coming to him. These two will vouch for me."

"Oh, well, that's all right then. Two unimpeachable sources."

"What can I tell you? I went through all this when he first got shot. Did you think I was gonna change my story?"

"Anything's possible. Can anyone any more reliable back you up?"

"You saying my bros are liars?"

Another crap accent. "Perish the thought. Interesting that you say Mr Clark had it coming, though. Maybe you didn't pull the trigger. Maybe you just made the arrangements."

"You got nothing." But the bravado rang false. Baines couldn't decide if that was because he had a hand in the shooting or was merely nervous about being accused of it.

Baines was about to retort when something moved in his peripheral vision. He turned his head, caught a flash of blue and white, and then it was gone. He fixed his gaze on the spot for a moment or two more and then became aware that everyone was looking at him.

"We'll speak to you and Noddy again," he told Sturridge.

"Or just Noddy," Bell added. "If we want an intelligent conversation."

Sturridge eyed them suspiciously. "Is that it? Why did you pigs come here?"

"To keep you on your toes, Michael. Don't let Gilbert and Sullivan tell you that a policeman's lot is not a happy one."

"Gilbert and who?"

"Ask Brandon," Baines threw over his shoulder as he and Bell walked away.

"So what do you think?" Bell asked once they were out of earshot.

"Either Clark or Sturridge, or both, are liars," Baines told him. "My gut instinct is that it's both of them."

"You believe Sturridge's two muppets then?"

"He hasn't got any other alibis, and I know those two wouldn't know the truth if it bit them. But I think I would."

"Still... Might be worth getting his place turned over."

"I'll talk to the new boss about a warrant, but I suspect even Michael Sturridge wouldn't be so stupid as to keep the gun at home. But you never know. He could prove me wrong. The question is, though - if neither of them is telling the truth, then someone else did the shooting. Someone Clark is scared of."

"Or protecting."

"That's hardly likely, is it? No, for my money there's a much bigger fish than either The Barracudas or The Bloods swimming in our pool. Maybe even a shark. We need to catch him before there are any more shootings."

* * *

DCI Gillingham had got wind of Archer's team meeting and decided to sit in. She decided to be charitable and see it as moral support. But it felt more like he was looking over her shoulder.

Baines and Bell walked in just as she was starting, and it was Gillingham who sarcastically thanked him for joining them. She was extremely irritated, as she'd known in advance that Baines would be pushing it to be on time. Now it would look like further unfair criticism, further undermining her as a manager.

As the two latecomers found seats, Archer began again.

"Stephanie Merritt," she said, pointing to the photograph on the wall. "Beaten to death, almost certainly with a hammer, some time around 8 o'clock yesterday morning."

She ran through Richard Merritt's story of leaving for work and the train disruption that led to him returning home and discovering the body sooner than he would otherwise have done. Then she mentioned Mrs Hathaway's sighting of a hooded figure disappearing into the alley at about the right time of morning before handing over to DC Collins.

Collins told the gathering about the CCTV footage, the figure that matched Mrs Hathaway's description, and the burned out car.

"Two new things, though, ma'am," she said. "First of all, I've gone back though earlier footage, and the car first appears in the car park at four in the morning."

"When he's least likely to be spotted breaking into the house opposite. And the second?"

"Our killer wasn't as clever as he thought he was if he imagined torching the car would remove any evidence of its involvement in the crime. The SOCOs have already collected some traces of blood, and they're sending it to the lab for comparison with the victim's."

"Any prints off the door handles or steering wheel?"

"Yes, but smudged. They've got partials, and they'll try to match them, but they think it's most likely they're the owner's and the killer wore gloves."

"DI Archer, you mentioned the empty house opposite the Merritts," said Gillingham. "Did the SOCOs find anything of interest there?"

"No, sir. Like the primary crime scene, they found no physical traces of the killer, but there were some tell-tale signs suggesting that the break-in was very recent."

"What sort of signs?"

"Such as the disturbance of dust. It reinforces the likelihood that Stephanie Merritt's murderer had used the property as a vantage point from which to choose his moment."

"Hold on," Baines said. He's in there from four until gone eight, and he didn't even use the loo?"

"If he did, he was very house proud about it," Archer replied, getting a chuckle from around the table. "DS Baines, did you get anywhere with forensics about the murder weapon?"

"They called me on my way back here." He turned to Gillingham. "I asked about the possibility of identifying the murder weapon from the victim's injuries, sir."

"Any use?"

"Pretty limited. They reckon they can work out what type of hammer it probably was, but that's about it. And they doubt whether even that would stand much scrutiny in a court of law. The best they could do is add a very small amount of weight to the rest of our evidence."

"If we found the hammer," Gillingham commented.

"If we found the hammer," Baines agreed.

"There's one other thing," Archer said, keen to crack on. "Richard Merritt has given me a list of names of clients that he knows Stephanie had trouble with, and he's also given me her diary with this year's appointments in them. I'm drawing up a short list of possibles to interview, although I want to liaise with Social Services first. I've got a meeting fixed for tomorrow morning."

"Okay," said Gillingham. "Progress of sorts, but it's early days. It looks as if this mystery hoodie is our primary line of enquiry for now?"

"It's always possible that he was just some sort of vagrant. He could have identified the house as a potential doss earlier on, stolen the car, had a few hours' kip, and then left."

"But you don't think so."

"Too coincidental. We've drawn a blank with the Merritts' neighbours, but somebody else may have seen something. I'd like to put out an appeal for anyone who saw him or the car. Especially if anyone caught a glimpse of his face."

"Agreed. Let's see if we can set up a press conference for tomorrow afternoon. If we can get a member of the family involved in making an appeal, so much the better, but not the husband. We can do without him having a second coronary on the telly."

10

Peter Nish stepped out of Walker & Scott's Aylesbury offices. The early evening sky had a Turneresque quality about it, a patchwork of different shades of grey. There might be rain in the air, maybe even thunder. He realised he had no idea what the forecast was. Every night, after the ten o'clock news, some bouncy weather man or girl would come on the screen, waving their hands over a map of the UK, but it mostly washed over him these days.

And Jenny never commented. She usually had her nose stuck in a book or a crossword. He strongly suspected that she wouldn't notice if they were forecasting the ten plagues of Egypt. God knows, it was a long time since she'd last really noticed him.

26 years of marriage. Two sons - one working in Scotland, the other away at University in Exeter. Neither of them could have got very much further away from their parents without going abroad. Peter and Jenny left in a mostly empty nest, leading almost separate existences.

He took out his phone and speed-dialled a familiar number. When he got an answer, he said, as he did every Tuesday around this time, "It's Peter. Are we still on for tonight?"

And, as every Tuesday evening, the voice on the other end replied, "Of course. Looking forward to it."

"I'm on my way."

He hung up, glanced at his car in the car park, and began the short walk to his destination.

As far as Jenny was concerned, he spent his Tuesday evenings having a drink with two former colleagues, Gerald and Dean. She had never met them, knew very little about them. She would occasionally ask him how they were, in a perfunctory sort of way. He would say they were fine, might even embellish it with a little story like, "Gerald's been on holiday. Greece again." Or, "Dean's had a little bout of the flu. He's fine now."

He wasn't sure why he bothered. Just because Jenny could occasionally be bothered to ask the question, it didn't mean she actually listened to the answer. He was becoming increasingly tempted to casually tell her that Gerald had joined MI5 with a licence to kill and that Dean's entire family had been kidnapped by pirates or white slavers. Just to see if she was paying attention.

But he didn't, because her lack of interest suited him fine. The thing about Gerald and Dean was that they didn't exist.

Jenny might not pay him much attention, but he didn't think she'd be happy to ignore what he really did on a Tuesday night, if she ever found out. He might not be happy in his marriage, but he had no stomach for divorce.

That was the effect that his years as a family law solicitor had done to him. Divorces, disputes over children, money and property, domestic violence. In the end, it all blurred into a single squalid mass.

Peter Nish's destination was only a ten-minute walk away. The street was quiet and respectable, and no red light burned outside number 11. Yet he found it hard to believe that the neighbours didn't know how Geraldine made her living. He was hardly the only gentleman caller she received in the course of her day, and she had once confessed to being a workaholic. She certainly went about her job with enthusiasm.

Nish walked up the front garden path, pausing to smell the flowers, and rang the front doorbell. He could hear the chimes echoing in the hall.

She answered almost immediately. Before he'd plucked up courage to answer her ad in the local paper, he'd always imagined that women in her profession would probably come to the door wearing a filmy black negligee.

Geraldine wore a loose cotton blouse and a skirt. She looked sexy but ordinary, which was what he liked about her.

She closed the door behind them and offered him both cheeks to kiss. He extracted an envelope from his inside pocket, a familiar routine by now.

"This is for you," he said.

"Thank you." She spirited it away into a room he assumed was her office and returned smiling. "So why don't you go and take a shower, and I'll open a bottle of champagne and meet you in the bedroom."

As he ran the shower, he stripped off his clothes, looking forward to washing away the grime of the day and to the delights that lay ahead. It was only three hours a week, but it made the rest of his week almost bearable.

He stood under the shower, imagining Geraldine setting the ice bucket on the dressing table and turning back the bedclothes. But she wouldn't undress until he was there. She knew how he liked to watch her taking her clothes off.

Showered and shampooed, he towelled himself dry, combed his damp hair, and slipped on the robe she had left for him. He sometimes wondered how many robes she owned, and whether she sent them to a laundry or washed them all herself.

He knew his way around the house by now. The study was out of bounds, and there was a second bedroom that he always assumed was for sleeping rather than business. The main bedroom, where Geraldine awaited him, was at the end of the landing. He let himself in, and she rose from the bed, where she had been lounging, came up to him and kissed him full on the mouth.

"We're going to have fun tonight," she said as she moved to the sideboard, removed the bottle from the ice bucket and began to pour. "I have a feeling this is going to be one of those nights to remember."

Peter sat down on the edge of the bed and she handed him a glass. Then her fingers moved to the buttons of her blouse, undoing them slowly, teasingly. Never taking his eyes from her, he sipped his champagne, little shivers running up his spine. As she dropped the blouse on the floor and unzipped her skirt, he raised his glass.

"A night to remember. Here's to that."

He did not know how true his words were.

11

DI Archer was sitting at a table reading a paperback novel when Baines showed up in the Holiday Inn's Hub Bar just after 9 pm. She had changed out of her work clothes and now wore a simple red shirt with dark blue trousers.

Baines himself was in jeans and a blue polo shirt, and he suddenly felt unaccountably awkward about meeting a female senior officer here in casual clothes. It had something of the feeling of a date about it, which couldn't be further from the truth, given the tension between them. He was happy enough to acknowledge that she seemed a very competent detective, but she needed to work on her people skills, as least as far as he was concerned.

He still seethed when he thought about her so-called advice. She'd obviously been telling him his card had been marked. He had especially not liked her reminding him of his 'disappearance from a crime scene' yesterday morning in Wendover. He hadn't forgotten she'd half-accused him of slipping into the Red Lion for a sneaky pint.

And the worst of it was, he could hardly tell her he'd been chasing the shadow of some phantom teenager he'd thought might be his missing son.

He shook off the thought as he reached her, determined to try and mend some fences tonight. Looking up, she pointed to a half-empty pint glass in front of her.

"I'm a bit ahead of you, I'm afraid. She handed him the little cardboard holder that held her room key card. "Get yourself a drink, and I'll have another half of Stella. Charge it to my room."

As he stood at the bar being served, he looked back at her. It was a shame about her scar, he thought. She would have been a very good-looking woman otherwise. He wondered what the story was. He supposed it must be to do with the injury she had suffered in the course of duty. Seeing as how she was clearly very touchy about it, there was no way he was going to ask her.

He opted for a pint of Stella Artois to go with her half and watched her expertly add her beer to the contents of the larger glass.

"Cheers, ma'am," he said, raising his glass.

"Cheers," she acknowledged, "but I think you can drop all that ma'am stuff. To be honest, I don't much care for it at the best of times. It makes me feel like The Queen, or someone's maiden aunt. Lizzie is fine off duty, or outside formal meetings. Okay?"

"Fine by me. So what did your last team call you?"

"Guv, usually. Boss, sometimes."

He tried them on in his mind. DI Britton had always been 'boss' to him.

"Tell you what," he decided. "I'll call you guv in briefings and maybe the team will drop the ma'am too. Probably not a good idea to make a thing of it."

"Thanks." She took another swallow of lager. "You never really got to tell me how you got on with Michael Sturridge."

He set his own pint down and watched condensation trickle down the side of the glass. "I don't exactly see him as a credible suspect. I have to say that the only people who can vouch that he was nowhere near the scene of the shooting when it occurred are two of his half-witted henchmen, but it still doesn't feel right."

"Worth tossing his home?"

"That's what Bell suggested, but I don't know. He must have known he might be a suspect. He was probably reading a comic upside down when the brains were handed out, but even someone as thick as Michael isn't going to have the gun on his premises. If he did do it, surely he'll have dumped the gun or lodged it with somebody else."

"So where does that leave us?"

He puffed out his cheeks. "Pretty stymied. I still think Brandon's hiding something. Maybe Sturridge too. I'm half-wondering if there's a new gang in town that we've yet to hear about. Maybe someone a bit scarier than the devils we know." He reached for his glass. "Did you get a chance to look over the file?"

"I've had a skim through. I'm not saying you've missed anything, but a couple of things puzzled me."

"Go on."

"Brandon was shot after buying cigarettes, right?"

"Right."

"Well, in the shopkeeper's statement, Brandon was in there with his little brother. Marcus? They left the shop and, about three minutes later, he and his customers heard the shot. While they dither over whether it was a car backfiring or whether to risk checking outside, Brandon staggers inside, blood everywhere, saying he's been shot. He collapses and the shopkeeper calls an ambulance."

"Sounds right."

"About three minutes, Dan? What was Brandon Clark doing outside the shop for three minutes?"

Baines sipped his drink, waiting to see where she was going with this.

"Then there's the statement by the brother. He says that after he and Brandon left the shop, he decided to run home to catch a TV programme. Brandon wasn't prepared to run. Marcus claims the shooting must have happened after he was round the corner and out of sight. He didn't see or hear anything."

"So?" But an alarm bell was sounding in his head.

"Do you really buy it, Dan? Don't you think it's all a bit too tidy?"

Baines' stomach flipped over as he saw her point.

"I didn't attend when the emergency call first came in," he said, perhaps a tad defensively. "I think it was only a couple of uniforms originally. But Marcus definitely wasn't there when they arrived at the scene."

"Maybe Clark sent him away. Maybe he waited for someone. A few minutes later, that someone arrived and, for some reason, shot him. Or maybe Marcus saw the whole thing and bolted, and now he's scared to say anything. You need to talk to the brother again."

Baines felt a flush creeping up his collar. He couldn't believe he'd missed that. In fairness to himself, DI Ashby had been the original Senior Investigating Officer, but DCI Gillingham had soon transferred the case to Baines, claiming pressure of work on Ashby.

In Baines' opinion, Ashby was a lazy, sloppy bastard who didn't know the meaning of pressure. He and Gillingham went back a long way, and the DCI seemed to cut him a fair bit of slack. Ashby hadn't covered all the bases properly, but Baines knew he had let himself down by not reading the reports carefully enough.

"Jesus," he said finally. "What a cock up."

"Don't beat yourself up until you know whether it's material," she said. "And, if it is material, I'll beat you up myself."

He tried to gauge whether she was joking and found that he wasn't sure.

"Amazingly, Marcus Clark has never been in any trouble," he said. "But then he's quite a bit younger than Brandon, so it's early days."

"How much younger?"

"He's nine, maybe ten."

"See him tomorrow afternoon, after school. In fact, why don't we both go? A woman might be a bit reassuring."

"You mean I can be the bad cop?"

"Why, Sergeant, I don't know what you mean." With a 'butter wouldn't melt' expression, she reached for her drink. "Anyway, this is a 'getting to know you' session, and so far all we've done is talk shop."

"And we haven't even got onto the Merritt murder yet."

She smiled faintly. "You know, I thought the pace of life would be a good deal slower when I came here. I didn't expect all this murder and mayhem. It's not like Aylesbury Vale is renowned as a hotbed of crime, is it?"

"We have our moments. I've attended some pretty grisly murders. And don't forget that one of the 7/7 bombers lived in Aylesbury."

A 19-year-old Aylesbury resident had been one of four suicide bombers who had wreaked carnage on the London transport system on 7 July 2005, detonating his bomb between King's Cross and Russell Square, and killing 27 people including himself.

"True," she acknowledged. "And then there was the Invisible Man, of course. What was that - about ten years ago?"

Baines could feel his jaw clenching. "Eleven."

"I don't suppose you happened to have worked that case?"

He stared at her, wondering if it was a cruel wind-up. But her response to his angry expression was visible confusion.

And then the penny dropped.

"My God." He was aghast. "He didn't tell you, did he? Gillingham?"

"Tell me what?" The words were barely out when her hands flew upwards as if she would stuff them back into her mouth.

"Oh, fuck," she said. "I remember now. There was an officer on the investigation whose own family were targeted. His little boy..." Her hands moved to her temples. "Oh, shit. That was you, wasn't it?"

He simply nodded.

"Oh, Jesus, Dan, I'm so sorry. You've got to believe I had no idea. I mean, Gillingham did say you'd lost your family a long time ago. He wouldn't say any more. He said you'd tell me yourself if you wanted. I'd just assumed it was a car crash or something. Not that that wouldn't be bad enough. But this?" Her distress was visible. "I don't know what to say."

He sighed, reaching for some sort of calm. "Like you say, you weren't to know. How could you? Gillingham should have told you."

Like he should have warned me about her scar.

"I know it was all over the news at the time," she said, "but I'd honestly forgotten the details, or the officer's name. I would never have mouthed off like that. Putting my sodding big foot in it. A thing like that... How do you ever get over it?"

"You don't," he said simply. "If you're lucky, I suppose you learn to live with it, although I'm not sure even that's true in my case." He looked her in the eye. "I'm still in touch with Neil Mahon, you know. His wife was the Invisible man's first victim, and his daughter Chloe was found at the second scene a week later. He said it had left scars on his soul, but I think he understated it. For me, the pain goes way deeper than that."

Archer unconsciously touched her own scar. The gesture wasn't lost on Baines.

"Bugger," he said. "Now who's saying the wrong thing?"

She touched the line that bisected her cheek again. "This?" She shrugged, trying, he suspected, to appear casual. "I know I'm touchy about it. I'm really trying not to be."

"Would you mind if I asked how..." He tailed off, afraid he may have overstepped the line.

She picked up her pint again, toyed with it, then put it down untouched.

"You know how it is. Wrong place, wrong time..."

12

So Archer told him about the lunchtime drink. The altercation at the bar. The broken bottle. Her intervention, and its disastrous consequences for herself.

What she didn't tell Baines was how lucky she'd been that the knife-like shards had somehow missed her eye and the facial artery. How she'd been less lucky in that some branches of the facial nerve had been damaged, which, despite the surgeon's best efforts, had left her with a slightly lopsided smile. How, after the initial surgery, during which the wound had been trimmed to remove the jagged edges and then carefully sutured layer by layer, she'd had to wait another nine long months before the surgeon was prepared to excise the scar and re-suture it.

That had been summer last year. She had been told then that the scar would continue to fade for perhaps another year to eighteen months, but would never become completely invisible. She had tried growing her hair long to hide it, but it wouldn't hang right and just looked like she was trying to cover it up - which she felt simply drew all the more attention to it. She had experimented with various makeups and spoken to experts in cosmetic cover-up, but hadn't been particularly impressed with the results. Whatever she did, the face that looked back at her from the mirror was that of a freak. A monster.

But what she especially didn't want to get into with Baines was how badly the incident had affected her. How it had destroyed what she had with Rob. The impact on her self-confidence around people, all of whom she was always convinced were staring at her in revulsion or, worse still, pity. And the way it had changed her attitude to dangerous situations.

Once she had been accused by her superiors of over-confidence bordering on recklessness. She had gone fearlessly into dark places where she knew menace and violence might be lurking. Now she was reluctant to do so, fearful of being hurt again.

Fearful that, next time, she might not be so lucky.

She hated it. And she hated that she might have lost her edge irrevocably. Before she was hurt, she had been a high-flyer, tipped as Assistant Chief Constable material. Now she wondered if she would even make DCI, especially now she was effectively starting her career over again in this unfamiliar place.

She picked up her glass and took a long drink, hoping Baines would change the subject now. But he didn't.

"Shit. What happened to the bastard who did it?"

"Malicious wounding. He got five years."

"He should have got life."

She really didn't want to talk about it any more. She didn't know why she'd told him at all. "Mm."

"So, what did the doctors say about it? The scar, I mean?"

"Can we talk about something else, Dan? You asked me how I got it, and I told you. I don't want to go into all the ins and outs."

For a moment, he looked slapped. Then remorseful. "Sorry Lizzie," Baines said. "A bit too nosy. Comes of being a detective."

They continued to drink in awkward silence, neither of them entirely sure how to get the conversation back on track.

* * *

Peter Nish had indeed had a night to remember. Geraldine had been at her voracious best, and still managed to come up with new ways of pleasuring him after all this time. Before he left, he had another shower to wash the smell of her off him.

"Same time next week?" she asked him at the door.

"Count on it," he said, and he walked back down to her front gate in buoyant mood.

Part of the subterfuge was the pretence that, after a few drinks with the fictional Gerald and Dean, he was well over the limit and thus unfit to drive. So, on a Tuesday night, he left the car at the office, got a taxi home, and got Jenny to drive him into work on Wednesday morning.

He always booked the taxi in advance and asked to be picked up from the corner of Geraldine's street. It was always possible that the local cabbies knew exactly what business was conducted at number 11, and it was also just possible that one of the drivers who picked him up might drive both Nish and his wife together on one of admittedly the rare occasions they went anywhere together. It could get a little tricky, and he didn't want to take a chance.

When he got to the corner, there was a slightly elderly Vauxhall Vectra waiting at the kerbside. It looked a bit downmarket for the firm he usually used, but there was no one else.

The driver wore a baseball cap. The face was vaguely familiar.

"This isn't your usual cab, is it?"

"No. The usual one's off the road. This is a spare."

He nodded in understanding and moved to get in the front passenger seat.

"Sorry," the driver said. "Would you mind sitting in the back?"

Nish shrugged. "I usually ride shotgun."

"New company policy."

"Christ," he muttered as he got in the back. "More red tape. You know where you're going?"

"Sure."

Peter Nish fastened his seat belt and sank back, savouring the memories of tonight's session with Geraldine. It didn't register with him that, the last time he had seen the person now driving him, they hadn't been behind the wheel of a car. Nor that the driver had not once looked straight at him.

And there was no reason at all for him to examine the steering column. A close inspection might have revealed that the car had been hotwired.

And it might have hit home to him that, this particular Tuesday night, he was in a great deal of trouble.

13

Stephanie Merritt had worked for the Children's Services Department at Buckinghamshire County Council as part of the Child Protection team. Accompanied by Baines, Archer showed up at the council offices in Aylesbury - a hulking grey lump of a building with the slowest lifts she had ever encountered - at around 10 am and were shown into the Chief Executive's office.

The office was small and modestly furnished. The CEO himself was a middle-aged man called Roger Frost. He had the beginnings of middle-age spread, hair that had seen better days, and the look of a man with one eye on retirement. He introduced the two colleagues he thought they would want to talk to for starters.

The Children's Director was called Hannah Hudson, and was about Archer's age. She looked more like a Vogue model than a senior social worker in what looked like a tailored Armani suit. Long blonde hair was tied in a ponytail.

The other person present was Stephanie's team leader, Elaine Staples. Staples was quite the opposite of the glamorous Ms Hudson. Her mousy hair looked as if she had butchered it herself with a little help from a pudding basin, her careworn face looked in desperate need of some makeup, and her clothes looked cheap and ill-fitting. She was thin and boyish, and her shoes were what once might have been called 'sensible'.

Roger Frost gestured them towards a round, dark wooden meeting table and offered them coffee. Baines looked about to accept, but Archer declined for both of them, not wanting them to be interrupted in a few minutes' time by a secretary fiddling with cups and jugs and sugar bowls. Baines looked disappointed.

Hudson slipped off her jacket and hung it on a hanger before joining them. Underneath she had on a low-cut, clingy white top. Archer observed Baines noticing her cleavage and hoped he picked up on her disapproving look.

When the five of them were seated, Frost spread his palms.

"You've come to talk about poor Stephanie. Everyone here's shocked and devastated by what's happened. It goes without saying we'll do whatever we can to help you bring her killer to justice. So what can we do to help you, Inspector?"

All eyes swivelled her way, and she resisted the urge to touch the left hand side of her face.

"What we're trying to do is get as full a picture of Stephanie's life as we can, and any ideas you might have as to who might want to harm her."

"For a start, we'd like to know which colleagues were close to Stephanie." Baines added. "Anyone she might have confided in."

"Hannah?" Frost prompted.

"I'm not really the one to ask," Hudson said. "I do try to take an interest in all my staff, but I don't follow who's mates with who." She turned to her colleague. "Elaine, you probably knew her better?"

Staples bit her lip. "I've only worked with Steph for about nine months. But she was really nice, you know. She's had some horrible cases to deal with, but she kept on believing in her job. All she wanted to do was help people." Her lip trembled and she fumbled in her bag for a tissue.

Archer resisted the urge to say they wanted information, not a testimonial, as Baines came back to the point.

"So would you call her a friend?" he wanted to know.

"Yes. We weren't especially close, but we got on well."

"Did she ever confide in you about her personal life? Or any fears she might have, connected with her work?"

She dabbed at her eyes. "She never said much to me about her life outside work." Staples pondered for a moment. "I mean, she talked about her holidays, what she'd done at the weekend, that sort of thing. But if she had rows with her husband, anything like that, she kept it to herself, as far as I was concerned."

"Was there anyone here she might have been closer to?"

"Well, there's Brian."

"Brian?"

"Brian Hughes. Another social worker. They sometimes go to lunch together."

Archer felt a stirring of interest. "As in just having the odd lunch? Or a bit more?"

"What do you mean?"

"I think the Inspector's asking if you think they might have been having an affair," Frost said.

It was an obvious question, Archer thought, but Elaine Staples seemed shocked. "No, not really."

"What does 'not really' mean?" Baines prompted.

"Well, there's always office gossip, isn't there? A man and a woman go out to lunch together, and there's the odd snide remark. But I thought it was just a friendship. Whether it was a particularly close one, I just couldn't say."

"Is he around today?"

"I saw him about ten minutes ago."

"We'll see him afterwards. Mr Frost, could you get your secretary to make sure he doesn't go anywhere, please?"

Frost went to do so. Meanwhile, Archer asked Elaine Staples how familiar she was with Stephanie Merritt's cases.

"All of them," she said. "I get regular progress reports from all my team."

"What about if it turns nasty?" Baines suggested. "Say someone gets aggressive or threatening?"

"It would be drawn to my attention straight away," she said carefully. "A note would be made on the file. It depends what you mean by aggressive, as to whether any action would be taken."

"So, do you think any of the cases Stephanie dealt with recently may have caused her to fear for her own safety?"

"No more than usual. You have to understand that we often deal with people at the worst time of their lives. Some expect us to make everything all right for them, and get frustrated when we can't. Sometimes there are child protection issues, or questions of domestic abuse, and things can get ugly whether the allegations are true or not."

"I get it," said Baines. "If there's one thing worse than being investigated when you are an abuser, it's being investigated when you're not."

"We often act on reports from relations or neighbours, or from teachers at the children's schools. I suppose no one likes to feel they're being snooped on."

"Still, actual violence is quite rare?"

"It's all too common actually, but not an every day occurrence, no."

"Yet I heard she was on the receiving end of some physical violence not so long ago," said Archer. "Did you hear about that?"

Staples nodded. "About eight weeks ago. Maybe longer." She looked awkward. "A mother slapped her and spat on her. I think there were threats of worse, too." She looked at Hudson. "I don't know if I can go into names, or details..."

Archer ignored that for now. "How did she respond to that? Did it make her scared?"

"She said it could have been worse and that it went with the territory."

Archer thought about this for a moment. "But was that a bit of bravado? Do you think it unsettled her more than she was letting on?"

"I suppose that's possible." She stared at Archer. "Do you think...?"

"I think we need to see all Stephanie's case files," said Baines. "Over the last six months, for starters."

Hudson frowned. "You are joking, right? I don't want to be obstructive, Sergeant, but that's a pretty broad request for people's personal information. Just handing you every file would break just about every data protection rule in the book."

He folded his arms. "Ms Hudson, this is a murder enquiry. There's a clear public interest in release of this information. The public haven't forgiven the Data Protection Act for allowing Ian Huntley to get a job at a school, despite all the red flags there should have been against him."

Humberside Police had deleted records of rape and sexual assault allegations against the Soham murderer, with the result that he had obtained a caretaker position at a primary school and went on to be convicted of murdering two of its pupils in 2002.

Hudson was unimpressed. "And you know very well that the police misapplied the Act, and were heavily criticised for it. Not a mistake I intend to make. It's hardly in the interests of the service users we work with for them to know the police can seize their data without good reason." She shook her head. "By the book, you'd need to make a written request through your Superintendent, naming the specific files you want. Then we'd seek a view from our legal department, and we'd probably have to seek the individuals' consent."

Frost had re-entered the room in time to witness the exchange. "Normally I'd agree with you, Hannah. But I think we can waive a lot of that red tape here. This is a serious matter, and one of our own has been murdered."

The Director held up her hands. "I was about to go on and say, Roger, that's doing it by the book, but we can move faster than that." She turned to Staples. "Elaine, how quickly can you get those files together? I'm thinking you can identify the ones the police are most likely to be interested in and then go through them with DI Archer or her colleague."

Archer had typed up the names on Richard Merritt's list with some dates based on what she had filleted from the diary. She handed it to Hudson.

"These will do for a start, but anything else you can add would be good."

The Director passed the note to Staples, frowning again. "Where did you get these names?" she wanted to know.

"We're detectives," Baines said with a smile.

"Obviously. Well, I hope I never do anything naughty." Hannah Hudson smiled at Baines, and Archer wondered if she could detect an irritating hint of flirtatiousness.

If Baines noticed, it was lost on him. "And how long will it take Ms Staples to go through the files?"

"We'll try to get back to you within 24 hours."

Archer decided she didn't much like Hannah Hudson. She didn't like her simpering at Baines, and she didn't much care for the whole glamourpuss image. Most of all, she didn't like her bureaucratic attitude or her apparent lack or urgency in solving the murder of a colleague.

"Close of play today," she told her, "We don't know why Stephanie Merritt was murdered, but her killer is still at large. We need to catch him, and quickly."

* * *

Brian Hughes must have been ten years younger than Stephanie Merritt, a fact neither Hannah Hudson nor Elaine Staples had chosen to mention to Archer or Baines. The latter was momentarily thrown by the case worker's relatively youthful appearance. He was handsome, with dark brown hair and grey-green eyes, his teeth just a little too white, his suit expensive-looking.

He tried to picture Hughes and Merritt as either lovers or just two people who had struck up a friendship at work and couldn't see it, although he acknowledged to himself that he would have had less difficulty if the man had been a decade older than the woman.

Archer and Baines joined Hughes in a small meeting room with a pot of coffee and a plate of chocolate biscuits. Hughes poured for them all and Baines helped himself to a biscuit. He was munching happily when he felt Archer's eyes on him and realised that she expected him to lead off. He hastily washed the mouthful down with coffee that was too hot. It brought tears to his eyes.

"Mr Hughes, this is just an informal chat," he began, and then he coughed behind his hand to dislodge a stray crumb from his throat. "Sorry. You'll have heard about Stephanie Merritt?"

Hughes nodded. "We're all shocked."

"You in particular. We gather you were quite close friends."

His gaze slid off to the side. "I wouldn't go that far."

"But you used to go to lunch together."

"Who told you that?"

Baines smiled at him. "I don't think that's really relevant, do you?"

"Well, if someone's saying -" Hughes looked just a little too affronted.

Archer stepped in. There was something about her body language that Baines was already beginning to recognise when she became impatient. He was sure he'd once heard some reference or other to some woman being like a galleon in full sail, and he thought the epithet rather suited Lizzie Archer when the mood took her.

"Mr Hughes, are you actually going to answer my colleague's question?" she demanded. "Only it seems very strange to me that we're simply trying to establish what sort of a relationship you had with one of your colleagues. She's lying in the mortuary, and all you're doing is answering questions with questions. And I have to wonder why."

He coloured. "It's just that -"

"As DS Baines says, this is just an informal chat, Mr Hughes. Don't make us get all formal with you. You won't like it, and we won't like the paperwork. It tends to annoy us."

Baines couldn't resist. "You wouldn't like us if we get annoyed."

Archer briefly rolled her eyes at him.

"All right," Hughes said hastily, "you've made your point. Yes, okay. I had lunch a couple of times with Steph. About once a month since Christmas. She looked a bit down in the New Year. She was letting a case get to her. So I suggested lunch at an Italian. About a month later, she said one of the local pubs had just gone gastro, and did I fancy checking it out. It was probably four times in all."

"What sort of thing did you talk about?"

"Work, obviously."

"Cases?"

Hughes shook his head. "Not so much so. She's a bit of s stickler for confidentiality."

"So..."

"Mostly office gossip, you know. Whether there were any office romances going on. Who was going on holiday where. Who might be up for promotion."

"Ever talk about difficult clients? Did she say any of them had been violent or abusive?"

"We might have swapped a couple of war stories. A certain amount of aggression from families is sometimes par for the course."

This was like pulling teeth. "Sure," Baines persisted. "So I understand. But did she confide in you about any case in particular where she'd been given a hard time? Maybe even been assaulted? Spat on, maybe?"

"Oh, that? It must have been around the end of March. She was looking into allegations of child neglect and the mother took umbrage. Slapped her and told her to get out. Spat on her just before she shut the door."

"Were the police called?"

"Do you know how many assaults on social workers there are each year in this country, Sergeant? About 50,000 and rising. Not many of them lead to prosecution. Steph didn't want the police called immediately, and the woman hand-delivered a letter of apology the next day. As far as Steph was concerned, that was it."

"And the child neglect?"

"You'd have to ask Eileen Staples. I don't know the details of the case."

Baines thought that, for a man who claimed to have had only had four social lunches with the victim and clearly didn't want it to be seen as much of a workplace friendship, he might have been more of a shoulder for her to lean on than he was admitting. At the same time, if her death had upset him overmuch, he was hiding it much better than Eileen Staples was managing.

"Mr Hughes, I'm going to come right out and ask you something. If you lie now, and we find out you were lying, it will raise some serious issues for us. Do you understand?"

Hughes made a show of sipping his coffee. His hands were shaking slightly, and Baines knew he had guessed what was coming. He also thought he knew the answer already.

"Do you understand?" he asked again.

"Yes, I understand. Do you need to be so heavy?"

"That depends on how much you piss us about, Brian. I think you're pissing us about."

"Language, Sergeant," Archer said primly.

"Sorry, ma'am. Here's the question, Brian. Were you sleeping with Stephanie Merritt?"

"I'm a married man."

"But were you?"

Hughes wore a wedding ring. He fiddled with it.

"No. Not on an ongoing basis. But yes, okay, it happened one time. We were on a residential training course together. A few drinks, it seemed like a good idea at the time. You know how it is?"

"I don't believe we do," Archer said. "Suppose you tell us?"

"Oh, Christ." He covered his face with his hands for a few moments. "Does this have to come out?"

"I really can't say at this stage," Archer said. "It depends on how relevant it is to our investigation. But we do need to know."

"It was only last month. We hadn't planned to go on the course together, it just happened. It was a two-day thing with an overnight stay. I suppose I got a bit flirty. We both did, really. It got out of hand. In the morning, we couldn't believe what we'd done. It was a bit awkward over breakfast. We agreed it couldn't happen again."

"And have you had lunch since?" Baines asked.

"No. We decided to knock all that on the head as well."

"So you had a fling?"

"I suppose."

"Do you think your wife suspects?"

"I don't think so."

The truth was, Baines suspected, that Stephanie Merritt wasn't Brian Hughes' first 'fling', and probably wouldn't be his last either. He wondered who had really been the most remorseful the morning after.

"And you're sure it was a mutual decision to break it off?"

"Of course." He stared at the table. "To be honest, Steph was horrified at what had happened. She seemed a bit low that night, and maybe that was why she had a bit too much to drink in the first place."

"Low in what way?"

"Hard to put a finger on it. Everyone loved her. She was kind and cheerful on the outside. But I got the impression there was a sad side to her she was hiding." He looked up. "Some of us social workers get a bit hardened to what we see in the job. I don't think that was Stephanie. I think some of her cases haunted her, and sometimes she just let the job get on top of her. Sometimes she couldn't let things go."

"Any case in particular?"

"I never asked and she never said."

Baines thought they'd got about as much as they were going to for the time being.

"One last question, Mr Hughes. Do you think Stephanie's husband might have suspected anything had happened?"

"I don't know. Maybe. She never mentioned it. But I doubt if she was much of a liar, to be honest."

Whereas Baines thought Brian Hughes was probably an accomplished liar.

Which cast doubt over every word he had said.

* * *

Whilst Archer and Baines were interviewing Brian Hughes, Hannah Hudson and Elaine Staples had repaired to the Director's office.

"Just the last six months?" Staples said. "I didn't like to say, but..."

Hudson cut her off. "That's what the police want, Elaine. That's what we'll concentrate on. And I'm sure they're right. If Stephanie's death has anything to do with her work, it's bound to be something fairly recent. There's no need to go dredging up ancient history."

What Hannah Hudson didn't say was that the sort of ancient history she had in mind reflected poorly on her department. Throughout her career, she'd always managed to avoid any mud sticking to her - hence her fairly meteoric rise. She intended to go further, and every time she saw Roger Frost she wondered how much longer he would be ignoring the call of his comfy slippers and his golf clubs.

The last thing she wanted was something rotten from the past breaking the surface once more, like a bloated corpse buoyed up by its own gases.

If the police wanted to go back further, she decided, that was fine by her, but she wasn't about to volunteer anything more than they were asking for.

Playing it by the book was the safest policy.

14

Considering that the press conference had been pulled together somewhat hastily, Archer thought it went remarkably well. Paul Gillingham went first, talking in surprisingly impassioned tones about the need to bring a 'brutal and sadistic' killer to justice. The CCTV footage of the hooded figure moving around Wendover car park was shown, together with shots of Menzies Drive, number 37 and the house opposite. The number plate of the car the hoodie had been using was displayed, as was a picture of the same make and model of car.

Then came the moment Gillingham, and Archer for that matter, had been dreading. Sitting alongside Gillingham and the Merritt's two children was Richard Merritt, just out of hospital, and who had insisted on speaking for the family against the DCI's and his doctor's advice. He looked terrible: drawn and haggard, as if he had aged a good twenty years in the two days since Archer had first spoken to him in the ambulance outside his house.

But when his turn to speak finally came, Merritt spoke calmly and clearly, and straight to the camera. He had refused to consider a script and spoke straight from the heart.

"On Monday morning, our family was destroyed when Stephanie was taken from us in the most horrific of circumstances. People talk glibly about something like this being every family's nightmare, and I can tell you they are right. It's something nothing can prepare you for.

"We're making this appeal because we don't want anything like this to happen again and for another family to have to go through what we're suffering now.

"Stephanie was a wonderful person: a devoted wife and a loving mother who had made her career in social services because she wanted to help people. All we want is justice for her and some sort of closure - if that can ever really be achieved - for ourselves.

"To the killer we say, whatever drove you to do this terrible thing, if you have any conscience at all, you'll be getting no rest right now, thinking about what you've done. Do the right thing and turn yourself in. We believe in British justice and that you will be treated fairly.

"To anyone who might have seen anything, however seemingly insignificant, that might be of help to the police and their investigation, we say please, please come forward.

"This is a nightmare for Stephanie's family. We are all in Hell, every moment of every day. Please help in getting justice for Stephanie so she can rest in peace and we can try to rebuild our lives."

He spoke with true dignity. His voice faltered slightly on the last sentence, and Archer, looking on, was surprised to feel a tear rolling down her cheek.

Gillingham said he would take three questions, although that was largely for form's sake. BBC Oxford asked whether the police were pursuing any other leads. He told them a number of leads were being pursued, but that it was an ongoing investigation. He used a similar formula when *The Sun* asked him if he thought Stephanie Merritt had known her killer.

The third question came from Claire King of *The Aylesbury Echo*.

"Chief Inspector, Mr Merritt said he didn't want another family to go though what his family is suffering. My question to you is this. Is this killer likely to strike again? And should Aylesbury Vale be afraid?"

"That's two questions, Claire," Gillingham said with the ghost of a smile. No one laughed. "Look. Obviously we don't know why Stephanie's murderer did what he did, or what's going on in his mind. I can't say absolutely certainly that he won't strike again, and we're trying to keep open minds about his motivation. As I keep saying, we're pursuing a number of leads. The important thing is to apprehend this man as soon as possible, and we need everyone's help to do so."

"I can see the headlines now," Baines murmured from beside Archer as Gillingham and the Merritt family left the platform. "'Psycho Beast Stalks Quiet Market Town.'"

"Maybe people should be a bit scared," she said. "We have no idea what this killer's agenda is. I thought Richard was impressive."

"Almost too impressive."

"You still think he might be the killer? Even after his heart attack?"

Baines gave an almost imperceptible shrug. "Maybe the pressure of being a hammer-wielding monster was getting to him. Maybe our interview made him think he hadn't been as clever as he thought. A day in hospital might have restored his composure. But what do I know? When will we get some forensics back on that burnt-out car?"

"If it wasn't for bloody budgets, we'd most likely have something by now. I think Joan Collins was pressing them for close of play today."

"Good. If we can definitely tie the car in to the murder, then I agree that Merritt's off the hook and it's our fashion victim in the anorak that we're looking for."

"We're looking for him already, Dan."

"Well, let's hope this appeal helps us find him." He checked his watch. "Are you still up for coming to see Marcus Clark? Fill the gap in his brother's file?"

"Why not? It'll be a few hours before this appeal goes out on TV and we start getting calls."

"At least half of which will be cranks, confessing or saying they saw a spaceship landing in Menzies Drive."

"At least we haven't mentioned the probable murder weapon to the media. I doubt any of the serial confessors will think of a hammer. Let's just hope we get one useful lead, Dan. Even if we can be sure the man in the anorak is the killer, we still don't have a clue who he is."

* * *

If the front of Michael Sturridge's flats had been a bit of a mess, then the outside of Brandon Clark's family home was like House and Garden in miniature. The doors and windows were well maintained and looked as if they had been fairly recently painted. The little strip of lawn beside the concrete drive was immaculate, and the front garden flower beds were well-stocked and seemingly weed-free.

It was just after 3 pm. Julie Clark, the boys' mother, invited them in and said she expected Marcus home from school within the next ten or fifteen minutes.

"He reckons he's a big boy now and doesn't need mummy to meet him," she said as she put the kettle on in a kitchen as pristine as the front of the house would lead one to expect. "Besides, the school's big on the environment and reducing your carbon footprint by walking to and from school."

She was a petite blonde whose hair colour probably came from a bottle, but certainly not any sort of stereotypical gang leader's mum. Indeed, when Baines had spoken to her before, he'd been at a loss to understand how any son of hers could have gone off the rails. She'd put it down to their father not being around - he'd been a gambler who'd got the family into debt and then killed himself. He hadn't even left them any life insurance.

The family had finally washed up on the Northfields Estate where Julie had done her best to bring the boys up decently. When the gang craze had sprung up, no one had been more surprised than her to see Brandon embrace it. He'd always been a good boy, and was far cleverer than the average kid in the neighbourhood. But Baines privately thought that was the point. Brandon Clark had leadership qualities, and the gang was something he could lead.

"So what's all this about?" Julie Clark asked them, dropping teabags into a pot. "Why do you want to see Marcus?"

"Just a loose end we want to tie up, Mrs Clark," Archer said. "We've noticed from one of the statements on our file that Marcus was with Brandon just before the shooting. We just want to make absolutely sure he didn't see or hear anything that would be useful to us."

Julie Clark looked confused. "He would have said."

"He must have parted company with Brandon only a couple of minutes at the most before the shooting happened," Baines explained. "No big deal."

The kettle began to boil and she switched it off. "So long as you don't frighten him. He's only nine." Baines saw her shoot a doubtful look at Archer's scarred cheek. Archer clearly noticed too, and she coloured slightly.

"We'll do our best not to," she promised.

Julie was pouring the tea when they heard a key turn in the lock. Moments later it opened, then slammed shut, and footsteps clattered through the little hall.

"Mum -" began Marcus Clark, and then he fell silent, looking uncertainly at Archer and Baines.

"Marcus," Julie said, "these people are from the police. They want to talk to you about Brandon."

Marcus's mouth fell open. He was small for his age, but well-proportioned - no puppy fat, but not too skinny either. His school uniform was typically scruffy.

"Let's all go in the living room and sit down," said Julie.

Marcus began to back away, shaking his head.

"Marcus -"

He bolted.

He had turned on his heel and hurtled back to the front door before any of them could react. Baines was first to move, but the boy was already opening the door.

"Marcus, come back here!" shouted his mother as he ran out of the house. Baines was giving chase already. He had longer legs, and was reasonably fit, but Marcus Clark had the makings of an Olympic runner. Every time Baines thought he was gaining, the kid seemed to find another gear.

Baines pursued him to the end of the road, where he turned left onto The Northfields, the main road that bisected the estate. As Baines himself reached the corner, he saw Marcus race across the road, narrowly dodging an oncoming car. Baines tried to follow, but the car hooted furiously at him, making him wait and allowing the boy to gain a few yards on him.

Panting, Baines glanced over his shoulder and saw Archer catching up with him. She was running in stockinged feet and carrying her shoes.

"Go!" she waved her arm. "Don't lose him!"

He plunged across the road. Marcus was just passing one turning on his right, sticking to Northfields. Baines had a sudden intuition about where the boy was headed. The next right, Driver Way, was a labyrinth of shabby blocks of flats, each with more than one entrance and exit, as well as interconnecting walkways. Once in there, Marcus Clark would be very difficult to find.

Sure enough, as Baines redoubled his efforts to close the distance between them, Marcus did wheel into Driver Way. Moments later, he had been swallowed up by the entrance to the nearest block of flats.

Baines didn't follow. He stood watching for signs of the boy's progress, some indication of where he might emerge. Archer arrived at his side.

"Where?" she gasped, gulping in air.

He pointed at the flats. "In there." His own breath was sawing.

"Why didn't you keep after him?"

"Because I couldn't keep up with him. By now, he could be on any floor, using the walkways to get to other blocks. Those flats are like a maze. I've chased villains in there before. Frankly, unless you've got an army of coppers to seal off every exit, it's like looking for a needle in a haystack."

"So... what? We wait?"

"I suppose you could take the back and I could cover the front. But we could be here a long time."

She was getting her breathing better under control now. She put a hand on his shoulder for support whilst slipping on first one shoe, and then the other. He was mildly surprised by the intimacy of the gesture, and not entirely displeased.

"So what's the alternative?" she wanted to know.

"Three options, I reckon. One - we wait here for as long as it takes. Although, after dark, he could probably slip out without us spotting him anyway."

"I haven't got time for that."

"Two - we get backup. A lot of backup."

"You know we haven't got the resources. And three?"

"He'll go home when he's hungry. We ask his mother to keep him there and give us a call."

She pursed her lips, clearly feeling defeated and not liking it. "All right. That's probably the least of all evils. But why did he run, do you suppose?"

"He could just be scared of coppers. Maybe Brandon told him we're the bad guys."

"Or maybe he knows something."

"Let's leave our cards with Julie Clark," he suggested. "I dare say we'll hear from her in a few hours."

Archer's phone rang. She answered it, listened intently, asked a few questions and hung up.

"You're going to have to phone our contact details through to Mrs Clark," she said.

"Why? What's up?"

"A body has been found on the canal towpath near Bescott, wherever that is."

"It's an arm of the canal just up to the north of Aylesbury."

"Well, we need to go there. This one's for us. The head and face have been smashed to pieces. Just like Stephanie Merritt."

15

Lizzie Archer sometimes wondered how many dead bodies would lie undiscovered forever if not for dog walkers and joggers. Somewhere along the line it had become a cliché that one or the other always stumbled across a murder victim and raised the alarm.

In this case, it was a female jogger who had been pounding along the canal towpath when she'd spotted what looked like a briefcase in some tall weeds. The jogger had stopped to check it out. As she had approached, she had made out a human shape just beyond the bag. She thought the person had perhaps been mugged and left for dead, but might still be alive, so she had gone to see if she could help. Then she had seen the blood, the ruin of the head and face.

She had told Archer that her vocal chords still hurt from screaming so much.

It hadn't taken a genius to work out that there was a probable connection between this victim and Stephanie Merritt. Different genders, and this one had apparently been killed outside rather than in his own home, but as Barbara Carlisle had said, "The fact that both their heads have been seriously rearranged is a bit of a giveaway."

She'd estimated the time of death as between 10 pm and two in the morning and also confirmed that the injuries looked consistent with the previous victim's - although, as usual, she emphasised that her findings were provisional until the post-mortem. She also commented that most of the teeth had been damaged, although she thought positive identification of the body through dental records was still a possibility. Otherwise it would have to be DNA or fingerprints off a toothbrush, a comb, whatever.

Archer and Baines had left the SOCOs still crawling over the scene, but they had already noted the considerable pool of blood under the bridge a few yards away. There was rather less blood where the corpse lay. The SOCOs had also found a trail of blood leading up to the road.

Phil Gordon, the Crime Scene Manager, said his reading was that the victim had been driven to the spot and the attack had started in the car.

"My guess is, he was rendered unconscious, or at least helpless, and then dragged or thrown down the bank. Then the killer dragged him under the bridge and the real fun began."

"Why would he do it in the open?" Baines had puzzled. "What if someone had spotted him?"

Archer had pondered. "I suspect this is a relatively quiet spot. If he was killed at the later end of Miss Carlisle's time of death window, that would be two in the morning. He'd have been fairly confident that nothing would come past."

"Even so. Maybe he's got a little bolder since last time."

They'd identified the body as Peter Nish from the driving licence in his wallet. Now it was getting on for 6 pm and Archer, Baines and a family liaison officer were seated in the living room of Nish's luxury home at Watermead with his shocked wife, Jennifer.

Watermead is a purpose-built village, a brainchild of the planners, situated about half a mile north of Aylesbury and only about six miles from Bescott, where Nish's body had been found. From the outside, the Nishes' substantial white house looked like a young mansion, and it had spectacular views over the village's man-made lake, originally created to reduce the risk of flooding from a higher-than-average water table, but now home to rare birds and other wildlife.

Jenny Nish had reported her husband missing that morning when it had become apparent that he hadn't been home all night.

"He goes out with a couple of mates on a Tuesday evening," she explained. "Gerald and Dean. Straight from work. He leaves his car at the office and gets a taxi home. Some nights he's later than others, and I've been known to go to bed without waiting up. When that happens, he usually sleeps in the spare room, so as not to wake me. So, when I woke up and he wasn't in bed beside me..."

"You assumed that's where he was?" prompted Archer.

"At first. But when there was no sign of him getting up for work, I went to hurry him and found the bed hadn't been slept in. That's when I knew something was wrong. I phoned his office after nine, but he hadn't turned up. That was when I rang the police."

"We'll need to talk to these friends he was meeting. Can you let me have their details?"

"That's the terrible thing. I don't know anything much about them. Not their surnames, where they live... nothing."

"No phone numbers?"

Jenny Nish sighed. "Look, Inspector. No point in beating about the bush. Peter and I haven't had much of a marriage for years. We just co-exist, really. He brings in a good income working as a solicitor, and I wash his boxer shorts and cook his meals. We barely talk. I ask him how Gerald and Dean are, and sometimes he gives me a bit of detail, but I never remember. I'm not really interested." Tears leaked from her eyes. "I didn't want this to happen, though. I wish now I'd shown a bit more interest."

Archer thought the tears were less to do with grief than with the guilt people so often feel when someone dies. They haven't paid them enough attention and now it's too late.

"Did Peter have any enemies?" Baines asked. "Anyone who'd have wanted to harm him?"

"He's a solicitor, Detective Sergeant. Didn't Shakespeare say something about, Let's kill all the lawyers?"

"Henry the Sixth," Archer supplied, noticing a raised eyebrow from Baines.

"But, as for anyone specific... I'm sure he must have had a few run-ins, but as I say, I didn't pay that much attention to him. I suppose that makes me a terrible wife."

"We're not here to judge you, Mrs Nish," Baines said. "We just want to catch the person who did this to your husband.

They asked if they could take Peter's pc away, but Jenny said he hadn't used one for years.

"He just uses his laptop, and that goes everywhere with him."

Archer remembered the bag that had first attracted the jogger to the body. With any luck, it might contain the laptop, together with a diary with some useful information in it, and a mobile phone containing the numbers of Gerald and Dean. Archer wondered if one of those two was the link between Nish and Meritt.

"I suppose I'll need to identify the body," Jenny said. "Will it be awful?"

"I don't think it would be a good idea, or necessary," Archer said gently. "You want to remember him as he was, not how he looks now. There are other ways we can identify him."

* * *

Back at the station, Baines found Phil Gordon, working late as ever, and asked him about the bag. There had indeed been a laptop, and Gordon had already handed it over to Ibrahim Iqbal for the civilian officer to work his magic on. There had also been a mobile phone, not in the bag, but in a jacket pocket. Gordon signed the phone out to Baines, who went first to make sure Iqbal knew what to look for.

"I'm already checking out e-mail accounts, to see whether there are any interesting messages," Iqbal told him. "Obviously his Outlook, but I'm also looking to see if there are any obvious Hotmail or Yahoo accounts that he would have accessed through the web. There's nothing of note so far."

"Can you check whether there are any recent messages from a Gerald or a Dean - and maybe see if they're in his e-mail address books?"

"Doing it now."

But ten minutes later it was apparent that no such names were associated with Nish's e-mail traffic. Baines was surprised. He would have expected old friends that the solicitor had seen regularly to have been in frequent e-mail touch, maybe even forward him the odd joke.

He went to report back to Archer, who was on the phone. As usual, there was no sign of Ashby, who had probably long since left for the evening.

"Got to go, Mum," she said, and hung up.

"Sorry," he said. "Bad timing?"

She smiled her lopsided smile. "Come in."

He brought her up to date.

"Have you checked out the mobile yet?" she asked.

"Next on my list."

"Well, there's no time like the present."

The phone was in a clear plastic bag and he was able to turn it on and manipulate the keys through that. He scrolled through the numbers stored in the memory. There was a Dean and a Gerald.

"Try them both," Archer suggested.

Baines dialled Dean's number first. It was a landline, a local number. It rang a few times and then a rather breathy female voice answered.

"Geraldine speaking. How may I help you?"

"Can I speak to Dean, please?"

"Dean? I'm sorry, you must have the wrong number."

He hung up, puzzled. "Wrong number. Yet I used the number in the phone."

"Mobile?"

"Landline."

"Maybe the guy moved and Peter never updated his phone. Try Gerald."

Even as the number was dialling, Baines thought there was something familiar about it. He wasn't entirely surprised to hear the same breathy voice announcing that she was Geraldine and asking how she could help.

"Hi," he said, thinking on his feet. "You don't know me, but my name's Dan. I've got your number through Peter Nish. I believe you know him?"

"I know a couple of Peters." She sounded suddenly cautious, but Baines was catching on fast.

"Tuesday nights?"

"Ah!" The penny dropped at the other end of the line. "Yes, of course. Well, he's a bit of a naughty boy, giving you my number. I thought this was our secret."

"Perhaps I could come and see you?"

Archer was staring at him, clearly a little confused by what she was hearing from her end of the conversation.

"That sounds lovely," Geraldine was saying. "When would you like to come?"

"I can get there in about half an hour."

"Oh, I am sorry. I have a client due any moment now. Can we make it a little later? Or maybe tomorrow?"

"No, we can't." Baines abruptly changed his tone. "I don't think you quite understand me, Geraldine. My name is Detective Sergeant Baines from Thames Valley Police, and I want to talk to you in connection with a murder enquiry. So you give me your address and get rid of your client, and I'll be there in half an hour. Or we can do it the hard way at the station."

He half-expected her demeanour to change, but she continued to speak politely in her rather pleasant tone.

"There's no need for threats, Sergeant. I'm always keen to help the police."

"Good. Well, just to put your mind at rest, we're not interested in how you make your living - not yet, anyhow."

"I'm pleased to hear it. Well, I'll send my client away when he arrives. News of your impending visit should do the trick."

She gave him the address and they hung up.

"What was all that about?" Archer wondered.

He shook his head, chuckling. "You're going to love this. It turns out that Gerald and Dean are in fact a prostitute called Geraldine. He was her regular Tuesday evening slot."

She snorted. "Gerald and Dean. How inventive. I gather you're off to see her."

"Want to come?"

"No, I need to drive down to London shortly. Take Collins or Bell, if one of them is still around."

He was surprised that she was about to call it a day, even though it was getting on for 8 pm. The enquiry had just become a double murder, after all, and no one got much sleep in such cases. He had just begun to re-evaluate her, and he was surprised to find that he was a little disappointed.

He turned to leave the office. "See you tomorrow then."

"Before you go," Archer said, "now you've got an address for this woman, why not see if you can track down the taxi firm that picks him up. Maybe their number is in the phone."

Wondering why the idea hadn't occurred to him, he scrolled through the numbers again. "Moonlight Taxis," he said. "Let's have a look at the call log and see if he rang them last night."

He found a call logged at 5 pm the previous day. "A creature of habit," he observed. "He must have known when his bonking session was going to end and had the taxi already organised."

Archer burst out laughing. "I hope he and Miss Whiplash never run late. Just imagine... they're getting to the interesting part and the taxi's outside hooting."

"Tootus interruptus," he agreed, dialling the number.

"Moonlight Taxis," a gruff voice answered.

Baines introduced himself. "I need to talk to the driver who picked up Mr Nish from 11 Gray Street last night."

"Last night? Hold on." He could hear the man riffling through what sounded like the pages of a book. Then he came back on. "He was booked for 10 pm, but he cancelled."

"Cancelled? Are you sure?"

"That's what my log says. Sorry. By the way, it wasn't number 11. We pick him up from the corner."

"Really? Why's that?"

"Because he asks us to, mate."

Baines hung up and relayed the conversation to Archer.

"Why would he cancel?"

She drummed her fingers on her desk for a moment and then looked at him.

"He didn't. The killer cancelled it. I'd lay odds he picked Nish up himself, posing as the cabbie."

"You think?" It sounded far-fetched.

"Think about it. The one night a week when our Mr Nish never goes straight home. I reckon when you speak to Madame Geraldine, you'll find he always left at the same time. Hence the prearranged taxi."

The implications of what she was saying began to sink into Baines' consciousness. "Dear God. You're saying he's studied Nish, probably over quite some time. He knew when, he knew where, and he knew who the regular taxi firm was."

"It eliminates any chance of random victim selection, don't you think?"

His mind was racing. "And Stephanie Merritt... her husband left for the station at the same time every morning, leaving her alone at home until it was time for her to go off to work. The same window of opportunity, every morning, to kill her in. He just picked his day."

"The empty house opposite, pre-selected." Archer's face was grim. "This is a patient, meticulous planner who had these killings all worked out way in advance. There's nothing random about it."

"Two killings, less than two days apart? I agree - he had to have been planning both of them for weeks, perhaps months."

"I'm not going to make it to London," she decided. "I can think of at least two questions we need pretty damn quick answers to. For starters, why these two victims?"

He nodded. "And second?"

Her eyes were bleak blue chips. "How many more are on his list?"

16

The hammer was still in its plastic wrapping in the pocket of the anorak, where it had been since the killing of Nish. It really ought to be cleaned of blood and hair, but just the idea of facing that mess set the stomach roiling.

The killings themselves were gruesome, sickening work to have to do. They required a detachment that could only be maintained for so long. Then the flashbacks, the all-too-vivid images. The copious vomiting.

Most people were able to choose the paths they followed in life, but sometimes the path chose them. These killings... no sane person would want to be doing this, yet what was the alternative? People had to understand how their choices - their spur-of-the-moment, thoughtless choices - had consequences. Destroyed lives.

So these people had to pay for what they had done. Pay in as terrible and brutal a way as could be imagined.

And maybe, just maybe, the end would justify the means. If just a few others learned the lesson that was being taught and thought before they acted, then all the planning, all the horrific execution - and the nightmares it unleashed - would be worthwhile.

It was to be devoutly hoped for. Because there were plenty more lessons to be taught before this was over.

17

Baines' visit to the prostitute Geraldine Williams added little to the sum of his knowledge. She seemed genuinely upset to learn that Peter Nish had been murdered, saying he was one of her favourite clients, always polite and gentlemanly. She had not seen the taxi that collected him, as it always met him at the end of her road.

"He said it was more convenient for the driver," she said. "But I'm no fool. He was afraid the firm might drop or collect other clients here and know what line of business I'm in. He didn't want them knowing he'd been visiting me. I'm afraid it doesn't help you much, though, does it, Detective Sergeant?"

He'd asked her what sort of mood Nish had been in. She'd said with a tinge of sadness that he had been 'the same old Peter'.

In other words, Geraldine might be a likeable tart with a heart, but she could add absolutely zero to the enquiry.

After he'd concluded the interview, he checked in with Archer, who was still at the office puzzling over what might have connected the two victims.

"I'm brainstorming with Joan," she said. "We're not getting especially far. Obviously both lived in the Vale, so there's a good chance that the killer's local. Both had patterns of behaviour that enabled the killer to pick his moment, but frankly that probably applies to most of the population. Tomorrow we need to go back to the families and get a better picture of where they tended to go, what they did with their time. Maybe there's an overlap. I also want to know whether they knew each other."

"There's their professions, of course," Baines pointed out.

"Yes, we need to talk to both their employers. If Nish specialised in family law, he might have come across Stephanie in a professional capacity. They may have a pissed off client in common."

"Mind you, good luck with that," he said. "If Nish's firm are anything like social services, they'll be so scared of the Data Protection Act, they could have Jack the Ripper on their database and say nothing."

Archer's close of play deadline for a decision on Stephanie Merritt's case files had come and gone without any contact from either Hannah Hudson or Elaine Staples, an outcome that had been entirely predictable, but still left a feeling of impotent anger.

"I also think we need to try and track down the people on Richard Merritt's little list," Archer said. "with or without social services' cooperation. Joan's going to go through the local phone book in the morning and see how many people there are with the relevant names."

"I hope there are no Smiths or Joneses."

"There aren't, and there's no Browns, either, so it's not all bad news. Still, it's quite a task, especially when most of the names appear to be the lady of the house. It means we don't know what initial will be in the book."

"Big job." A thought struck him. "One other thing we should look into..."

"Let's have it."

"Well..." He paused, arranging his thoughts. "You're right about the meticulous planning, but I wonder if these two murders are almost too perfect."

"In what way?"

"We think Stephanie was his first victim. What if she wasn't?"

She looked astonished. "We'd know."

"Maybe not, if he's previously worked outside our jurisdiction. We've been keeping the hammer theory under wraps, and there could be another force out there that's been doing the same. Meticulous planner or not, he hasn't made a single mistake, as far as we can tell. Is that really likely for a beginner?"

She instantly picked up on where this was going. "You think he's tried it before, but less successfully? Like a trial run?"

"Not necessarily a trial run. But yes - he might have made one or more previous attacks and made a slip or two. Learned from his mistakes and got it right with Merritt and Nish."

"It's serial killers who do that, Dan, and it's too soon to say that's what this is. All we have at the moment are two murders that we think are linked. For all we know, Stephanie met Nish through work and they had an affair. Maybe she confided in Brian Hughes and he killed them both out of jealousy."

He weighed the idea in his mind. "Could be, although it doesn't feel right to me. I'll get someone to check Hughes' alibi. But don't forget you talked yourself about a 'list'."

"There might not be one." There was an edge to her voice now.

"There might not. Or there might be quite a long list. All I'm saying is, let's keep an open mind. The amount of groundwork involved so far, I'd say we're dealing with a man on a mission. And there's something else."

"What's that?"

"If our guy did botch an earlier attack, there could be someone alive out there with some useful information."

Archer paused for a moment, then sighed. "All right. I still have my doubts, but we'll circulate all other forces and see if we get anything back." She paused. "I don't suppose we've had any local hammer attacks?"

"I'd been thinking the same thing. None recently, as far as I know. A guy attacked his best mate last year - broke his arm, I think. An altercation over a car or something. But he's still in jail, to the best of my knowledge. There was a woman who killed her kids two or three years ago, but she killed herself." He frowned. "There was another one a bit further back."

"Go on."

"This guy... what was his name? Edmunds? Edwards, that was it. Clive Edwards."

"This had better be good."

He had a mental picture of her rolling her eyes. "Do you want to hear this?"

"Preferably before I'm drawing my pension, though."

He sighed. "All right. Well, this Edwards comes home from work early and finds his best mate in bed with his wife. There's an altercation, the ex-mate leaves with his trousers round his ankles, and the wife goes with him. Next day she's starting divorce proceedings. A couple of days after the divorce goes through, the wife's new squeeze is found dead in an alley. Blunt force trauma to the back of the head."

He had Archer's attention. "And? Was this Edwards arrested?"

"Oh, yeah, but nothing proved. We weren't even a hundred per cent sure it was a hammer."

"So... Edwards wasn't charged?"

"No evidence."

"And was the other man's face smashed like our latest victims?"

"I'd have to check the file."

"How long ago?"

"Not sure. A year or so?"

"Better check him out," Archer said. "Find out if he has any contacts with our victims. Maybe to do with the divorce." She paused, long enough for him to think he'd lost the connection.

"Hello?"

"Sorry," she said. "I was thinking, was your Clive Edwards the sort of organised planner we're dealing with here?"

"It wasn't my case," Baines said. "But I do seem to remember he'd held down a fairly decent professional job of some sort. And, if he did it, he got away with it."

"Interesting. We'll need to check him out for alibis too."

There was a beep on Baines' mobile indicating that another call had come through and gone to voicemail. He ignored it for now.

"If you ask Joan to pull Edwards's file, she's bound to remember it," he said. "Do you want me to swing by the office before I go home?"

"No, you go off. See you in the morning."

He hung up, recalling that she had intended to drive down to London that evening and was now still in the office at getting on for 10 pm. Maybe he had misjudged her when he thought she lacked commitment.

As he dialled into his voicemail, he pondered on the contradictions of Lizzie Archer. There had been the friction between them when they had first met. After three days working with her, he had to admit she was very good at what she did, and so his resentment towards her had begun to soften. He was hoping the ice was breaking in both directions, but every now and then she said or did something that showed there was still some edginess. He wondered if that would fade with time, or whether their working relationship was always doomed to be prickly.

There was also her touchiness over her scar. She had been prepared last night to tell him how she had come by it, but not in any detail. When he'd attempted to ask about her treatment, the walls had come down. He had always assumed that plastic surgery could easily repair that sort of damage like new, but maybe that was only the case in fiction. Surely she would have gone for such treatment if it was available?

In truth, once the scar had made its initial impact, you soon ceased to really notice it so much. But he suspected she knew it was the first thing anyone saw when they met her. It probably meant that she felt the scar defined her in some people's minds.

Just as a number of his friends and relatives clearly still saw him as 'poor Dan', more than a decade after tragedy struck his family.

The worse thing was, that was sometimes how he also saw himself.

His voicemail was telling him he had one new message, and he retrieved it.

"Mr Baines, it's Julie Clark. You know - Brandon and Marcus's mum? You asked me to let you know when Marcus came home." There was a silence, and for a moment he thought the message was over. Then the rest came out in a rush. "Mr Baines, I'm ever so worried. Marcus still hasn't come home, and it's dark now. I don't know what to do. Can you call me or something?"

He groaned. This was all he needed on his plate. A vulnerable missing person. He knew that children who absconded were often just testing the boundaries, but he wasn't sure Marcus Clark fitted into that category. His impression was that Brandon's younger brother was a decent kid cut from rather different cloth to his sibling.

He also knew far too well what it feels like not to know where a child is.

Baines was on the point of ringing Julie back when he decided he could get to her house in not much longer than it would take to make the call.

* * *

Julie Clark prowled her living room like a caged tigress. Her hair had been as immaculate as her home the last time Baines had seen her, but now it was a mess. Five minutes in her company told the story. She kept raking her fingers backwards through her tresses. Each time she did it the result was more straggles.

Within minutes of arriving, Baines had called the station to report the boy's disappearance, relaying details from Julie so that all the necessary information could be circulated on the Police National Computer. Aylesbury Vale was keeping the PNC busy this evening. Baines imagined Archer, or more likely Collins, feeding it information about the two hammer murders. In both cases, once the information was on the system it could be accessed by all national or international police forces within 48 hours.

Baines had been thrust into the role of Initial Investigating Officer almost by default, although he was hoping that either Marcus would show up by midnight or another officer would be assigned to deal with the enquiry. Fears would soon grow for Marcus Clark's safety, and then the investigation would take on a life of its own. The public would be asked, through the media, to keep an eye out for the missing boy, and the press and the TV cameras would descend.

He cringed at the idea of being involved in a high profile missing child enquiry. It would not take long for the media machine to recall his own tragedy, thrusting it into the spotlight again. It had been bad enough last year when the local papers had run a piece on the tenth anniversary of Jack's disappearance. He'd cooperated rather than have them write something without his input, and then had to endure sympathetic looks from colleagues and friends all over again.

Worst of all, it had brought all the feelings he had tried to bury bubbling back to the surface. Looking back, it was then that the dreams had really started. What he couldn't explain was why they had grown in frequency and intensity lately.

Once he had made his initial report, Baines' next task was to get Julie to focus. She was so distracted, he half-wondered if she'd forgotten he was there. It was not so surprising. To have a child go missing was worrying enough, but this was a mother whose other son was in hospital recovering from a gunshot wound.

"Julie, you've got to listen to me," he urged, and she finally stopped making a mess of her hair and looked his way, her eyes wide and haunted.

"Okay," he said. "We'll be needing some recent photographs of Marcus, and something we can get his DNA off of. His toothbrush will do."

"DNA?" There was panic in her eyes. "What do you need DNA for?"

He knew what she was thinking. To identify a body, if and when one was found.

"It's just procedure," he said. "I've also asked for a couple of constables to come over and search your house. That's just procedure, too. There might be something that gives a clue to where Marcus has gone. And, if he has a computer, they'll need to take that too. You'll be asked to consent to all that, obviously."

"Of course. I just want him back."

He racked his brains for anything else he might need. "You're sure you've rang all his friends' parents?"

"I've rung everyone I can think of. You know boys, Mr Baines. You can't be sure you know who all their mates are."

"Does he have any medical conditions? Anything he needs to take medication for?"

"No, he's fine."

"And you're sure you've rung all his friends' families?"

"I told you. None of his mates has seen him since they went their separate ways on the way home from school."

Now the awkward question.

"Do you know why he would have run off like that?"

"You scared him, Mr Baines. You and that Inspector. Maybe she scared him, with that face of hers."

He sighed. "Julie, neither of those things is going to make him run off and still not be back. We'd come to talk to him about Brandon's shooting. Do you think he knows something about that? It seems he was with his brother a matter of minutes before it happened, yet it's obvious that he hasn't mentioned that to you."

She shook her head, then gave her hair another rake. "Until you came round here, I didn't know about that. I've no idea what he knows. If he knows anything at all." Her face crumpled like tissue. "What if he's run into a paedophile?"

He couldn't do this. Couldn't handle trying to reassure this woman when she was voicing all the fears that had tortured him in the aftermath of Louise's death and Jack's abduction. There had been so many times when he had imagined what the Invisible Man might be doing to his son and had almost hoped the boy was already dead.

Privately, he thought the paedophile scenario a relatively minor risk. He was more concerned about what Marcus Clark might know about his brother's shooting, and whether the people responsible thought he posed a threat to them. They had already gunned down one young man. Would they balk at a second boy?

Baines rearranged his face into the best smile he should muster. "You don't want to think like that, Julie. It's still most likely that he's hanging out somewhere and will come back when he's ready. Maybe he's trying to work up the courage to come home."

But 11 pm came and went with no sign of the boy. A thorough search of the house had predictably found no trace of him, and a more extensive search was being swiftly cranked up, responsibility for the hunt mercifully passed to another officer.

He had waited until Julie's sister Paula arrived, having persuaded her to get someone to stay with her tonight. As he left, she told him with a twisted smile that Brandon was expected to be released from hospital tomorrow.

"We were going to be a proper family again," she said, breaking down once more. "All together. Who says God doesn't have a sense of humour?"

Around midnight, he stepped out of the house and into a chilly night, fatigue washing over him like a tidal wave. He yawned and moved towards his car.

Beside the Mondeo stood a gangly figure in a blue and white hooped shirt. The face was expressionless, but he looked as real and solid as the car.

"Jack?" Baines croaked, his voice a hoarse whisper. "Is that you, son?"

Tears flooded his eyes, blinding him. When he had wiped them away, the boy was gone. The feeling of new loss hit him like a kick to the stomach, so hard that he almost doubled over. He tried to rationalise that Marcus Clark's disappearance had brought everything flooding back with a vengeance, but he knew that he was fooling himself. The feelings had never gone away, not even for a moment.

He just wished he could understand why this fourteen-year-old version of Jack had begun to haunt him lately. He was certain that it must mean something, but whatever that meaning was, it remained tantalisingly beyond his grasp.

He drove home to Little Aston, fighting sleep all the way. When he got indoors, the display on his answering machine was informing him that he had a message. He pressed the play button.

"Hi Dan, it's Karen. Just wondering how you are. Call me, drop me a text or an e-mail. Whatever. I think matters somehow took a bit of a heavy turn the other night, and I don't want things to be weird between us. Just get in touch, okay?"

It was much too late to call her, so he dropped her a text:

Got yr msage. Nothing weird here! Job mental, will call when calmer ha ha. X

Nothing weird here, he thought. Other than he seemed to be having confused feelings for his dead wife's identical twin sister. No matter how hard he had tried to deny it to himself, the truth was that it had hurt to be told they would never be more than friends.

Did that mean he'd had feelings for her all along? That he'd simply been suppressing them since that one time they'd slept together? Or had they developed over the years from feelings of friendship into something deeper?

Or was it what both of them feared the most? Simply a matter of trying to replace Louise with the next best thing.

More confusingly, he couldn't help wondering whether the whole thing had been triggered by the way Jack had started insinuating himself, first into his father's dreams, and then his waking moments.

Nope. Nothing weird here at all.

And now, suddenly, there was another missing boy, one who had been seemingly swallowed up by the Driver Way flats and not been seen again. Baines was glad not to be leading the search. He wasn't sure he could be objective right now.

As it was, the overlap with his own investigation into Brandon Clark's shooting was probably highly relevant. He was still sure Brandon had been hiding something when he had last seen him, and that something had him scared. Now his brother, who might well have witnessed the attack, had vanished. Wherever Marcus was now, Baines was convinced that the key to his disappearance lay in whatever the elder boy feared.

Julie Clark had said Brandon would be coming home tomorrow. Baines decided he would pay him a visit and try to persuade him to talk. For his brother's sake.

18

Lizzie Archer crawled out of her hotel bed, feeling grumpy from lack of sleep again. She should have seen her mother last night, and felt pangs of guilt about cancelling, despite the assurances that it was all right, she understood.

It went without saying she understood. Archer had followed her father into the Met. He had retired as a uniformed sergeant, and he had lived long enough to see her make DI. She would always remember him saying he felt his buttons would burst with pride when she gave him the news of her promotion.

Alan Archer had spent long hours on the job. Archer's mother, Jane, had called herself a 'police widow'. Six months before his daughter's disfigurement, the joke wasn't funny any more. Alan, a heavy smoker, succumbed to lung cancer. Although Archer missed him unbearably at times, at least he'd been spared seeing what happened to his 'beautiful angel'.

Now history seemed to be repeating itself. Her mother had just been diagnosed with a brain tumour. The prognosis was not looking good. Jane Archer had sounded devastated when she had called her daughter, and had clearly been putting a brave face on it when her daughter cancelled her promised visit last night.

Archer's brother, Adam, lived nearby with his young family, and she knew that he would do all he could to support Jane, but he had his own job, and a wife and two children. She suspected that he resented bearing the burden alone, just as after their father's death he had made little effort to conceal his bitterness about having to comfort their mother and organise the funeral without any input from his sister, who always blamed the pressures of her job for not pulling her weight in the family.

She filled and switched on the courtesy kettle in her room and spooned coffee into the courtesy cup from her own jar.

While the kettle bubbled away, she went into the bathroom and got the shower going. She paused by the bathroom mirror and, as she often did, checked out first her left profile, then the right. The reflection of her right side showed, she had to admit, a good looking young woman. The left side reflected an ugly parody of a human face.

As she wandered back into the bedroom, she wondered why she kept doing this. It made her miserable, and things were never going to change.

She looked around the small room, wondering when she might find time to sort out her own place. As a police officer, she was eligible for the government initiative to provide affordable accommodation to key workers, and she would have the money from the sale of her own flat in London if a buyer ever materialised. In theory, she supposed she could sleep at the flat and commute to work, but in practice the 40-plus mile journey was too far for the needs of the job and too long a drive at the end of the long and punishing days she tended to work.

One thing she knew, as she finished making her coffee and left it to cool down while she showered. Living out of a hotel was not going to work as even a medium term option. The government scheme allowed interim rental of accommodation, which would at least afford her somewhere to have her things around her and cook her own meals.

She stripped off her tee-shirt and knickers and stepped under the shower, hoping the jets of hot water would wash some of the tiredness away. With a double murderer to track down, and no way of telling whether the killer had yet finished whatever he had set out to do, she needed to be a whole lot sharper than she felt.

* * *

She had barely reached the office, and hadn't even got her jacket off, when DCI Gillingham summoned her to his office.

"Have you heard from Baines this morning?" he asked.

"Dan? No."

"What did you do to that little kid you both went to see yesterday?"

Her head was full of Stephanie Merritt, Peter Nish, and the next steps in progressing the case. "Little kid?" She mentally rewound her Wednesday. "You mean Marcus Clark?"

"The one you and Baines terrified yesterday."

She frowned, not sure what he was getting at. "Hardly terrified, boss. He walked in his front door, took one look at us, and scarpered."

"This is getting to be a habit, Inspector," he said. "First you interview a grieving husband and give him a heart attack -"

She felt her colour rising. "Now that's not -"

"- and then you scare a nine-year old so badly that he runs away from home and hasn't been seen since."

"Not seen..." The truth dawned on her. "You mean Marcus has disappeared?"

Gillingham nodded gravely. "Like I said... what did you do to him?"

Her stomach tensed, and now the heat in her face owed nothing to embarrassment. She knew that she'd done nothing wrong, yet her boss was laying the blame on her. "Who says I did anything?" Baines? Had Baines been saying something?

"Marcus's mum seems to blame you." His gaze suddenly slid away from her, as if he had suddenly seen something fascinating in a corner of the room. "Lizzie, do you think it's wise to go frightening children?" he said softly.

There was something about the way he said it. Her hand moved towards her left cheek almost of its own volition. As his meaning sank in, outrage overrode her natural instinct to avoid an angry confrontation with the boss.

"What did you say?" she demanded. It was as if her mouth had disconnected from her brain.

"Look, it's not that-"

She was shaking. Her hands had clenched into fists so tight that the nails were actually cutting into her palms. The pain seemed only to goad her on. "How dare you," she snarled. "How fucking dare you?"

He wouldn't look at her. The coward. "Look," he blustered, "Mrs Clark's son has been in hospital with a gunshot wound and now her younger son is missing. She's very upset about it, and she thinks it might be to do with..." he trailed off, seemingly not even having the guts to complete the sentence.

She filled the gap he left, self-control scattered to the winds. "And you agree with her? Well, guess what? Now there are two of us who are upset." She jabbed a finger at him, wanting to punch him. "You listen to me. *Sir*. DS Baines and I were completely professional in our approach to the Clark family. Julie Clark seemed to have no issues with the way I look while we were waiting for Marcus to come home. In fact, she gave no sign of even noticing. Whatever he ran from, it wasn't my scar."

At least *she* wasn't afraid of the word. "He had something to hide. DS Baines thinks his brother has something to hide, too. Someone was in our district with a gun not so long ago, and he wasn't afraid to use it on a young boy - and these two kids know more than they're saying." She knew she had lost it, groped for some sort of calm. "So if I were you, Paul, I'd worry about that - not some narrow-minded shit that a distressed mother is pedalling."

She didn't give him a chance to reply. She surged out of her chair and out of his office, slamming the door behind her. She was shuddering with anger and humiliation.

She stalked back to her office and found Steve Ashby there, his feet on his desk and chewing gum. At least he wasn't smoking, she told herself.

"Good morning," she said with as much enthusiasm as she could muster.

He responded with a knowing smile. "Hear you've just been in to see the boss. He can be a hard taskmaster, can't he? Especially where bad PR is concerned."

She did her best to look unconcerned, but inside she was seething. Had Gillingham told Ashby he was about to bollock her? Surely he wouldn't be so unprofessional?

But another, even more unpleasant, possibility came to her. Ashby seemed like a lazy officer who came and went as he pleased and did as he pleased. He seemed to spend very little time at his desk, and she couldn't believe all that time away was spent on the job. He claimed to have a network of contacts and informers, but she wasn't convinced.

Everything about him was disorganised. He never seemed to use a note book, preferring to scribble on silly little yellow stickers, peeling each jotting from its pad and sticking them to his phone, his computer, the inside of his wallet - anywhere that reduced his chances of finding them when he needed them. She wondered how many he lost by the end of each day.

And then there was the smoking. He was like something out of Life on Mars in reverse. As if something had happened to Ashby in the 1970s and he'd found himself in a 21st Century that was alien to him. The idea that someone would think they could still get away with workplace smoking in 2012 was staggering.

Gillingham couldn't have not known, so he must have tolerated it. Why? The reason was obvious. Whether it was the old pals act or for some more complicated reason, it seemed the DCI was prepared to cut Ashby a great deal of slack.

So when Archer had told Steve Ashby she wasn't sharing an office with a workplace smoker, and that he could either take it outside or explain to the health and safety team, maybe he had gone moaning to his boss.

She switched on her computer, ignoring Ashby's cynical smirks, and asked herself if she was being paranoid. After all, when the governor had given her a hard time over Richard Merritt's heart attack, she had never even met Ashby, much less ruffled his feathers.

Maybe there was some truth in Ashby's words. Perhaps Gillingham was sensitive to any possibility of a bad press and his knee-jerk reaction to complaints was to give the officer in question the third degree. If that was so, then he and Archer were going to have a very awkward working relationship, especially if he was going to bring her scar into it - or allow others to.

Whatever was going on with Gillingham, there was little doubt that Ashby knew she'd been in the DCI's office and that it hadn't been to receive praise.

She suddenly couldn't bear to be in the other DI's company. It was all she could do not to grab her bag and run out of the office, but she managed to make her exit as casual and dignified as she could manage.

She found herself out in the car park, breathing deeply, clawing for some sort of self-control. She couldn't do this. At least at the Met, all she'd had to cope with was looks - imagined or otherwise - and sympathy. Here she was meeting downright hostility at every turn - Gillingham, Ashby, Baines half the time - and she was also feeling real anxiety about being out of her depth in a double murder enquiry.

It would be so easy to get in her car, drive down to her mum's and never come back.

Her phone rang, and she answered it with the greatest reluctance.

"DI Archer? This is Elaine Staples, from Children's Services. Apologies for missing your deadline yesterday, but I've been over Stephanie's case files and I can go through them with you whenever suits."

Archer hesitated. This was a job she could delegate to Baines, maybe even to Joan Collins, who was clearly good at detailed stuff. Then again, she could hide and feel sorry for herself, or she could do something.

She glanced at her watch. 8.55 a.m.

"There's no time like the present," she said.

* * *

It was less than a mile from the police station in Wendover Road up to the Council Offices in Walton Road, so Archer decided to walk it. It took her less than twenty minutes and by 9.25 a.m. she was seated next to Elaine Staples in a small meeting room, with a pile of files on the table.

"I'm not sure we'll need to refer much to the files," Staples said, "but let's see how it goes."

She opened up a well-used black-covered A4 notebook. The pages were covered with small, neat handwriting.

"The first thing to say is, however you came by that list of four names, I can't really add to it. You're sure you only wanted to go back six months?"

Archer looked at her. "I was thinking that would do for now. Why? Has something else occurred to you?"

Staples broke eye contact hastily and made a show of running her finger down the page at which she had opened her notebook.

"Ms Staples?" Archer urged.

"No," the other woman said. "It's nothing at all. Just making sure, that's all."

Archer continued to stare at her for a moment longer, weighing up whether anything was being concealed, then let it go.

"So what can you tell me?"

"Right. First of all, you can eliminate Tracey Jenks. She died of a drugs overdose three weeks ago, so she couldn't have killed Stephanie."

"She made threats, didn't she?"

"All sorts. She was pretty unstable, and I think she reduced Stephanie to tears on more than one occasion. But, as I say, she couldn't have made good on them. The irony is, Stephanie was doing all she could to keep her kids from being taken into care, and that's what will probably happen now."

Archer made a note. "Are there any other family members who might have shared her hostility? Or maybe blamed Stephanie for her death?"

"There's no suggestion of that on the file. Tracey was a single mum. It seems there were several candidates for the kids' father, but none of them wanted the job. She was trying to get her life together and Stephanie was trying to help her. Drugs rehab. A proper job..."

"A proper job? Had she been financing her habit through prostitution?"

"That was what neighbours asserted more than once, and one of the reasons we kept going back there. Our first concern is for the children."

"And was she?"

"She denied it, and there was no proof. Said she had a lot of boyfriends. Stephanie thought she probably picked up a guy here and there. Some paid for it, some didn't."

Archer nodded reflectively. "Okay. Who else?"

"There's just the one male on your list. Tony Plater, a veteran of the Iraq war and a double amputee. All Stephanie ever accused him of was a bit of shouting and verbal abuse, mostly born of frustration. I don't see a man with no legs in a wheelchair as being equipped to carry out a brutal murder, do you?"

"Not unless his victim knelt down and kept still," Archer concurred with a smile.

"Then there's Gina Hunter. She threw hot coffee at Stephanie one time, but missed. That was just about within your six months window, but I don't think she's your killer, either."

Part of Archer wanted to ask Staples who was the detective around here, but she rather liked the woman's methodological approach.

"Why would that be?"

"She seems to have turned her life around since then. Stopped drinking, got a job, met a man, whirlwind romance. The wedding was on Saturday and there's an invitation on the file."

"Did Stephanie go?"

"Not to my knowledge, but you'll want to check with her husband, Richard. I'd guess she's on honeymoon even as we speak."

"We'll check." Archer made another note to herself, one side of her brain wondering how Steve Ashby survived with just a series of sticky notes. "So, that leaves one. Dawn Dulac, the slapper and spitter."

"She hand-delivered a letter of apology the very next day, and that was the end of it as far as the file is concerned."

"That's as may be, but she still used actual violence, and she's the one person on your list who might have been physically and logistically capable of doing it. Do you have contact details for these people?"

Elaine Staples passed her a typewritten sheet with four names and accompanying addresses and phone numbers.

Archer hesitated, then threw in casually, "I don't suppose she dealt with a Clive Edwards at all?"

"The name doesn't ring a bell, and he doesn't figure in Stephanie's case files. Why do you ask?"

"Just someone we might be interested in."

Staples looked pensive. "Remember I'm relatively new here. I was in Cambridgeshire before. He could have been before my time, and I suppose she could have had some peripheral contact with him but not been the lead case worker. Do you want me to do some digging?"

"Please. And you're sure there's no one else in Stephanie's files we might want to take a look at?"

"You're welcome to look through all the files, Inspector, but I doubt it."

"No, that'll do for now. Thanks, Elaine, that's really helpful. Is there anything else at all?"

Staples was silent for a moment, and then looked about to say something. At the same moment, the door opened and the Children's Director breezed in.

"Good morning, Detective Inspector," purred Hannah Hudson. "I just thought I'd look in to see how things were going."

"We're about done," Staples said quickly.

Too quickly? Archer glanced at her. "Elaine has been very helpful. I was just asking if there was anything else we ought to know."

"No," Staples said. "There's nothing."

"Only I thought..."

"No. No, that's everything."

"Do let us know if you need anything else, Inspector," Hudson said. "No one wants you to catch this person more than us."

"There was one other thing, as a matter of fact," Archer said. "Have either of you come across a family solicitor by the name of Peter Nish?"

Hudson and Staples exchanged glances, their expressions blank.

"I mean we've heard of him, obviously," Hudson said. "He's been on the news, poor man."

"He hasn't crossed my radar," Staples said.

"Nor mine, to the best of my knowledge," agreed Hudson. "Although there's no real reason why he should, at my level."

"Well, thanks for your time," said Archer. "Give me another call any time if there's anything else that occurs to you."

"Of course," Hudson said, a little too smoothly for Archer's liking.

And that was the trouble. Afterwards, as Archer waited for the lift to crawl its way to her floor, she couldn't help reflecting that Hannah Hudson was altogether too smooth by half.

19

Archer returned to the station with little enthusiasm. On her way back to her office, she almost ran into Baines.

"I've been looking for you," he said. "Joan has pulled that Clive Edwards file we talked about."

"And?"

"He was actually a chartered surveyor, so he might well have the sort of organised mind you were talking about. Sadly, there's nothing on the file to suggest that he had any connection with our victims."

"But presumably nothing to indicate that he didn't, either. Let's get him in."

"I've asked Joan to check his current address, but you might want to hold off pulling him in. Joan has tracked down the woman who spat on Stephanie Merritt."

"Dawn Dulac?"

"How do you know her name's Dawn?"

"I've just got her details from Elaine Staples in Social Services."

He looked a bit deflated. "Oh, well. We've done it the hard way. It's not exactly a common name and there's only one Dulac in the local directory. Joan rang her first thing and asked if she'd had any dealings with Stephanie. She didn't deny it. She works for McDonald's in the High Street and says she can meet us in her lunch break, around noon."

"Sounds too cooperative. How did she sound to Joan?"

"Too cooperative," he agreed.

She pursed her lips. "Well, we'll see her. If it yields nothing, we can get hold of this Edwards." She briefly outlined what Elaine Staples had told her.

"Interesting," he said.

134

"I half-sensed that she had something else to get off her chest, but she said not. She hadn't come across Peter Nish."

Baines frowned. "I'm wondering if we should take the list to Walker & Scott, the firm where Peter Nish worked, and see if there are any common denominators."

"Good idea. Get Bell to do that, if he's not too tied up on other things. And get him to ask them generally if they've had dealings with Stephanie. We shouldn't fixate on the cases Mr Merritt told us about. Definitely get Jason to mention Edwards. Better get someone to track down Edwards' ex, too. She's likely to be on the list."

"Maybe he's saving her for last." Baines paused. "Do you want to sit in on the meeting with Dulac?"

"Anything to get me out of here," she said, and then immediately regretted the self-pitying note in her voice.

"Why?" Too late. He had picked up on it. "Problems?"

"No. It's just that it's a nice day out there," she lied. "So what have you got on this morning?"

"Brandon Clark's coming home. I want to talk to him urgently. Have you heard about Marcus disappearing?"

She winced mentally. "The boss did mention it, yes."

"Well, I think he and Brandon know something they don't want to tell us, and that's why Marcus bolted from us. I think he could be in a lot of trouble, and Brandon needs to tell us what he knows before it's too late. You said you wanted to have a go at Brandon - I could do with your involvement, if you can spare me some time in half an hour or so."

"I don't think that's a good idea," she said.

"Why not?"

What the hell? "I'm already in trouble for scaring off one Clark boy."

"Scaring -" He stared at her, mouth open. "Julie was moaning to me about..." He appeared to be grappling for any words but the obvious. "... about how you look. She thought you might have frightened Marcus, but I told her that was bollocks." He shook his head, his mouth a thin line of disgust. "Don't tell me she made it official?"

"Apparently. DCI Gillingham asked me if I thought it wise to 'go round scaring children', as he put it."

"He said that?" Baines' eyes widened in outrage. "Unbelievable. I thought he was better than that, even if he does like covering his arse."

"Apparently I ought to be a bit selective about which members of the public I see," she said bitterly, her vow not to sound self-pitying scattering to the winds. "Or rather that I allow to see me. Avoid those of a nervous disposition."

"And you're standing for it?" He shook his head again. "Look. It's not for me to tell my governor how to do her job, but I wouldn't put up with that. I'd definitely come to talk to Brandon Clark if it was me. Just to bloody show them."

She hadn't expected such a show of support. Had even wondered if he'd said something to Gillingham. She blinked twice, hoping the prickling behind her eyes didn't produce tears in front of him.

"Fuck it," she said, decision made. "You're right. An hour it is. Can you find me a big paper bag though?"

"Paper bag?" He looked mystified.

"To put over my head."

* * *

Julie Clark was pale with worry when she opened the door to Baines.

"Have you found him?"

"I'm sorry," he said. "No news yet. We've come to see Brandon."

She seemed to suddenly register Archer's presence and went several shades whiter.

"I'm not having her in here," she snapped, stabbing a finger in the DI's direction.

He sighed. "Julie, we're doing all we can to find Marcus. You've probably heard the helicopters overhead all morning. But we both need to talk to Brandon."

"Why both of you?"

"Because I say so. Because it's best."

She wrapped her arms around herself. It was another warm day, but she was wearing a cardigan. Her eyes looked everywhere but at Baines or Archer.

"He's only just come home. He needs rest."

"This really can't wait. We think he might know something about why Marcus has gone missing."

Her shoulders stiffened, making her stance more hostile. "How can he? He was in hospital when you came round here scaring everyone."

"I know that. Look, I might be completely wrong, but I think it's to do with the shooting. I think he knows something about what happened to his brother. Maybe he saw something. He could be in danger. Now, are you going to let us in?"

She shrugged. "You can come in, Mr Baines, but I don't see why she has to be here. I've already told your boss -"

Another woman appeared behind her. Baines recognised Julie's sister, Paula, from last night. She was blonde like her sister, but chunkier with slightly pointed features. "What's going on, Jules?" She looked from Baines to Archer, her gaze settling on the latter and taking in her disfigurement.

"Is she the one?" She spoke to Archer. "You ought to know better than to come round scaring a nine-year-old with that thing."

He'd had enough of this, even allowing for the strain they both must be under.

"Now, listen to me, Julie. I know what you told our boss, and it wasn't helpful. DI Archer has to be here because I say she does. Because I think talking to Brandon will help us find Marcus, and I think she can help us get some answers."

Julie wrung her hands. "I don't know..."

He shrugged. "Come on, DI Archer, we're wasting our time. You can see where Mrs Clark's priorities are."

He turned as if to go.

"Wait!"

Julie Clark was crying.

"I'm sorry," she said to Archer. "What with Brandon, and now Marcus... Do you really think he's in danger?"

Archer made a non-committal face and left her to fill in the blanks. "Obviously, if he's able to identify the gunman in any way - then yes, he might be."

Her shoulders sagged. "All right. Come in, both of you."

Paula scowled and disappeared into the kitchen.

Brandon Clark was stretched out on the sofa, watching daytime TV. Or at least, the TV was on, but on closer examination he was reading a paperback.

"Hi Brandon," Baines said. "Still Dickens?"

"Nah." The boy held the book up so Baines could see the cover. "Orwell. 1984. Big Brother."

"A bit different to the reality TV show," Archer observed.

"Just a bit, yeah. He wasn't far off the mark, though, was he? All the CCTV cameras? Someone's always watching you. And all that political correctness if someone steps out of line. It's like the thought police, man." He looked at her steadily. "What happened to your face?"

Baines saw her flinch, then she shrugged. "Someone tried to rearrange it with a broken bottle. Didn't make a bad job of it, did they?"

"That's harsh," Clark said. "Does it still hurt?"

"No. But it itches sometimes."

"Mum thinks Marcus was scared of you. But it takes more than something like that to scare him."

"We think he knows something about what happened to you," she said. "Either he thought he was going to be in trouble with the police, or he thought something bad would happen to him if it was known he'd been talking to us."

Somewhere along the line he had broken eye contact. He was holding his book, his finger marking his page, and staring at the cover.

"Brandon," Archer pressed. "Your brother's been missing all night. Everyone's worried about what sort of trouble he might get into, and we need to understand why he ran. Now, we know he was with you just before you were shot. But he wasn't there when people came out to see what had happened. The question is - where did he go? Could he have seen anything?"

He stared at the book for a moment or two more, then sighed heavily and looked at her.

"It's complicated," he said.

20

Brandon Clark is striding along The Northfields, heading for the newsagent's to get some ciggies. He is thinking about the feud with Michael Sturridge's mob, and how boring it has all become. He had started the gang for something to do to relieve the dullness of life on the estate, and the emergence of a rival had added some extra spice to the whole thing for a while. But now he has outgrown it. It's all a bit too like a kid's game, and he has no desire to take it to a more serious level.

Even bunking off school has lost its appeal. He is finding many of the lessons interesting, especially history and the novels his class is studying. He hasn't told anyone yet, but secretly he would quite like to be a teacher one day.

He hears feet running up behind him, and then his brother, Marcus, falls into step with him.

"Hey, bro," Marcus says. "How's it hanging?"

He is amused, as always, with the kid's attempts at street talk. He has picked most of it up from the telly, and he does it with an American accent, not the cod London Caribbean lilt Brandon and his mates employ.

"Hey, bro," he responds, not especially annoyed to have his little brother tagging along. Marcus is a nice kid who hero worships Brandon, but the older sibling won't let him do anything that will get him into trouble.

"You'll never guess what I found?" chirps Marcus.

"You're right there, man. I'll never guess in a squillion years."

The younger boy giggles. "Not even in a trillion billion squillion?"

"Not even then." They are nearly at the shop

Marcus starts slipping his school duffel bag off his shoulder. "I'll show you."

"Not now, mate. I've got to get my smokes. Afterwards, yeah?"

"Yeah, mate. You'll never guess."

Marcus follows him into the shop like his shadow. Mr Mohammed knows Brandon's way under age but sells him the cigarettes anyway. Brandon suspects that Mr Mohammed knows his reputation and doesn't want any trouble. While the shopkeeper gets the cigarettes down from the shelf and takes the money, he keeps an eye on them, making sure the boys don't steal anything.

There is a woman in the shop, studying the magazines on the shelves. As they leave, a man comes in, greeting Mr Mohammed and commenting on the weather. Outside, the street is deserted.

"So what's this big secret you've found?" Brandon wants to know as he wrestles with the cellophane on the cigarette packet.

Grinning shyly, the younger boy delves in his duffel bag. The gun is a revolver, Brandon can see that much. It's blue-black with a polished wood grip. The barrel is about four inches long. It looks heavy.

"Fuck!" he gasps. "Where you get that?"

"Found it on the way back from school," Marcus says proudly. "It was in amongst the flowers on that big roundabout."

Brandon realises that the boy's finger is on the trigger, which isn't a good idea. Plus, if someone comes out of the shop and sees the Clark boys messing with what looks to him like a real gun, they could be in really big trouble.

"Okay little man," Brandon says, "you need to give that to me."

He can see by Marcus's face that his brother doesn't like his tone.

"Why should I?" he demands. "It's mine. Cool, innit?"

"Yeah." Brandon tries to stay calm. "Real cool. But you don't want to be waving it about where anyone can see. Best put it back in the bag."

For some reason, Marcus looks agitated. Maybe he wanted his big brother to be impressed and is disappointed by his less than enthusiastic response. Whatever the reason, he starts waving his hands about, which of course means he is also waving the gun.

"I thought you'd be pleased. I was gonna give it to you anyway, so you could be a real gang banger, like on telly. Get some respect -"

The gunshot, when it comes, is louder than Branson would have expected. It makes his ears ring. He feels something like a punch in his side and then a burning pain. He puts a hand to the place and it comes away bloody.

His brother's eyes are wide, his mouth open in a silent O.

"Sorry," gabbles Marcus. "Sorry, Brandon."

Already the world around him is turning grey. He leans against the shop window, thinking fast.

"Quick, man," he gasps. "Put the gun in your bag and run. Get rid of it, soon as you can. You'll get in real serious trouble, a thing like this. They'll lock you up."

"But -"

"Go! Go now. Fast as you can." He feels woozy, his legs barely able to support him. "RUN!" he manages to bellow.

And Marcus does run, pausing only to stuff the gun back in his duffel bag. He runs like an Olympian. Only when he is out of sight does Brandon stagger back into Mr Mohammed's shop. The woman customer is at the counter, talking to the shopkeeper, looking worried. The man is halfway to the door.

"Please can you help me?" he says, his voice half-whisper, half-croak. "I've been shot." And he sinks to the floor.

The woman looks at him, her eyes darting to the rapidly spreading patch of red on his tee-shirt. "Oh, God, it was a shot. Look at the blood!"

"Who shot you, son?" the male customer wants to know.

It's amazing. They obviously heard the shot and yet dicked around over coming out to investigate. Probably scared the gunman might still be there. Brandon feels like he's dying, and these two muppets want to have a discussion about it. But he sees Mr Mohammed take down the phone behind him and dial a number. After a moment, the shopkeeper says, "Ambulance, please."

In a moment, the shopkeeper will finish his emergency call and, showing great presence of mind, run upstairs and come back down with some towels, which he will stuff into the wound, probably saving Brandon's life. Meanwhile, the boy knows help is on its way. Now he can start to lie.

"It was a drive by," he groans. "Someone in a car shot me."

21

"Let's get this straight," Archer said to Brandon. "Your brother shot you?"

"It was an accident. He don't know nothing about guns. It just went off. I thought he'd be locked up, or taken away from us, or Mum would get into trouble." He looked at Baines. "I meant what I said, Mr Baines. I want to give up The Barracudas and make a go of school, and I don't want Marcus getting mixed up in no trouble."

"But you said Michael Sturridge shot you," Baines said, looking confused. "You identified him as the shooter."

"You weren't letting it drop," he said. "Marcus told me all about his lame story about running off to watch the telly. I thought someone would push him about it and that'd be it. He's rubbish at lying, and it would have come out. But no one ever pushed him. I thought it'd be all right, but then you wouldn't let it go. I thought I'd give you Michael. You might believe it."

"Oh, Brandon." Julie Clark spoke for the first time. "I can't believe you'd do that. Blame someone for something they didn't do."

"It was Sturridge or Marcus, Mum. And, since Michael didn't have the gun, I didn't think you could prove anything against him. All I had to keep saying was it was a drive-by and I thought it was him. In the end it would all go away. Lack of evidence, you see." He looked confident in his plan.

Archer felt suddenly very old. "It was never going to go away," she said. "And now Marcus is out there all alone, and scared. He might even have the gun still."

"Nah." Brandon insisted. "I told him to toss it." But there was doubt in his eyes.

"You'd better think hard, Brandon," Baines said. "We want to know every single place you can think of where your brother might be hiding. We've already got a mess. We don't want a bigger one."

He looked about to refuse, but his mother was suddenly kneeling by the sofa.

"You do as you're told, Brandon. Right now. You've caused enough trouble with your lies. Now tell the officers what they want to know. Help your brother."

* * *

James Baxter lifted his face from the kitchen work surface, wiped away any traces of white powder around his nose, and let the high kick in. Now he felt sharp, and ready to go to work.

As he shrugged on the jacket of his Paul Smith linen suit, he looked around his handsome new apartment, part of a recently converted former coach house in the heart of Old Aylesbury. Everything was top spec, and he had a Maserati GranTurismo outside in his personal parking space.

On the face of it, most of his neighbours were much like himself. Young, upwardly mobile. A few lawyers, a lady doctor he had the serious hots for, a couple of entrepreneurs.

That was how Baxter described himself whenever he got chatting with a neighbour. An entrepreneur. When they asked him to elaborate, he was sometimes tempted to say he was in pharmaceuticals, but he knew that wouldn't be wise. Better to keep it vague. It wouldn't do for them to know that he was one of the most successful drug dealers in Buckinghamshire.

He had come a long way in a short time, treating drugs as a commodity, buying and selling at a profit, and making sure he never got caught. It was absolutely essential to stay one step ahead of the law, and he knew how to do that. On the couple of occasions the police had come sniffing around, he had been cleaner than a nun's knickers. Now he had a very nice lifestyle, with very nice neighbours, it was important to him that the law didn't come to his door at all.

He stepped out of the apartment, enjoying the solid feel of the front door as he closed it. He was on the second floor, and he took the stairs briskly, emerging into sunlight. The building

was set in over an acre of grounds, nicely maintained. Many of the flowers were in full bloom, and their colours and perfume always gave him an extra lift.

Baxter got in his car and started the engine. It responded with a throaty roar as it fired up, and then he was rolling down the gravel drive to the high, wrought iron gates that flanked the entrance. He emerged onto Chapel Street, heading off for this morning's round of deals. He turned on the CD player, and Mumford and Son's folksy sounds filled the car. He sang along, oblivious to the scruffy Peugeot that pulled away from the roadside and followed him.

* * *

Brandon Clark's list of his brother's haunts had been passed onto the search coordinator, together with a warning that Marcus might be in possession of a gun. DI Steve Ashby had been put in overall charge of the search, and SOCOs were combing the well-planted roundabout where Brandon claimed the youngster had found the weapon.

Meanwhile, a boy answering Marcus's description had been reported running off with some chocolate bars and drinks from a shop about a mile from his home, less than an hour after he fled from Archer and Baines. If it had been Marcus, then at least he wouldn't be starving for a while.

Ashby was going to put out an appeal to Marcus to come home, assuming he heard it. He would stress that neither he nor his brother were in any trouble. That everyone knew what had happened was an accident. Baines had serious doubts that someone like Ashby was ideal to make such an appeal, but it wasn't his call.

Meanwhile, Baines and Archer still had two murders to investigate, and DCI Gillingham had made it clear that this was their top priority. At noon, they showed up outside Costa Coffee in Aylesbury, a stone's throw from where Dawn Dulac worked at McDonald's.

Dulac was slightly overweight with hair that looked as if it was made out of scouring pads and a very red complexion. At the same time, she had the look of the permanently fatigued about her. She looked as if she had the strength to swing a hammer, but possibly not the energy.

"You can buy me a latte and a chocolate twist," she informed Baines, "since I'm helping you with your enquiries."

He had taken an instant dislike to her, and knew when someone was taking the piss, but it was true that he needed her help. He bought what she had asked for, an espresso for himself and a cappuccino for Archer. It was a bit early for the place to fill up with lunchtime trade and they had a choice of tables.

"So," Dulac said around a mouthful of pastry, "you want to know about my run-in with Mrs Merritt? Who told you about that?"

"I can't tell you that," he said.

Dawn Dulac snorted as if she didn't believe a word of that. "If you say so. Well, as to this argument, there wasn't much to it really. My ex's parents decided I was neglecting the kids and reported me. Mrs Merritt came round wanting to see them and asking all sorts of nosy questions. She caught me at a bad time, and I didn't take kindly to her."

"We understand you slapped her and spat on her."

Dulac took a monster bite out of her chocolate twist, chewed, swallowed, and chased it down with a swig of coffee. "That's a bit exaggerated."

"Which part?"

"The slap barely connected. And I spat at her, not on her. Well, I tried to spit on her, but it missed her completely."

"Oh," Baines said. "That's all right then."

"Yeah, well. I knew I'd been out of order, and I didn't want her to make a big thing of it, so I wrote her a letter of apology afterwards. She came back to see me, and she asked her questions. I answered, and that was the last I heard of her until it was on the news that she'd been murdered."

"Where were you around eight on Monday morning?" But he asked only for form's sake. Unless the hoodie in the CCTV footage was a total red herring, there was no way this large lady could be the person they were looking for. Although he supposed it was just possible that the hoodie wasn't the killer after all.

"I was getting my kids ready for school, and myself ready for work."

"And have you ever heard of a solicitor called Peter Nish?"

She nodded. "He's been on the news, too. Wasn't he murdered as well?"

"Did you know him?"

"No. Never heard of him before he was all over the news. Do you think it's the same killer?"

"It's one of a number of avenues we're exploring," Archer said.

"Yeah, well I didn't do it."

"Just for the record, what were you doing on Tuesday night? Between 10 pm and 2 am?"

"Watching the telly or asleep. Like I say, I didn't kill anyone. I don't know this Mr Nish."

They left cards and extracted a promise to contact them if anything occurred to her.

"That was a waste of time," Archer said on her way back to the car. "I guess we can at least cross her off the list for now."

"Unless she sent a friend to do her dirty work."

"We wouldn't be able to make that connection unless we had someone in custody, Dan. What we really need to do is cross-refer Stephanie's cases with Nish's and see if there's any overlap. Bell was talking to Nish's firm?"

"He was going there this morning."

"Well, see if you can catch him and tell him not to be too ready to let them play the data protection card. We need him to emphasise the need for cooperation with the police. While you're doing that, I'll check in with Joan and get her to send some uniforms to pick up that surveyor, Clive Edwards."

He made the call to Bell and caught him just as the DC was parking his car. At Archer's suggestion, he also asked ~~the~~ Bell to make himself available for a team meeting in the afternoon to take stock of where they were with the hammer killings, even though they knew they hadn't got very far at all.

Everyone was hoping that, however Nish and Merritt were linked, the solicitor's death marked the end of the killer's spree. But, Baines knew, if that wasn't the case then the clock was ticking. And that another victim could be literally moments from death.

* * *

James Baxter parked the Maserati at the end of the alley and began walking. He never particularly liked these drop-offs in this run-down part of town on the edge of the Northfields estate. Experience had told him the place had a much exaggerated reputation - he had never been mugged here, and his car had never been vandalised - but he always felt nervous here, and this walk down a long, gloomy alley invariably made him uncomfortable.

But the client he called Mister Indigo in his own code - whoever he or she really was - had proved extremely valuable to him, despite the cloak and dagger of their arrangement. He had received a text three months ago stating what was wanted and asking him to name a price. He had done so, and another text had directed him to the shabby disused yard at the other end of this alley. He had been told he would find the money in an envelope in an old dustbin and that he should leave the goods there.

It had all worked like clockwork, and Baxter had made certain he was being neither followed nor watched before he made the drop, to ensure that this wasn't a police trap.

Since then, it had been the same procedure every week on a Thursday. If he was honest, he had now become a lot more relaxed about the possibility of being observed. If it was some sort of police sting, he'd have long since been in custody, with his brief trying to talk him out of it.

He emerged from the narrow alley into the gloomy yard, which was awash with mouldy litter. He'd never been too sure, or very interested for that matter, as to what business used to go on here. He only knew that it was no longer possible to access the yard by car - hence the walk along the alley.

His footsteps echoed a little as he approached the bin, which stood waiting for him like a faithful pet. He liked to think that echo marked the quality of his well-polished brogues - solid and dependable.

As always, the envelope containing the cash was near the top, under a layer of old newspaper. Insects crawled in the bin, and he half expected you would find maggots if you excavated deeply enough. He always wore gloves for this operation. Not his good leather ones but a pair of surgical latex ones. They also ensured he left no fingerprints, although he doubted it mattered,

He slipped the envelope into his inside pocket, not bothering to count it. He trusted this client. He removed the package of drugs from his Leonhard Heyden Windsor briefcase and placed it where the money had been. He replaced the bin lid and the job was done. He turned to return to the alley, and immediately froze.

A silent figure stood watching him. A figure in a black hoodie. There was something menacing about the stance, and he was unable to see any sign of a face beneath the hood. It was like being confronted by some sort of faceless phantom. But this was not what really scared him.

What turned his guts to water was the hammer that the figure held in its right hand.

* * *

Archer and Baines returned to the station and checked with Collins on progress with Clive Edwards. It was not good news. Four uniformed constables - mob-handed in case of any trouble - had pitched up at the address in Butler's Cross where records stated he lived, but had not found him at home.

"The next door neighbour said she hadn't seen him for months," Collins told them.

"So where is he?" Archer wanted to know.

"She said she hadn't a clue, and by all accounts she didn't seem that sorry. She said he never said so much as a good morning to anyone. Even refused to take parcels in for neighbours, according to the postman. Then, three months ago, she sort of realised she hadn't seen hide nor hair of him for some weeks, and nor had the other neighbours."

"Three months?" Baines was incredulous. "What - and she hasn't reported him missing?"

"She said everyone was glad to see the back of him. His car was gone, so she assumed he hadn't been quietly decomposing in the house. Said she thought the house might have been repossessed."

"Sweet," Archer remarked. "Is this the village community spirit I keep hearing so much about, Dan?"

"I tracked down the ex-wife," Collins said. "She's been living in France for a while, and hasn't heard anything from him. Said she'd kill him if he came near her. Neither of our victims' names meant anything to her."

"That doesn't necessarily mean anything," Archer said. She drummed her fingers on Collins' desk. "So he could be anywhere. We should have thought of him before."

Baines felt he was being got at again. It didn't help that she was probably right.

"The timescale fits," he admitted. "He could have spent the time following the victims home from their offices. Stalking them, finding out the patterns in their lives, deciding when to strike."

"Elaine Staples couldn't give me a connection with Stephanie Merritt," said Archer. "Let's hope Bell has more luck with Peter Nish's office. It's about time we got a break."

22

Archer passed Steven Ashby in the corridor on her way to the major incident room for the team briefing on the hammer killings. For once, Ashby cracked no sarcastic smile. Being asked to co-ordinate enquiries into Marcus Clark's disappearance seemed to be weighing heavy on him, and perhaps he was nervous about his TV appeal this afternoon. Either that or it was hurting him to have to do some work for a change.

Once again DCI Gillingham was joining the briefing. He looked a little tense. So did they all. Two people were dead, their heads almost completely destroyed. There was someone out there with a whole lot of rage and no one knew if he'd finished his work yet.

Joan Collins was last to join the team, and Archer thought she detected a hint of excitement about the young DC - as if she had some news and was eager to impart it.

"All right," Gillingham said when Collins had settled, "we need to start making some progress in this case. I can tell you the top brass are nervous about this one. Some of them still remember the Invisible Man." He glanced at Baines. "Sorry, Dan. But having had a serial killer who was never caught still rankles with them, and they don't much like the idea of history repeating itself here. They sort of feel it could be career limiting. So, if they're feeling the heat, you can bet we're going to feel it too."

He smiled grimly. "No pressure then, DI Archer. What have you got for us?"

"Okay," she began. "First up, we have a possible suspect." She walked up to the wall board and indicated an A4 sized photograph of an unremarkable-looking man in his forties. "Clive Edwards."

She brought the team up to speed on the surveyor's history.

"I remember," Gillingham said. "But surely we don't even know he did one murder, let alone these new ones. So why do we think he's a suspect?"

She suppressed a sigh, realising that what she had thought was a good lead was going to be a hard sell to her superior. "Not much of a reason, sir. As I said, he's no more than a possible suspect at this stage. But the thing is, he went missing about three months ago. The neighbours were glad to be rid of him, and there's been no contact between him and his ex-wife since the divorce. Maybe he's living somewhere under an assumed name and stalking his victims."

"And maybe not. Frankly, I'm not hearing anything that interesting so far," the DCI remarked.

"I know, I know. But if he did kill his wife's lover, it's just possible he came into contact with Merritt and Nish during his divorce and took a dislike to them"

"I don't buy it. It sounds like you're clutching at straws. I mean, he could be working away, shacked up with a woman. Anything. No proof that he has previous form. No connection with the victims..."

Frustrated, she interrupted him. "Not so far, sir. But DC Bell has been to Peter Nish's employer this morning to see if they knew of any connections between him and Stephanie Merritt. Any luck, Jason?"

Bell was a gangly Scot with a shock of red hair. "Nothing definite, ma'am." At Baines' instigation, Archer suspected, most of the team had started to call her 'guv', instead of the hated 'ma'am'. For Bell, it seemed that old habits died hard.

"So what have you got?"

"Well, as we know, Mr Nish was a family solicitor. It seems Mrs Merritt is known to the firm. They've agreed to go through his cases and see where there's been an overlap."

"Do they think there definitely is one?"

"Best I could get out of them was 'most likely'. But not for a while, as far as anyone knows, so they'd have to review the files to be sure. They've at least promised to give it some priority."

"And did you mention Edwards?"

"Yes, ma'am."

"And?"

"Good news and bad news. The good news is that there is a link. The firm represented Edwards in his divorce. But the bad news is that Nish wasn't his solicitor. They couldn't rule out his having some involvement, perhaps when the person dealing was away. They're checking."

Archer turned triumphantly to Gillingham. "There's one connection, sir."

"Yes, I'll give you that, but it's pretty tenuous, isn't it? And why would he murder his own solicitor - let alone someone else on the firm?" objected Gillingham.

"Perhaps he didn't like the settlement," Baines said. "And maybe he's got a down on the whole firm as a result."

"Maybe, and maybe not. I'm not sure I want to tie up resources looking for him on such shaky grounds."

Archer felt her confidence ebbing away. She could see Gillingham's point. There wasn't so much to go on. Yet Edwards had form with a hammer and there was at least a tentative link with Nish. Instead of urging her to follow it up, her boss was making her look a fool in front of her team.

Seething, she turned to Bell again.

"Okay, Jason, let's park that for now. Did you give them Mr Merritt's list of names?"

"Yes, ma'am, but I told them not just to look for them. I thought if Edwards wasn't in the frame, then the link could be anything."

"Quite. Well done, Jason. How far are they going back?"

"I thought... six months?"

"No," she decided. "After we break up, can you call them and ask them to make it a year?"

He nodded. "Straight away."

"So there could still be a connection, and we just don't know what it is," Gillingham said complacently.

Baines held up a finger. "Sir, I wonder if we should bring the nature of the killings out into the open? I mean, we're looking at someone whose favoured weapon is a hammer.

Maybe if people know how our victims died, it will jog a few memories."

Archer had been intending to say the same thing. So her heart sank when the DCI shook his head decisively.

"I see what you're saying, Dan, but not quite yet, I think. It will give the serial confessors something to get their teeth into, and it might jog memories in the wrong way."

Archer looked at him. "The wrong way, sir?"

"I don't want them focusing on hammers and not on people. It's people and their motives that kill people, not weapons. If everyone fixates on who might be into battering skulls with hammers, they may disregard anyone they don't see in that way. And putting it into the public's mind that there's a maniac on the loose bashing heads in might panic everyone."

"Maybe a bit of panic's healthy, sir."

"No, DI Archer, panic is never healthy. It makes people do silly things. I don't want some poor sod of a carpenter lynched in Friars Square shopping centre, just because he stops off there with his toolkit to buy his kids some sweets." He said it pleasantly enough, but it still felt like yet another rebuke. "So, what else have we got?"

Archer turned to Collins. "Okay, Joan. I can see you're dying to tell us something."

"A couple of things, guv. The burned-out car we thought had been used in the Merritt murder?"

"Go on," she urged, interested. "The forensics guys managed to find some blood traces on the front seat that survived the fire, didn't they?"

"That's right. Well, they've matched the DNA to Mrs Merritt, so it's certain that the driver we saw on CCTV is the killer."

"At least that gives us a definite height and build to home in on," Archer said. "It's not much, but it's something. By the way, Edwards' build probably fits the bill."

"Three of the names on Mr Merritt's list were women, ma'am," Bell said. "There was only one man."

"It wasn't him," Archer said. "According to Eileen Staples, Tony Plater's stuck in a wheelchair."

"So we're at another dead end," groaned Gillingham.

"Apart from Edwards," she pointed out.

"Apart from Clive Edwards." He drummed his fingers on his chair arm, then gave a resigned sigh. "All right, then. I've got my doubts about him, but follow it up. But I don't want all the attention on him."

"Thank you, sir," Archer said, relieved.

"I don't want us fixating on a professional link between Nish, Merritt and the killer, either." He frowned. "Maybe the reason we're struggling to find one is that it doesn't exist. What if it's something else?"

"You think it might be random, sir?"

"Not really, no. But there are other ways they could be connected, surely?"

He looked at her expectantly, as if she was going to snatch a solution from thin air. Her mind went blank, devoid of ideas.

"For instance," offered Baines, coming to her rescue, "we know Stephanie had an affair with her colleague Brian Hughes. Well, a one night stand, by all accounts, but still... What if she had professional dealings with Nish a long time ago? Then she bumped into him more recently and had an affair with him too. We know Nish was seeing a prostitute, so he's got form for playing away."

"So then who has motive for killing them both?" Gillingham wondered. "His wife? Her husband? Richard Merritt could barely stand after that heart attack, much less kill Nish. And my money's still on it being a man, which would rule out Mrs Nish. What about this Hughes? Does he have alibis?"

"We're checking," Baines promised. "But here's a hypothetical scenario for you - Hughes finds out that Merritt is seeing Nish, doesn't like it, and kills them both."

Collins put her hand up like a little girl in school. The teacher's pet. Archer felt herself smiling.

"Sorry, sir, sorry guv. It would have to be a bit more complicated than that."

Archer gave her attention. "Because...?"

"Sorry," she said again. "I shouldn't have saved my most interesting news till last."

"No, Collins, you probably shouldn't." Gillingham agreed with a withering glare. "This is a murder enquiry, not a game of suspense."

"No, sir." The young DC was squirming.

"Let's hear it now, Joan," Archer said, trying to smooth the situation. She already had a lot of time for Collins, and didn't like to see her being knocked back. She'd seen young officers having their confidence rocked before, and ultimately it did no one any good.

Collins swallowed. "Well, guv, you know we circulated the details of both murders to all forces last night? Well, just before I came to the briefing, I picked up a call from a DI Baker in Norfolk Constabulary. It seems they had a murder three weeks ago with a similar MO. Like us, they kept the details about the probable use of a hammer out of the press. He was going to e-mail me a picture of the victim, and he's happy to speak to you, guv, or to you, sir," she looked Gillingham's way.

"Could just be a coincidence," Baines remarked.

"Let's see the picture, and then decide," Archer said. "If the face is completely obliterated, I'd say it's certainly our killer's style. Did he mention who the victim was, Joan?"

"That's what's most interesting, guv. Her name's Susan Downes. She retired to King's Lynn eighteen months ago. Before that, she was a solicitor here in the Vale."

* * *

Detective Inspector Ian Baker had such a strong Norfolk accent that it would have been easy to dismiss him as a bumpkin, but Archer had sensed even before dialling his number that it would be a mistake to do so. He'd moved swiftly when he'd seen the details of Archer's two cases, and seemed keen, judging by his e-mail, to share information. Even in the technological age of the 21st Century, there were still plenty of coppers intent on protecting their turf and keeping their cases to themselves, preferring the chance of glory if they solved a case to the chance of solving it quicker and sharing the spoils.

The jpeg attachment to his e-mail was sickening, even though Archer had twice seen sights all too horribly similar, at closer quarters than she would ever have wished. She was immediately convinced that she was looking at an earlier victim of her killer, perhaps the first victim.

"So you agree?" Baker said, once they'd got the pleasantries out of the way. "You think we're dealing with the same killer?"

"I certainly think everything points to it," she said. "We've got two solicitors and a social worker from the Aylesbury Vale area, their heads and faces pulverised. Your pathologist and mine both favour a hammer as the murder weapon. The trick's going to be connecting the victims, but now we have three of them, there can't be that many common denominators. I'm thinking it's most likely a case they've got in common."

"I'd imagine you've been checking out whether anyone saw or heard anything, and on the victim, their contacts, their habits." he said. "We started off the same with Miss Downes."

"She wasn't married?"

"Preferred the ladies, actually. She was in a civil partnership with a Lesley Pope, but they both used 'Miss', rather than 'Mrs'. When Miss Downes retired, the couple sold up and moved to Norfolk. It had always been a dream of theirs."

And, less than two years later, the dream had turned into a nightmare.

"So what happened to her, exactly?"

"It was a Friday. Every Friday morning, Miss Pope goes to an art class and Miss Downes used to catch up on the household accounts while she was out. It seems they used to come and go by the back door to their cottage, and never locked it when one of them was at home."

Archer felt the hairs on her neck prickle. "So anyone watching them over a period would have known that?"

"That's the assumption. Our theory is that he just let himself in, cornered her in her study, and..."

"I know how it goes," she said, not needing the details. "Did he make any slip-ups? We were hoping that, if there was an earlier victim, he might have made some beginners' mistakes."

"Not that we can really see. I mean, he had to walk across the garden to get to the back door, and we found two sets of size nine prints."

"Two sets?"

"Both trainers, both the same brand, but different tread patterns. One set going in, one coming away. We reckoned he changed footwear after the murder, in case he had any blood on his shoes."

Archer had the office to herself. Ashby was off somewhere, presumably in connection with the search for Marcus Clark. She was holding a ball pen, making the odd note, and now she tapped it on her desk while wheels went round in her head.

"He didn't leave any prints at either of our scenes," she said, "so I've no idea if he changed his shoes. Size nine. I don't suppose they're a rare and expensive trainer only a handful of people possess?"

He laughed. "Two types of bog standard Nike, I'm afraid. You'll find them in any good sports shop. Definitely a man's shoe, for what that's worth."

"A bit, perhaps. It all fills out the picture."

"I could copy the file and send you, if it helps. You might see something we've missed, with your own experiences. Or I could bring it to you and we could compare notes face to face."

"Sounds a good idea, if you don't mind the journey. Let's make a date before we hang up." But something had been bugging her. "Meanwhile, can we backtrack? You said you started by checking out possible witnesses and finding out about the victim. It sounds as if you moved on to something else."

"We did. When we'd exhausted all those avenues, we started thinking about the killer. Why use a hammer? Why keep on smashing the face and skull up long after the victim must be dead? Any thoughts?"

She squirmed awkwardly in her chair and rubbed her scar. "To be honest, Ian, with two murders in two days, we've not really taken the time to focus on those questions, although we probably do need to. There's obviously considerable rage behind the attacks, and you obviously feel the motive must be in some way personal. Have you got any theories?"

"A couple, actually. The ferocity of the attack really disturbed me, and I wanted to bring a profiler in, but my bosses wouldn't hear of it. Only one victim, and all those budget cuts.

But I've got an old school friend who studied psychology, so I took him out for a beer and chatted to him about it. I had to swear him to silence on the details of the murder, of course."

"And what did he think?"

"Look, I've got to stress that he's not a forensic psychologist. He doesn't even practice psychology. But he came up with two thoughts. Someone's face is what you recognise them by, physically. So by utterly destroying a person's face, you could be said to be obliterating their identity. Sort of totally erasing them."

"So the motivation would be serious personal hatred of the victim?"

"Or what they represent - especially now we've got three."

"Yes, but our killer went all the way to Norfolk to target your Miss Downes. She was from here originally, so the key has got to be on my patch. No, Ian. He wasn't looking for types of victim. He wanted these specific three."

"Fair point," Baker acknowledged. "I'd go along with that. You think they must have all worked a particular case. That makes sense too."

"You said your tame psychologist had two thoughts. The demolition of the face is one. What's the other?"

"Oh, yes. Well, why a hammer? As opposed to, say, a baseball bat? I mean, a hammer's heavy and awkward to carry. My guy wondered if it could be symbolic of something. Maybe to do with why he hates these people so much."

She wanted to meet Baker face to face as soon as possible and talk about his case with the file in front of her. She was especially interested in seeing the crime scene photographs so she could visualise the earlier crime more easily. A part of her wanted to drive across to King's Lynn and see for herself, but there was too much kicking off here in the Vale. Plus she still hadn't seen her mother.

"When can you come?" she asked.

"I can clear tomorrow, I think," he said. "If that's soon enough. It'll take me - what? - a couple of hours, maybe three. E-mail me the postcode and my satnav will find you. I'll get there as early as I can."

"I'll look forward to it," she agreed, then a thought struck her. "This crosses our jurisdictions. How shall we handle it?"

He gave a low chuckle. "Lizzie, you're welcome to it. Yesterday, I had one nasty unsolved crime. Now you have a potential serial killer." She noted his emphasis of 'I' and 'you'. "Tell you what. If you solve the crime, it was a fine example of inter-force collaboration."

She saw where this was going. "And if it goes tits up?"

"You're on your own, obviously."

"Why am I not surprised? One last question."

"Go ahead."

"Has the name Clive Edwards come up in your enquiries?"

There was a pause while Baker considered the question.

"I don't think so," he decided. "Why?"

She shared the local speculation with him.

"I'll speak to the partner, Lesley, if I can. See you tomorrow."

As she hung up, she heard a gentle tapping behind her. Baines was leaning on the doorframe.

"That was our man from Norfolk?"

"Yes. He's coming across with the file tomorrow, but I'd say it's pretty certain we're now looking at three victims."

Baines was shaking his head.

"What?" she demanded.

"Actually," he said, "it's four."

23

The yard stank of piss and decay and was somehow dark and gloomy, even though it was a not unpleasant May day. At the same time, the atmosphere seemed warmer, more oppressive than the streets beyond the alley they had trudged down to reach the latest murder scene.

The yard was overlooked by a long-abandoned building that might have been a factory or a garage at some time. Baines had lived and worked in the Vale for years, but had never known it was here.

It was equally impossible to divine what possible purpose the alley might have served. It was far too narrow for a car. At one time, that approach to the yard had been defended by a high metal gate, but that now hung off rusty hinges. However the victim had wound up here, he would have lain undiscovered if not for the Maserati parked by the alley.

A member of the public had spotted it and sensed there was something wrong with an expensive-looking car apparently abandoned in this God-forsaken part of town. Their assumption had been that it had been stolen and dumped, and they had dutifully reported it to the police. It was not unusual for such reports to take a while to respond to, but it happened that a patrol car was a stone's throw away. Its occupants had likewise assumed that the car had been dumped, but one of them had suggested they investigate the alley.

By the time Baines and Archer arrived, Barbara Carlisle was already kneeling by the ruined head of the well-dressed corpse, and the car's registration had been linked to one James Baxter, a name that matched the credit cards in his wallet.

Baines squatted beside the pathologist. "I take it we don't really have to ask?" he prompted.

"Not if the question is whether he's another victim in our series, no Dan." She blinked behind her glasses. "It's your call, but I'd say it's official - you've got yourselves a serial killer, and a pretty nasty one at that."

"Time of death?" Archer posed.

"Some time from mid morning to lunch time. It's so warm here, it's going to take some complicated sums to be as precise as I'd like. Not that I think you'll be swamped with potential witnesses. This is a bit of a last outpost, isn't it?"

The Crime Scene Manager, Phil Gordon, joined them, holding up a transparent evidence bag containing a package.

"What have we got here?" Archer asked.

"Drugs. Quite a selection. Found them in a bin, right at the top. If this was a one-off, I'd think it was a deal gone bad."

"Do you think he was dropping off or picking up?" Baines wanted to know.

"Search me. No sign of a big wad of cash, but you wouldn't expect the killer to leave that behind."

"Nor a bag of goodies like that one in your hand. My hunch? This is a perfect killing ground, where our murderer doesn't expect to be disturbed. He posed as either a buyer or a seller - depending on what this guy's role is - and lured him here."

"I think you're probably right," Archer concurred. "Smart clothes, flash car? Maybe he's another lawyer. One with a pricey habit?"

"A lawyer might fit with whatever vendetta our killer is pursuing. But how would the killer know about his drug habit?"

"How does he know anything, Dan? He watches and waits. One thing's for sure, though. We need to move our frame of reference back quite considerably."

Baines wasn't sure what she meant, and said so.

"I told you about the Norfolk victim," she said. "On the way here?"

"Yep. Retired lawyer. Used to be local."

"Used to be. That's the point. If we still think the most likely link between these victims is some legal matter, with the killer or their family at the heart of it... well, Susan Downes retired over a year ago. Whatever grudge the killer is working out, it happened at least that long ago, if not longer. This maniac could have been planning his campaign for a whole lot longer than we thought."

* * *

Archer was quiet on the drive back to the station, which suited Baines well enough. His mind was a jumble of thoughts, and not all of them were on the case.

He remained hopelessly confused about Karen, and exactly what his feelings were for her. He'd heard no more from her since her message last night and his texted reply, and he wondered what was going to happen. They had become close at a time of intense mutual pain, and had been nothing more than friends for over a decade - something that their early mistake in sleeping together had not dented at the time.

Now, suddenly, it was a lot more complicated than that. What he had genuinely thought was a tasteless off the cuff remark had suddenly, and unintentionally raised the question of a change in the nature of their relationship - a question that clearly scared and unsettled Karen. Now he wondered if they had reached a crossroads. Maybe the friendship had run its course in its present form and needed to evolve.

But evolve into something deeper, or simply peter out into something more distant? That was the question.

He understood why the first option frightened Karen. It had scared him at first, but now he wasn't so sure. The rational side of him argued that maybe it was just that his bed had been empty for too long. But he knew that if all he wanted was sex, he would never insult Karen by using her as some sort of fuck-buddy.

The reality was that he was torn between what he really wanted, and what he was most afraid of. He thought in his heart that he probably wanted much more than friendship from her, but at the same time he was terrified that pursuing that desire would ultimately destroy what they already had. That fear had prevented him from making that leap into the dark.

And what if they did take that step into becoming lovers and, for whatever reason, it didn't work out? He would risk losing her anyway.

A van pulled out in front of him and he had to brake hard, knowing as he did so that he should have reacted sooner. Everything he had on his mind was killing his concentration. He mumbled an apology to Archer, who simply pointed out that the van driver was a wanker before returning to her own thoughts.

This complication with Karen couldn't have come at a worse time, he thought. Two - now three - murders to solve, a missing boy he felt some responsibility to... and then there was Jack. He couldn't quite let go of the crazy notion that - assuming he wasn't simply on the verge of some sort of breakdown - in some way the boy was trying to tell him something. He clung to the idea that his son was still alive somewhere, but accepted intellectually that, if he was being sent a message, it might be from beyond some lonely shallow grave.

Maybe it was his personal anguish over Jack that forced his thoughts to keep returning to nine-year-old Marcus Clark. The child had now been missing for almost 24 hours, and Baines had little confidence that DI Ashby was the man to find him. When he had first learned that it was Marcus who had shot his brother, albeit by accident, he had been relieved that the child had nothing worse to fear than getting into trouble over the incident.

Now, he was not so sure. The boy had found a gun by chance. Who had it belonged to? And did they want it back?

If all those things weren't distraction enough, then there was DI Lizzie Archer, lost in her own contemplations beside him. The flame of resentment about his missed promotion had dwindled to a bare flickering, and none of it was any longer directed at the woman who had filled the job he coveted. He also sensed that the ice might be gradually melting between them. But for all that, she had so far remained self-contained and slightly remote. She had told him only very briefly how she came by her scar. As for her private life, she had kept that book entirely closed.

On the other hand, he knew her life outside work was none of his business, if she chose to keep it private. They were only colleagues. They didn't have to be friends as well. And it wasn't as if he had done much opening up to her, either, when they had shared that awkward, stilted getting-to-know-you drink.

Still, he told himself, it was early days yet. He had enjoyed a superb working relationship with DI Britton, before his old boss had become ill. There was no reason why he couldn't forge something similar with Britton's successor, given a bit of time.

As he drew close to the station, he turned his thoughts back to the murders. Clive Edwards was a promising line of inquiry, but then the latest victim, this Baxter, had been killed close to the Northfields estate. Given the apparent drugs connection, and the fact that at least one of the two gangs vying for supremacy on the estate was trying to carve out a niche in the drugs market, maybe they should take a look at The Bloods and The Barracudas.

Yet he was damned if he could see what might link Merritt or Nish to the gangs, unless both had also been into the drugs scene, unbeknown to their families. More to the point, why would the Bloods or the Barracudas drag their backsides all the way to Norfolk to murder a retired lawyer?

But then, why would anybody?

He swung the Mondeo into the station car park and squeezed in between two sloppily parked patrol cars. They got out and walked together into the building.

"I'd better update Gillingham," Archer said, looking a bit like a soldier about to go over the top for the umpteenth time. He watched her for a moment as she strode off towards the DCI's office, then went to the water cooler to get himself a drink. There he found DC Collins.

"Definitely the same killer?" she asked.

"Not much doubt. This time, a guy called James Baxter. We've got the licence number of what we think is his car. Could you check it with DVLA and see if you can get an address?"

"Sure." She watched him copy the number from his notebook onto a separate scrap of paper and took it from him.

"We think there's a drugs connection and that the killer knew. That's how he lured him to his death."

Her brow creased. "Baxter and drugs... Why does that ring a bell?" She shrugged. "Maybe it'll come to me. I'll chase this address down." She turned to go, a plastic cup of water in her hand. As Baines moved towards the cooler, she stopped.

"Dan, I was thinking about that gun Marcus Clark is supposed to have found."

"What about it?" he said, filling his cup.

"The roundabout he told Brandon he'd found it on. That's less than a mile from where that petrol station holdup took place."

"So?" He shrugged. The holdup had been the stuff cartoons are made of, a total botch by as inept a bunch of villains as he'd heard of in a long time. With Brandon Clark's shooting, three murders on their patch, and Marcus's disappearance, that crime had barely featured in his thoughts lately. He supposed three idiots with a gun really ought to be taken a bit more seriously.

Collins was undeterred by his apparent lack of enthusiasm.

"Look, the bullet recovered from Brandon was a .38, yes?"

"Sounds right."

"And the ballistics expert who looked at the CCTV footage of the holdup recognised the gun as a Bruni Olympic. Which is a .38."

That got his interest. "Go on."

"Well, we know that the Olympic's actually a starting pistol..."

"Yep, and a growing number of Olympics have been converted to fire live ammo for criminal purposes." The revolver had recently been classified as a prohibited weapon under Section 5 of the Firearms Act 1968 and not so long ago owners had been urged to hand them in under a national amnesty. "So what are you thinking?"

"We've been assuming the three men who held up the petrol station were first-timers. Sounds like they were even more scared than the kids behind the counter."

Baines remembered. The staff had said the guy with the gun had been shaking so badly, it was a wonder he didn't get a round off by accident. They'd demanded money from the till and, when there wasn't too much of that, they'd demanded cigarettes. One of them had helped himself to a few DVDs on the way out. The CCTV footage had shown them dropping half the cigarettes as they legged it for the car.

Collins sipped her water. "So I'm thinking maybe they were just scared kids, not criminal masterminds. About the only sensible things they did were to use a stolen car and wear Disney masks. Maybe they so lost their bottle that they chucked the gun into the flower bed on the roundabout on the way past?"

"So when we find Marcus and the gun, we might get some prints or DNA off it and catch the petrol station robbers?"

She nodded. "What do you think?"

"I think you should get DI Ashby to show Brandon pictures of an Olympic starting pistol and see if he can recognise it."

Collins made a face. "I tried that and he didn't want to know."

"Didn't want to know?" Baines echoed. "Ashby?"

"He said the petrol station job was still yours, and so was the Brandon Clark shooting. Said he was sorting out the mess you and DI Archer made with Marcus and that was all."

Tempted as Baines was to condemn Ashby as an idle sod who would do anything to wriggle out of actually doing some work, he was loathe to rubbish a senior officer to a DC, even though Ashby's reference to his and Archer's mess made his blood boil. Especially as he was doubtless responding to DCI Gillingham's claptrap about Archer's scar. Perhaps he'd even done his bit to fuel that in the first place.

He hoped Gillingham wasn't mouthing off about it all over the station. Just coping with her disfigurement was challenge enough for Archer, without the boss telling people it prevented her doing her job properly.

Still, Baines didn't think he could spare the time to investigate the matter right now. Plus the question of whether it was the same gun was academic until they recovered both it and the child who either still had it or had dumped it sometime since the shooting.

"Let's leave it for the moment then," he said finally. "But it's a good thought. Don't let's lose sight of it. If you could get us that address meanwhile?"

"On it. Oh, by the way, it looks like we can eliminate Brian Hughes from our enquiries."

"Oh?" Baines had almost forgotten about the social worker who'd had a one night stand with Stephanie Merritt.

"I called him on his mobile and he said he was at home with his wife when Peter Nish was being murdered. He seemed unhappy about giving me her number to check, but she confirmed his story. He's also got work colleagues who'll swear he was in the office when Baxter died."

Baines shrugged. "Can't say I'm surprised. Drugs and a Norfolk lesbian doesn't sound like him."

"You never know. I'd hate to be in his shoes tonight though. Mrs Hughes wanted to know why I was asking. I didn't say anything apart from some guff about normal procedure, but I think our office Romeo may have been rumbled."

"Tough," Baines retorted. "He should have kept it in his pants."

* * *

An hour later, Archer and Baines, with some uniforms and a couple of SOCOs in tow, were letting themselves into James Baxter's smart apartment with the set of keys found on the body.

They knew nothing of the latest victim of the hammer killer - some smartarse had made a comment about Hammer horror and been warned of dire consequences if anything like it appeared in the press - and had no idea whether he had a spouse of partner at home. So they had rung the doorbell and knocked first, only resorting to the keys when they got no reply.

Archer sought out the master bedroom, went to the wardrobes, and took a cursory glance at their contents.

"No sign of a woman living here," she remarked.

"All nice-looking gear," said Baines, indicating the quality suits and jackets, the hand-made shirts. All had been carefully placed on hangers, the shirts grouped together by shade. "All a bit fussy, though. Maybe two gay guys living together?"

Archer looked inside the en suite and then found the main bathroom.

"Only one toothbrush out. I'd say our Mr Baxter lived alone. Dan, get one of those uniforms to start knocking up neighbours - although I'd be surprised if anyone's at home at this time of day. These places have got 'executive pad' written all over them. Still, we might get lucky. I want to see what they know about him."

A uniformed constable had followed them into the room, and Baines sent him off on the errand. All the other uniforms were busy turning over the rest of the apartment. Archer had seen one of them in the second bedroom, which appeared to have doubled as a study for Baxter, bagging a slim Apple laptop, which she would get Ibrahim Iqbal working on later.

"We might as well have a nose in here," she told Baines. Both had pulled on latex gloves before entering the apartment, and they got to work.

"Whatever he did for a living, he was doing pretty well," she commented as she rifled through drawers, noting the labels on the silk boxer shorts and even the neatly folded pairs of socks.

"Either he's pretty house proud himself," Baines shot back at her from beneath the bed, "or he's got the only cleaning lady on the planet who pulls the bed out to vacuum. Hello," he added suddenly, "what have we got here?"

"I don't know, Dan," she replied. "My x-ray vision's a bit below par."

"Lizzie, can you help me move the bed?"

"Why, have you spotted a speck of dust that Mrs Mop has missed?"

He crawled out from under the bed and rose to his feet. "It's on wheels. Shouldn't be too difficult."

"I'll just supervise then," she said smugly.

Baines sighed and set to work manoeuvring the super king sized bed to his satisfaction. When he had finished, Archer could see a metre square section of carpet that had been carefully cut out and replaced. Baines rolled it back to reveal a hatch with a pull loop and a lock. He tugged experimentally on the loop.

"Locked. Somehow, I don't think there's a Mrs Mop after all. Or, if there is, I'd guess he's definitely told her not to bother cleaning under the bed."

She fished Baxter's keys out of her shoulder bag. "See if any of these fits."

Baines had an unerring eye for the right key and had the hatch open in seconds. He looked inside and gave a low whistle.

"Well, well. I think we know what side of the drugs deal he was on. I don't think this lot was all for his personal use."

Archer looked down into the compartment Baines had uncovered. Clearly home-made, but neatly finished, it was perhaps half a metre deep, and an Aladdin's cave of packets of white powder, packets of what was obviously cannabis, and packets and jars of pills.

She stared at him. "We checked him for a criminal record before we came here, and he hasn't even had a parking ticket. How can that be?"

"Unless he's got some friends on the force, I'd say he's been very good at being careful, up to now."

"What, drops in dustbins in grotty old yards?"

"Pretty safe. Who's going to go there? I'd guess he did something similar with a number of his clients. At least half of them probably don't even know his name."

"But..." She shook her head, frustrated at the thought that, in a town like this, someone could be making an extremely good living out of drugs and not even appear on the police radar. "His luck was bound to run out eventually."

"It just did," he said soberly.

Archer let out a despairing sigh. "A drugs dealer. Hard to see a link to Clive Edwards."

"I agree. But let's not rule him out."

"I'm not. But Gillingham might. Damn." She pointed into Baxter's secret chamber. "Empty it out."

"Maybe we should leave it to the SOCOs."

"They're busy and this isn't the primary crime scene. I want to see if he's got any diary or whatever stashed away. A fastidious guy like James Baxter is going to keep some sort of records, I'll guarantee you."

As Baines carefully removed the packets and jars, Archer tried her best to stack them reasonably tidily. Under the first couple of layers, he unearthed a black, hardbacked notebook.

"Gold dust," she said, leafing through it. "Dates of all his transactions. No names, or descriptions of the merchandise though. Look - Mr Pink, three Mars bars. Mrs Green, two pkts Maltesers."

"He's seen 'Reservoir Dogs' too many times. Seriously, though, maybe he has codes for the clients but he doesn't know much about them either. Safe all round."

"He was dropping off some sweeties for Mr Indigo today. 10.30 am." She leafed backwards through the book. "Same two weeks ago. And two weeks before that." She kept flicking through. "Mr Indigo seems to go back to March. A couple of months. Not always the same day or time."

"But you see how it was? The other victims had set habits for how they lived their lives, and our killer cashed in on that by knowing the best time and place to strike. Every couple of weeks, a drop off for Mr Indigo. He must have been following Baxter for months."

That sounded probable, but something wasn't right.

"I'm sure he followed him, but wouldn't he have been taking a risk?" she mused. "What if Mr Indigo showed up early and caught him in the act?"

"A calculated risk, though."

"Maybe, but he doesn't seem to leave much to chance. He wouldn't be able to control Mr Indigo's behaviour." Archer frowned. "Suppose the killer is Mr Indigo? He posed as a client and actually created a habit for Baxter."

Baines paused contemplatively, then nodded. "It sounds like his style, doesn't it? Much more foolproof. I don't suppose there's a phone number?"

"No, nothing like that. But I wouldn't be surprised if there are numbers in his phone - maybe coded, but they're there, for all the good it will do us."

"How do you mean?"

"This killer's not going to hand over a number he intends keeping beyond the murder. You'll find it's a disposable pre-pay. Untraceable and probably on a skip or at the bottom of the canal by now."

He looked grim. "How many more, Lizzie?"

"Who knows? Maybe this was the last one. Maybe there are dozens on the list. Two lawyers, a social worker and a drugs dealer. Surely we can find some sort of link with that little lot?"

"We'd better. Someone's life may depend on it. Three in the last four days. He's not wasting any time, is he?"

"Maybe he's got plans for a long weekend away," she quipped, but her heart wasn't in the joke. Who knew how many more might be dead by next Monday?

24

Clive Edwards tilted his head back and emptied the contents of his water bottle down his throat, hoping that in some way he might dilute the pain that was now racking his skull. It was as if his head was being stung from the inside by a swarm of angry wasps. Coloured lights kept exploding in front of his eyes, and there was a metallic taste in his mouth.

He wondered if he'd made the right decision, simply abandoning his home like that. At the time, when everything had been coming to a head, it had seemed his only option, but living rough wasn't exactly proving a good alternative.

He was sitting on a park bench, flicking through a discarded newspaper and consuming his usual subsistence rations of crisps and water. The story about the local murders was on page five, and he devoured it with considerable satisfaction. Social services busybodies and money-grubbing lawyers. Those people had a lot to answer for. Cleaned out by his wife in the divorce, let go by his firm, who didn't appreciate having a murder suspect on his books, his life had spiralled downward rapidly.

Okay, so he'd been lucky to get away with what he'd done to his wife's fancy man. By the time Edwards had finished rearranging his face with a hammer, he hadn't looked so fancy any more. But the man had got what he had deserved. And so had the people whose faces stared at him out of the paper.

He read on, enjoying the story, and then stopped with a start. The police were keen to interview one Clive Edwards. And, sure enough, there was an incredibly bad photo of himself at the foot of the page. He suppressed a chuckle. Well, good luck to the police if they imagined anyone would recognise him from that.

He folded the paper and slid it into his rucksack. If the police were after him, he'd have to think very carefully about how to respond.

Very carefully indeed.

* * *

The evening briefing was a grim affair. The latest killing had turned everything upside down.

"How the holy fuck does a drug dealer fit into the picture?" Gillingham said despairingly. "For a moment there, we had a social worker and two lawyers, and there was at least some sort of speculative link. We even had a connection of sorts between Peter Nish and that Clive Edwards you're so keen on, Lizzie. But surely this Baxter blows all that out of the water?"

"I don't think we can say that, sir," Archer replied. "Baxter has managed to keep his business dealings completely off our radar for who knows how long. There could be any number of ways he could have pissed off Edwards."

"Or anyone else," growled the DCI.

"Or anyone else," she conceded. "I think we do need to notify anyone who could conceivably have been involved with Edwards' divorce that they could be in danger. The wife, obviously, in case he's found out where she's living and hopped on Eurostar. Nish's firm. Have you got any of the partners' mobile numbers, Jason?"

Bell confirmed that he had.

"Good. Joan, see if there's an out of hours contact for the Council. Maybe they can contact the Children's Director. Get her to contact us."

"I'll give it a go," Collins said.

"She said Edwards' name didn't ring a bell, but make sure she understands that, if anyone there did have anything to do with Clive Edwards, they could be in danger."

* * *

Elaine Staples loaded her two Tesco carrier bags into the back of her Vauxhall Corsa, got into the driving seat, and started the engine. One of the luxuries of living alone was that you could do what you liked, when you liked - if you discounted the demands of three cats, that was. For Elaine, this included late night supermarket shopping when she was less likely to be subjected to crowds and queues. Tuesdays and Thursdays were her regular evenings.

She thought about the bottle of New Zealand Merlot in one of the bags, pricier than what she would usually buy, but then she rarely drank alone. Tonight, she had a lot of thinking to do, and she hoped something nice in the booze department would free up her brain cells a little.

Two more murders since Stephanie Merritt had been killed on Monday morning, and the police had admitted they were linking them. Elaine was wondering if she should have acquiesced quite so easily to Hannah Hudson's instructions not to rake up old cases.

And it did seem unlikely that any of the more embarrassing cases Elaine was aware of had anything to do with the wave of killings. She wasn't even sure that Stephanie had had any involvement in most of them. Still, perhaps the police might have at least wanted to eliminate them from possible lines of enquiry.

She remembered arriving in the department just as the dust was settling on an internal enquiry into its handling of one case that had gone horribly wrong. It had raised a stir in the local press at the time, but had somehow avoided the national headlines, precisely because the Children's Department had done all the right things, as far as she had understood.

Still, it was a forbidden subject at the office, and it was part of Hannah Hudson's regime that no one ever spoke about it. The Director's approach was to celebrate successes and bury disasters, even the most minor ones.

Now Elaine was wondering whether to break ranks and talk to the police about it. Just in case.

Her terraced house in Princes Risborough was less than ten minutes drive from the local Tesco. She pulled into her drive, opened the car boot, and went to open the front door before bringing the shopping in.

She squinted at her keys. The front and back door keys were very similar in appearance, and it was always hard to tell them apart once dusk had fallen. As she turned the key in the lock, she heard footsteps behind her.

She wasn't expecting anyone.

Heart pounding, she wrenched the key out of the lock, clenched it in her fist, ready to jab it into the face of an attacker, and spun round to face whatever was coming.

* * *

Gillingham had insisted Archer and Baines go and get some rest while they could. Baines had felt a little guilty about leaving Collins and Bell in the office, still making calls, but he hadn't objected. Now he was drawing up outside his house in Little Aston, thinking about a glass of whisky, and thanking God that he was still able to have a drink when he felt like one.

He knew how easy it could have been, after the Invisible Man had come calling, to dive into a bottle and never find his way out again. Either that, or face a long battle with booze, culminating in a life on the wagon and the constant temptation to have just one drink, knowing it would never stop at the one.

He had seen it a few times with colleagues. The job wrecked marriages, or officers saw more horrors than they could handle without a little liquid assistance.

It was Jack who had saved Baines, or rather the possibility that Jack was still alive. The same fragile hope had made him keep this house, haunted though it was by the horrors inflicted on it all those years ago. Everyone, even Karen, thought he was mad to stay there with those awful memories.

It wasn't even that he was that keen on the house, or the village. It was Louise who had fallen in love with the idea of being part of a small community. She'd joined the Mothers and Toddlers and got Karen to babysit Jack once a month when she went to her WI meeting. She'd been the youngest member by at least 15 years, staunchly ignoring her friends' cracks about jam,

Jerusalem and middle-class old ladies . She made cakes for the church fête.

The outpouring of local grief and the mountain of floral tributes and soft toys left outside the house after tragedy struck had taken him by surprise.

Just the thought made Baines want to smile and cry at the same time, which was why he tried not to think about it more than he could help. He had never found the time to engage with village life. Everyone knew that.

When he had said - back in the days when he allowed himself to think about his missing son - that he couldn't leave the house because Jack wouldn't know where to find him, he got the strangest looks.

He knew it was entirely illogical to suppose that a three-year-old boy would be able to find his way home, and eleven years on it was highly unlikely that, even if Jack was alive, he would have any real memories of his father, let alone his own house. But still Baines clung to some superstitious instinct that, if ever he moved from here, then Jack would really be dead.

It was ridiculous, even to him.

He was powerless to feel otherwise.

He let himself into the empty hall, threw his jacket over the banister rail, and went in search of a drink and something to eat. The whisky was easy enough to locate. He kept his little stock of drink in a corner of a kitchen cupboard. Food was more of a problem. Somehow last weekend had slid by without him making it to the supermarket, and the weekdays had been far too full-on to do anything as mundane as shopping.

He found some sliced bread in the freezer and decided it would be toast again. There was no cheese, apart from a lump of unidentifiable mould wrapped in foil, which he binned, but he did find a jar of strawberry jam. Dan Baines, the tough copper, tucking into jammy toast. There was also a packet of custard creams, not too far adrift of their use by date, to complete his feast.

Whilst he waited for the toaster to pop, he wandered into his living room to see if he had any phone messages. There was another message from Karen, asking him to call her back when he got this, whatever time it was. The agitation in her voice was unmistakeable.

Concerned, he called her immediately.

"Can I come round please?" she urged. "I need to see you."

She still sounded strange.

"Sure," he said. "Is everything all right?"

"I'm fine. Look, it really is best that I come round. I'll be about twenty minutes, yes?"

"Okay. Should I be worried?"

Her answering laugh was shaky. "I hope not."

* * *

When Joan Collins typed 'Bucks County Council social services emergency duty team' into her computer's search engine, she was immediately rewarded with a phone number for out of hours emergencies.

She explained that she was the police, and that she urgently needed to contact Ms Hudson, the Director of Children's Services.

"I'm afraid she will have left for the day," the person on the end of the line told her. He had announced himself as 'Martin'.

"Yes," said Joan, "I'm sure she has."

"I dare say she'll be in tomorrow."

"Yes, but I urgently need to contact her now."

"Perhaps if you tell me the nature of your emergency, we can send one of our team round to see you."

Joan ground her teeth. "Martin, I don't need a social worker. I need to speak to Ms Hudson, and I need to speak to her urgently. As in urgently?" She failed to keep the sarcasm out of her voice. "You must have some contact details."

"We can't just give them out over the phone." Martin sounded shocked by the notion. "I mean, how do I know you're the police?"

"How about you call the station and ask for me?"

"I still couldn't give you Ms Hudson's personal phone numbers without her consent."

"Then call her yourself and get her to ring me."

"If you give me some idea what it's all about..."

"I can't just give that out over the phone," she mimicked. It was a mistake. Martin got huffy.

"There's no need for that. I'm only doing my job, Constable."

"Let's try this another way," she said, exasperated. "What's your surname, Martin?"

"It's Martin Giles, but -"

"Well, *Martin Giles*. This is a matter of life and death. Literally. So you get off your arse, phone your director, and get her to ring me immediately. Tell her what I said. A matter of life and death. And Martin, if you don't do this for me, and someone dies as a result, I will make it my mission in life to get you sacked. Are we clear on that?"

"It's not as -"

"Are we clear?"

"Sure. Let me have your number."

She gave it to him and hung up, cursing all jobsworths. Then she continued searching the web for any references to Clive Edwards. Hoping for hints about possible victims. So far, she was finding nothing she didn't already know.

Before he had hung up, Baines had told her he thought DCI Gillingham, and maybe DI Archer too, were hoping Edwards' list of victims may have been exhausted. She could tell he was less certain.

It was going to be another late night.

* * *

Hannah Hudson downed the last of her fruit juice, said goodbye to her friends, and headed out to the car park.

Thursday night was gym night. Local government may not pay spectacularly well, but she was able to afford membership of a decent health club, and Thursdays worked well for her. Her partner, Robin, had a regular lads' night out on a Thursday, so it made sense for them both to be out for the same evening.

Hannah had made a small group of friends at the health club, and her workout always ended with a few soft drinks and some feminine chat. A lot of the things she dealt with in her day job were pretty harrowing, and it was good to chill out and switch off her brain for a while.

There were three women whom she saw regularly on a Thursday - Rebecca, Annie and Lisa. Two high-powered professionals like herself, and a businesswoman. They had made it a rule not to talk about their day jobs, nor about politics or religion. Instead the conversation revolved around families, love lives, films and television, clothes and accessories. She normally despised women who dwelt on such shallow concerns, and suspected that the others were much the same. But somehow it was fun to deliberately become someone you usually were not.

She was always the first to leave their gatherings. 9.30 pm on the dot. She liked to be home, showered again, and changed out of her work clothes when Robin came home. All the testosterone of his own evening often meant that sex was part of the Thursday night ritual, and she had to admit she was looking forward to it tonight. There was still a gloom cloud hanging over the office as a result of Stephanie's death, and she needed something to take her own mind off it.

She crossed the car park to her beloved Mazda RX-8, got in and turned on her Blackberry. That was another little rule when she was with the other girls - no phones. So hers had been turned off, along with the others'.

She was always slightly uncomfortable about that. A fatalistic streak in her sometimes imagined that something bad would happen and she would be unreachable when she was most needed.

So, when the Blackberry chirruped the little fanfare that told her she had a new voice message, a small, superstitious fear invaded her, as if any bad news would have been caused by the act of switching off her phone

But it was only a message from nerdy Martin Giles, who had apparently pulled the emergency duty team shift for tonight. Could she contact a Detective Constable Collins as soon as possible?

She felt a twinge of irritation. It wasn't that she didn't take the investigation seriously, she told herself. She had co-operated with that pushy female detective - her name hadn't been Collins, though - and had thought that would be the end of it.

Now she was being chased, and through the out-of hours team. Maybe something had come up - a breakthrough on the case. Then again, it was probably just some footling further request for information - maybe even one that would involve delving further back and some embarrassing cases being dragged back into the light of day.

She knew she ought to ring this Detective Constable Collins, but that would probably mean going to the office at this time of night, doing some grunt work and trying to come to a decision. Robin would be coming home, loosened up by a few drinks and undoubtedly feeling horny. Surely it wouldn't make that much difference if she didn't make the call until the morning?

She slipped the Blackberry back in her bag and started the car.

25

Brian Hughes stood a few paces away from Elaine Staples, his face contorted with fury.

"You fucking interfering bitch," he snarled.

She took a pace back, the keys still held out in front of her as a somewhat pathetic makeshift weapon. She wondered now whether she could have got the door open, ran inside and slammed it behind her, before he caught her. But something had made her prepare for fight rather than flight - something she would never have expected of herself. Now she was faced with an angry male, just a few days after he had been questioned in connection with Stephanie's murder.

It couldn't be a coincidence.

"What do you want, Brian?" she asked, trying to keep her voice steady.

"What do I want?" He took a step towards her. Then a second.

She brandished the key. "Keep coming and I'll hurt you."

He laughed. "Really? What, you're going to unlock me to death? I don't think so."

Panic got the better of her.

"Help!" she yelled. "Help me please!"

"Christ!" he yelped, immediately beginning to flap his hands in a 'shushing' motion. "Stop it. There's no need for all that. I've had enough of the bloody police for one week."

No one came rushing to their door to see why a woman was shouting for help. Fantastic. But her yells seemed to have made an impression on Hughes. He held his palms up placatingly, backing off a pace or two.

"All I wanted," he said, "was to ask you why you had to tell the police I had an affair with Steph."

She stared at him. "Did you?"

"Well, more a one night stand really."

She shook her head. "I had no idea."

"No? One minute you and Her Highness are talking to the police, the next minute they're giving me the third degree. I had to tell them about me and Steph. It was a mistake, that's all. We both agreed. But the police seemed to know already. Now they've been asking my wife to confirm my alibis and she's put two and two together. There's been the most horrendous row..."

She sighed, finally lowering the key. "All I said was that you and Stephanie had lunch together occasionally and she might have told you things I wasn't aware of. As a matter of fact, they asked if I thought there was anything... you know, going on. I said no. I still can't believe it."

"It just happened, Elaine. It was like some silly holiday romance."

Elaine had always thought Hughes fancied himself as a ladies' man. He always smelt of grooming products and was always saying flirty things to women. Not her, obviously. She doubted he normally noticed her.

"Did you admit to your wife that you slept with Stephanie?"

"No. I told her she was being ridiculous, then I stormed out."

Feeling like an old mother hen, she said, "Then go home, Brian. Go home and lie to her. Convince her it didn't happen. And try to make sure nothing like it ever happens again."

He nodded. "Okay. Yeah, you're probably right. Sorry. I shouldn't have come here shouting the odds."

He turned to go.

"Brian," she said on impulse, and he turned back to face her.

She hesitated and then named the case that had been so much on her mind. "I don't suppose Stephanie was involved in any of that?"

He frowned. "Well... yes and no, really."

After a moment's hesitation, she invited him in.

* * *

Hannah Hudson swung the car into her drive, activating the remote control garage door as she did so. She waited while the double-sized up and over door swung up, and then drove in. She cut the engine and pressed the button to close the door behind her before climbing out, ferreting in her bag for her house keys.

There was a personal door to the side of the garage which opened onto a path up to her front door. The key was on the ring with her front door key. But Hannah never got that far. She wasn't even aware of the figure looming up behind her from one of the garage's shadowy recess.

The first blow felt as if her head had exploded. She fell awkwardly to her knees, her hands instinctively reaching up to the seat of the excruciating pain she felt, her vision blurring. She almost cried out, but all that emerged from her throat was a half-hearted bleat. For a moment, she thought perhaps she was experiencing the mother or all migraines, or perhaps a brain haemorrhage. In a sense, the latter was true.

The second blow smashed the tips of several fingers, causing new pain to scream through her hands, in company with the fresh agony in her head. This time, she instinctively knew she was under attack, but the third blow fell before she could do anything about it.

And then a fourth.

* * *

9.55 pm. Aylesbury nick would be closing in five minutes and was already like an alien abduction scene from a sci-fi movie.

Joan Collins took a last look at her desk and nodded in satisfaction. Everything was organised the way she liked it, so she could get straight down to work in the morning. Her colleagues sometimes teased her, accused her of being anal, especially when she berated them for rummaging on her desk when her back was turned and ruining her system. But she didn't mind. In a way, they were probably right.

She picked up her bag, slung it over her shoulder and, suppressing a yawn, called it a day.

Out in reception, there was a minor altercation going on. A scruffy, tramp-like individual was confronting the desk sergeant and getting rather overwrought.

"You mean you really have no idea who I am?" he was bawling incredulously. "Christ, why did I bother?"

Joan decided she wanted no part of it. Probably some deluded nutcase who imagined he was the Prime Minister or heir to the throne. She edged her way past the desk and was making a bid for the exit when the tramp called out to her.

"Oi! You, miss! Are you a police officer?"

She thought about denying it, but couldn't bring herself to lie.

"How can I help you, sir?"

"Have a look at my face," he commanded, stepping up to her and presenting it for inspection. "Familiar?"

There was something.

"I'm not sure," she said. "Suppose you help us out and tell us your name, and we'll take it from there."

He sighed. "A word of advice, officer. Next time you're looking for someone, make sure you have at least a half-decent photo." He shook his head. "Oh, well. Edwards is the name. Clive Edwards? I understand you want a word."

* * *

Baines opened the door and let Karen in. She seemed to be shivering, her arms wrapped around herself, even though it was not especially cold.

"Is everything ok?" he asked as he stood aside for her to walk into the living room. She didn't kiss him, nor offer her cheek to be kissed. His stomach churned at what that might mean.

She turned to face him. "I honestly don't know any more, Dan."

She looked utterly miserable.

"What's the matter?"

She drew a ragged sigh. "I just keep thinking about Monday. What we said, how we left it."

Monday felt like a million years ago to him now.

"I thought we left it that you didn't want to be anything but friends," he said. "We weren't going to talk about being anything more than that ever again. Were we?"

He noticed how pale and tight her features were. There were dark smudges under her eyes.

"Maybe I lied," she said, her voice barely a whisper.

He stood looking at her, confused and uncertain.

"Lied about what, exactly?"

She shook her head despairingly. "Oh, Christ. I'm just so mixed up. I've got this feeling that maybe I'm in love with you after all. That maybe I have been for a very long time, but I just couldn't see it. Maybe I've been deliberately ignoring what was right in front of me. That was why I made such a big deal when you joked about me being up for a shag."

He opened his mouth, but she silenced him with a gesture.

"It isn't right, surely? I mean, you're my brother in law. Louise's husband. We should be more like brother and sister. And then Louise's my identical twin. I look like her, think like her, talk like her. Maybe that makes me love like her, I don't know. But don't you think it all makes the idea of anything between us way too weird, Dan?"

He knew he should be overjoyed at what she was saying, the possibility that she had real feelings for him. But all he could think was, Oh, Christ. Not now.

Not when he was in a race against time with a mass murderer and also feeling in some way responsible for a missing boy. Now it came to it, he didn't know if he had the emotional resources to have this conversation.

"What are you saying, Karen?" he asked, perhaps a little too harshly. "That now you do want something between us? Or that you don't?"

She blinked. "I just don't know. I'm so scared of being hurt." Tears leaked from her eyes. "You said you wanted to take it to the next level. It being our friendship." She laughed nervously. "I mean, it all sounds a bit teenage - like getting to second base or something." She swiped the tears away with the backs of her hands.

He couldn't bear to see her cry. He wanted to sweep her up in his arms, but he still wasn't sure what she was trying to say. He felt that if he did attempt to hold her - to kiss her - it would seem like he was forcing things. So he stood there, arms at his sides, saying nothing.

"I guess, what I'm saying is this," Karen said, filling the vacuum, her voice now very small. "I know I feel something much more than friendship for you. I'm just a bit mixed up. Is it some sort of deep, sisterly love or, something more intense?"

"I don't know," he heard himself say, not trusting himself to say more.

"I think it's proper love," she said. "Not just the sisterly kind. Or it easily could be. But at the same time, I'm absolutely terrified by the idea. That one time we went to bed - can you honestly say you were making love to me and not to Louise?"

"You know I can't say that," he told her quietly. "But that was then, and this is now. I'll never get over Louise, but that doesn't mean I'm looking for a clone, either." He shook his head, a realisation dawning on him. "You know, when Louise died, I was 27. We'd been married five years, and you were nothing more than the sister in law who looked just like her. What you and I have - that's been eleven years now. Twice as long as my marriage. So, whatever it was in the beginning, whatever we've got has been just about you and me for an awfully long time."

"So you're saying you really do want to be more than just friends?"

There. It was out there. The question. He sensed the future of their relationship depended on his answer. If he got it wrong, the result could be disastrous. Did he really want to risk losing what he already had, the person who knew him better than anyone in the world?

The question hung in the air. And then his mobile shrilled in his pocket.

"Fuck," he snarled.

"Don't answer it," she urged.

"I've got to."

"Please don't." She was practically begging him.

But he was already hitting the receive button, barking his name. He listened intensely for a few seconds, asked a couple of questions, and then said, "I'll be there asap."

He hung up. Karen was staring at him, stricken.

"I'm so sorry," he said. "Fucking awful timing, but I've got to go."

"What?" Cold fury flashed in her eyes, so much like Louise in a strop that it hurt. "You can't just leave things like this."

"I'm really sorry," he said again. "Something's come up. There's a body..."

"There's always a fucking body. It's not like it's going anywhere, is it?" She was almost sobbing now, tears of frustration rolling down her cheeks. "It's a very simple question, Dan. Do you want to be more than friends or not?"

He sighed. "It's not a simple question, Karen. It's a very complicated question, and the answer isn't a simple yes or no."

She stared at him, all sorts of emotions in her expression. One of them bordered on utter contempt.

"Jesus. I don't believe this. You started all this on Monday night. You can't look me in the eye and say it was an entirely throwaway remark. You were the one who hinted at taking our friendship to a new level. I've been thinking about it, going over and over it in my mind. I haven't been able to sleep. And now I've come here to say I think I'm ready if you are, and you tell me it's complicated?" She shook her head in disgust. "Well, fuck you, Dan."

She walked towards the door. He reached for her and she shook him off.

"Call me when you know what it is you want," she said. "Maybe I'll be interested, maybe I won't. In the meantime, you fucking stay away from me."

He was left with the slam of the front door ringing in his ears and a mass of conflicting emotions. Maybe he'd been a fool. Maybe he should have just said yes, that was what he wanted too. For them to be lovers. Now he was afraid that, having opened that particular door, the one that led back to mere friendship and to safety might have slammed shut forever.

Everything churned inside him as he reached for his jacket. He somehow had to put aside what had just happened and concentrate on being professional. Because now the Children's Services Director, Hannah Hudson had joined the ranks of the killer's victims. And that meant that it was a long way from over.

26

Clive Edwards' gaze was steady. There was a vaguely amused look in his eyes.

"How many more times?" he said. "I didn't kill those people. If I had, there's no way I'd be here now."

Archer and Baines sat across the table from him. Of the three of them, only Edwards showed any sign of having had any sleep. Which was hardly surprising.

Last night had been a nightmare. Collins had phoned Archer just after ten to say that their suspect had just walked into the station. She'd driven straight over, planning to assess the situation before dragging Baines in. But she'd barely arrived when the news had come in that Hannah Hudson's partner had found her dead in her own garage, her head smashed to pulp like the others.

Archer's first thought had been that Hudson must have been the final victim on Edwards' agenda before he turned himself in, and she had immediately arrested him on suspicion. He seemed happy enough to sign up for a night's bed and breakfast, courtesy of Thames Valley Police, but had declared himself completely innocent of all the current spate of deaths.

"I've come here as a good citizen," he had assured them. "You've been on the wrong track looking for me and I wanted to put you right, so you can invest your time and resources in more profitable lines of enquiry."

She had met up with Baines at Hudson's home, and Gillingham, who she had also notified, had turned up too.

"Jesus," he had muttered as he stared at the body, which was only recognisable to Archer by the blonde mane. "Will this never stop?"

Now it was a little after 4 am. Archer listened to Edwards' latest denial, blinked, and took another swig of foul-tasting black coffee.

"You know, it's funny, Clive," she said. "As we've said, another woman was killed tonight. Well," she looked at her watch, "last night really. According to the pathologist, the sort of time she would have died would have given you just enough time to get yourself round to the station by 10 pm - which is about when you arrived."

"But why would I?" he said again. "You're not listening to me, Inspector. If I'd killed however many people it is you're accusing me of, this is the last place I'd be."

"Not if you'd been on some sort of revenge mission," Baines pointed out. "If Hannah Hudson was -"

"Who?"

"Hannah Hudson, Clive. Director of Children's Services at Bucks County Council."

"But I've never had anything to do with children's services, let alone this Hannah Hodgson."

"Hudson."

"Whatever. I don't have children. What could I possibly have against Children's Services?"

A nasty little doubt nipped at Archer's insides. They had focused on Edwards' wife and her affair and hadn't given a moment's thought to children. If there were none, then there was something of a question mark over why either Stephanie Merritt or Hannah Hudson would have been targeted. It came of being too stretched. With other cases on the go, and a body turning up each day, it was a detail easily missed.

But stupid. Hudson herself had denied any knowledge of Edwards. What if Archer had, after all, found a possible suspect and grabbed at him like a reed on the edge of deep water?

Yet there was something so knowing, so smug about the man's expression, that she parked the doubt.

"What would you have against Children's Services, Clive? You tell us. We know Peter Nish's firm represented your wife in your divorce."

"Her solicitor was Tom Pocock."

"You disappeared from your home around the time these killings started."

He slammed his hand on the table. "Why do you think that was? You lot tried to pin a murder on me. Even though nothing could ever be proved, I lost my job because of it. Clients don't like to work with murder suspects, apparently. I had no income and had payments to make to my adulterous bitch of a wife."

"Who fled abroad to get away from you."

Edwards sighed. "So she might say. The point is, I was in arrears with my mortgage. I was going to lose the house anyway. I took to the streets. Maybe that was stupid, but that's what I did. I saw in the paper that you wanted to interview me in connection with these murders, and I did what any good citizen would do. I came in to talk to you."

"You deserve a medal, sir," Baines sneered. "Really you do. Now why do you suppose we saw all those corpses and thought of you?"

Edwards shrugged. Archer saw where this was going and decided to let Baines go there.

"Because," the DS went on, "there are certain similarities between the murder of your wife's lover and these deaths."

Gillingham had been adamant from the start that the use of a hammer as the murder weapon should be kept under wraps, but Archer had hoped that mentioning it now would rattle Edwards. She was sorely disappointed. Far from shaken, he actually laughed.

"You mean they were hammered to death? That's it? And because of that, you're suspecting me? Even though nothing has ever been proven against me?"

The smirk playing around his lips made her want to throw the remains of her coffee in his face. But something he had said grated on her.

"You know," she said, "you keep saying that. Nothing has ever been proved. It's not quite the same as protesting your innocence, is it now?"

"I don't have to protest anything. There's not a stain on my character. Yet I've lost my job, my home, my financial security..."

"That must make you very angry," Baines observed. "It must make you want to take a hammer and smash someone's face in."

Edwards grinned openly. "That it does, Sergeant. And yet - have you found a hammer on me? No. And the plods who tried to fit me up last time never found a murder weapon either."

"Because you hid it well. Maybe you've put it back in the same place after each of your latest killings."

The suspect leaned back in his chair, arms folded. "Well, if that's so, it must be somewhere near this Hannah Hudson's home, or somewhere between there and here. Because, as you said yourselves, there would have been just enough time for me to leave there straight after the murder and get to the station at the time I did. And I have no hammer with me. Or any other murder weapon."

"Do you know what I think, Clive?" offered Baines. "I think either you came here to confess and then had second thoughts. Either that, or you're playing mind games with us."

"You find that weapon," Edwards retorted. "Then we'll speak again, with the duty solicitor present. I want to sleep now."

Sensing she wasn't going to get much further with him for now, Archer had him escorted back to his cell, then told Baines to go home and get a few hours' sleep.

"We'll get the duty brief in first thing and start again." she said.

"What do you think?"

"I think he's altogether too cool, Dan. I think he's having a good old laugh at us. What I can't decide is whether that's because he got away with one murder, or whether he thinks he's got away with five more."

* * *

Detective Constable Jason Bell started his day at the law practice Susan Downes had worked for when she had lived in the Vale. Archer had given him Ian Baker's mobile number, and the Norfolk DI had obliged with the details. It turned out to be Mason's of Princes Risborough.

The news that Clive Edwards had turned himself in was a bombshell, and apparently Archer and Baines were interviewing him again at this very moment. Bell had been asked to turn up something, anything, that could give them a more concrete link between Edwards and the murders.

Bell turned up at Mason's offices on spec, asking for some assistance in connection with their former employee's murder in her home in King's Lynn. The senior partner, one Frank Mason, immediately made himself available, and his attitude was very helpful and positive, especially when Bell explained they were looking for a connection with four other murders.

"Does the name Clive Edwards mean anything to you, sir?"

"Not immediately, no," Mason said. "We'd have to check her old case files, of course, but I'll get someone on it straight away. Everyone liked Susan. She took her work very seriously - a little too seriously, some might say."

"In what way?"

"Have you spoken to her partner, Lesley, about why Susan took early retirement?"

"We've only just become aware of Susan's murder, sir - Norfolk Police have been dealing with it. I knew she'd retired, but I didn't know she'd gone early. But I would have supposed it was to relocate to Norfolk while they were still relatively young. I gather it was a dream of theirs?"

Mason shook his head. White-haired, tanned and craggy, he had to be in his sixties but looked in pretty good shape. Bell imagined him playing golf and squash, maybe ten lengths before breakfast in a private swimming pool.

"Yes," he said, "Norfolk was their dream, but it's more complicated than that. Sue retired after a case she'd worked on went horribly wrong. After that, she said she had no stomach for the law any more."

Bell looked at him with interest. "What case was that, sir?"

* * *

The morning team meeting took place later than usual, but no one was complaining about that. Everyone knew there had been progress of sorts. There had been the interviews with Edwards, and the buzz was that Jason Bell's enquiries might have borne some fruit.

"First of all, Edwards," Archer said. "He's insisting he's just a good citizen, helping us with our enquiries. He insists that these hammer attacks have nothing to do with him, and he's challenged us to find the murder weapon."

She re-ran Edwards' argument that, for him to have killed Hannah Hudson and arrived at the station, he would have had to stash the murder weapon either somewhere between the two locations or somewhere near to one of them. Some uniforms were conducting searches.

"No news yet, and I still can't quite decide whether he's playing games or not."

"What does your gut tell you?" Gillingham asked.

She sidestepped that question neatly.

"I think we should hear what Jason has to say," she replied.

All eyes were on Bell. The team wanted to hear what the young Scot had found out, and being so much the centre of attention made him blush to his red roots. Archer remembered that gauche feeling, even though it was a long time ago. Before her father's losing battle with lung cancer, before her own argument with a broken bottle.

Before her mother's own illness.

Last night was another night Archer hadn't made it to London. Adam had sent a couple of texts and left one message on her mobile, making it unsubtly clear that she could make more effort to spend time with their mum. He clearly thought she could drop everything, even though a serial killer had kicked off on her patch in her first week in the new job.

"It's only forty-odd miles, Liz. That's what? An hour's drive? You could come down, spend an hour with Mum, and be back again, all within about three hours. Surely you can manage that?"

She tried to put away the nagging pangs of guilt as she focused on Bell's words. Didn't wholly succeed.

"According to the senior partner at Mason's, Susan Downes was very popular, and a first-rate solicitor," Bell was saying. "She specialised in family law, including divorces, and it wasn't uncommon for both parties in a divorce to compliment her on her handling of their cases. It seems she had the knack of making a hellish situation resolve itself with as little pain as possible. Frank Mason said more than one divorce had started out acrimoniously and ended up amicably, thanks to Susan's magic touch."

He took a swig of official coffee and grimaced. Archer made another mental note to do something about the beverage situation.

Bell set his mug down. It was blue with 'Rangers Football Club' emblazoned on it. Presumably he was a Glaswegian. She vaguely recalled that Rangers were in all sorts of financial trouble, then forced herself to concentrate.

"It seems all that changed a couple of years ago," he continued. "She was representing a woman called Sharon Morgan. Sharon and her husband, Shaun, were in dispute over parental responsibility for the two kids - Emily, aged eight and Oliver, six."

"Emily and Oliver Morgan." DCI Gillingham frowned. "I know those names. Go on."

He looked as if he knew what was coming and didn't much like it.

Bell continued. "Sharon was adamant that they should live with her, but Shaun was arguing that she wasn't a fit mother because she had a history of drug taking. Apparently she'd had a couple of bad trips that had scared Shaun and the children.

"Susan confided in her colleagues that she didn't like or trust her client, but she was able to produce evidence from Sharon Morgan's doctor that the woman was clean, she was no longer using. Sharon was also holding down a job as a cleaner while the children were at school, and there was testament from her boss about how reliable she was.

"Statements from the kiddies' school didn't suggest anything awry either. In the end, Shaun didn't get the sole custody he wanted. The judge ordered that the children should live with their mother on weekdays in term time, with Shaun having them at weekends and school holidays divided between the two parents. Just ten weeks later, Sharon Morgan killed both of the children when she was on a bad trip."

"I remember." Gillingham snapped his fingers. "She killed them with a hammer. Just like our serial killer's victims." Then he looked doubtful. "But... she's dead herself, surely. Didn't she kill herself?"

Archer glanced at Baines. He had already confirmed that this was one of the cases he had mentioned to her when she had asked about previous hammer attacks. They had both dismissed it back then, precisely because the woman was dead and because of the passage of time.

"Coincidence?" Baines wondered.

"Let Jason tell it," she said, having already heard the story once from Bell.

"That was effectively the end of Susan Downes' career," Bell went on. "She found it hard to live with the guilt that she'd helped put two young children in the hands of a woman who would go on to murder them so brutally, despite the husband's warnings. She feared she might make the same mistake again - that she might already have done so. She told Mason she used to lie awake at night, wondering how many ticking bombs she'd helped to plant in homes where children were living with the wrong parent after a divorce."

"But it wasn't her fault," Joan Collins protested. "She was just doing her job. Presumably the woman's doctor, the judge, everyone - they were taken in."

"I remember it all now," Gillingham said. "It was one of those child killings that doesn't capture the imagination of the national press, although there was a bit of a stink in the locals for a week or so. I always thought the poor kids weren't quite photogenic enough for the nationals to care much, and the husband wasn't an especially charismatic character either."

"No?" queried Archer. "What makes you say that?"

Gillingham frowned again. "You know, I've no idea why I said that. I can't remember a thing about him, to be honest. I can't even remember what he looked like."

"Well, anyway," Bell resumed. "Susan Downes took early retirement soon after the murders. Worked her notice - all very proper - and moved with her partner to Norfolk. The office had a letter and a couple of postcards, and that was that."

Archer swept her gaze around the room, checking expressions, seeing for whom the penny had dropped. She could see enlightenment on Baines' face, and Collins's. Understanding was also dawning on Gillingham.

"Now tell them about Peter Nish, Jason," she said softly.

He took another sip of coffee, made another face, and cleared his throat. "Nish's firm were quite helpful when I spoke to them, and promised to look out his old cases. But when I phoned and asked them if he'd worked on the Morgan divorce, they confirmed that he'd represented Shaun Morgan. They remembered it, obviously, because of how it had turned out. They did a case review afterwards, even though Shaun Morgan never complained about Nish's handling of the case."

"How did the review turn out?" asked Baines.

"They looked into it, decided Nish had done all he reasonably could in the circumstances. Family courts are still generally minded to place the kids with their mother, and there seemed to be good evidence that she'd got off the drugs and got her life together. It was no one's fault. Sharon Morgan bamboozled them all. Nish did his best to get custody for Shaun, but there was only so much he could do."

"And his firm didn't think to mention this, when you first approached them?" Gillingham looked incredulous.

"No, sir. They'd heard nothing more, and a lot of water has flowed under the bridge since then."

"We've all been thinking of a more recent motive, sir," Archer pointed out. "Plus we've kept the nature of the murder weapon to ourselves, to help filter out the nutters who might come forward confessing." She didn't think it was politic to remind her boss that he'd repeatedly rebuffed her suggestion that they go public about the hammer.

"And Stephanie Merritt?" Baines was leaning towards Bell now, eager for as many of the pieces of jigsaw as possible to fall into place. "Hannah Hudson? I take it they fit in somewhere?"

Bell shook his head. He seemed more relaxed than when he started his report. "Not that anyone seems to know of. There was a CAFCAS officer involved in the case."

"CAFCAS?" queried Collins.

"The Children and Family Court Advisory and Support Service." Baines supplied.

"Yes, sir," confirmed Bell. "In cases like this, the judge relies on someone independent from the local social services - a sort of independent senior social worker specialising in children's affairs. The CAFCAS officer would have seen both parents and the children to form a view on the contact arrangements. They were taken in by Mrs Morgan, too. Supported her petition for custody."

"And no involvement at all by local social services?" Archer asked.

"Not at the time, no."

"No, but wait," Gillingham said. "It's coming back to me. After the murders, there was an enquiry because the father had actually warned social services that his wife was back on the drugs. I can't remember any more than that."

"What about yesterday morning's victim, Jason?" Collins wanted to know. "Has anyone mentioned James Baxter?"

"No," said Bell. "But someone must have been supplying Sharon. Perhaps Shaun knew - or found out - that Baxter was her dealer."

There. Someone had named their new prime suspect.

Collins creased her brow in a frown. "There's still something about that name. Baxter, I mean. Why can't I remember?"

"Too much booze," Bell opined. "Fries the brain cells."

That got a laugh, but didn't really lift the tension.

"This is excellent work, Jason," Archer said. "Well done."

Bell blushed again.

"But there's more to do, I'm afraid. Can you and Joan work together and try to identify and warn everyone who was involved in the original custody battle? And anyone Shaun Morgan might have subsequently voiced his concerns to?"

"I don't get it, though," remarked Baines. "I mean, we're assuming Stephanie Merritt and Hannah Hudson fit in somewhere here. Yet Hudson and her colleagues said nothing about it."

"Why should they?" Archer pointed out. "For all we know, several of Stephanie's cases have ended in tears. This one was two years ago. We simply didn't go back that far in our questioning. Without knowing about the hammer, there's no reason why they would make the link. We don't even know how involved social services were."

She imagined a broken man, one she couldn't yet put a face to, first crushed by grief, then burned by anger, and finally consumed by a determination for vengeance on all those he considered responsible for his losses. She no longer hated the man who had scarred her, although she would always bear a grudge. What must it take to spend the best part of two years stalking your prey, learning all their habits and routines, planning their deaths and identifying places of execution?

"We'd better pick Morgan up," Gillingham decided. "Have we got an address?"

"I left Ibrahim finding that out," Bell said. "If I know him, he's got it by now."

"Good. Let's get him into custody before anyone else gets hurt. However long his list is, he's moving it along much too fast for my liking."

"And Clive Edwards?" Baines asked.

"We can hold him for a while yet," Gillingham said. "Let's do that. His brief won't like it, but sod him. Meanwhile, Morgan's our chief line of inquiry now. That's where we concentrate our resources."

27

Shaun Morgan's home was in Deacon Road, one of a row of modest, terraced houses. Gillingham, Archer and Baines were all in stab vests and helmets, and they had brought an armed response unit as backup. Given what Morgan was suspected of, Gillingham was taking no chances.

Baines and Archer flanked the DCI as he strode up to the door and pressed the bell. He stepped back and waited. When there was no reply, he went to the door again and rapped loudly with his fist.

"Mr Morgan? This is the police. Can you open up please? We'd like a word with you."

Again there was silence. Baines began to have a bad feeling about this. It was seven in the evening, and there were myriad reasons why Morgan might not be at home.

Like polishing off yet another victim, for example.

Collins had been left trying to find out what she could about the murder of Morgan's children, and whom he might consider bore a share of the blame. His wife, who had actually done the deed, was dead. But Shaun Morgan's campaign seemed to be against those who, in his view, had created the circumstances in which Emily and Oliver had met their horrendous deaths.

So, Susan Downes, who had supported Sharon Morgan's request for the children to remain with her, had been victim one. Stephanie Merritt, number two, had to have been involved somehow. Number three had been Shaun's own solicitor, Peter Nish, who had failed to prevent the decision. Number four was James Baxter, who had presumably supplied the drugs that induced Sharon's disastrous trip.

No doubt Morgan was the mysterious Mr Indigo.

Baines had commented on the way here that he was surprised that the judge who had decided in Mrs Morgan's favour had not yet been targeted.

"He seems to be going through them in an order," he mused. "You'd have thought everyone involved in the original custody decision would be dealt with first, then Baxter." He was driving, Gillingham alongside him, and Archer in the back.

"If it was that simple, the judge would have been number four, the CAFCAS officer five, and Baxter number six," Gillingham replied.

"And that might even have been the end of it," Archer had added. "Everyone he could blame. In fact, who's to say he hasn't targeted the judge and the CAFCAS person as well? Maybe that's two more bodies yet to find."

"Or maybe, like Susan Downes, they were killed in other forces' jurisdictions and they've just been slower to join up the dots than Norfolk were," Gillingham suggested.

Baines had thought it a fair point, but had also thought it might be wishful thinking to imagine that this killer was going to stop any time soon. He had a feeling that Shaun Morgan would be capable of finding plenty more people to blame yet.

"Well," Gillingham had said as Baines drew up a few doors down from number 19, Morgan's home, "if he's in, we can ask him."

Only now it appeared that he wasn't in.

Gillingham gestured to one of two uniformed officers standing by Morgan's front gate. The constable held a battering ram known affectionately as 'the enforcer'.

"Break it down," he commanded.

The uniform stepped up to the door with obvious relish and made short work of smashing the door open. Gillingham shouted another warning to Morgan, stating again that they were the police and they were coming in. But his voice echoed in the hall, and the pile of post, junk mail and free newspapers on the doormat added to the story the unkempt front garden had already been telling Baines.

Shaun Morgan was long gone.

He thumbed his way through the post. "Earliest postmark's the 24th of April. He's been gone the best part of a month."

They separated, moving from room to room in pairs. Everything was covered in a fine layer of dust. Baines had felt tense as he opened wardrobe doors, half-expecting a hammer-wielding madman to leap out, despite the evidence to the contrary. But he had been met only by clothes.

There were only two bedrooms. Archer checked drawers.

"No underwear," she remarked. "No pants or socks. I'm thinking he took the clothes he wanted with him and left the rest.

"So, he might want to change his smalls whilst he's on a killing spree, but not necessarily wear a suit," Baines agreed, half-pulling a grey two-piece out of the wardrobe.

"Or sweaters," she said. "There's a drawer full here."

"It's Spring. He probably thought he didn't need them. Or maybe he's brought clothes specially for the job." He frowned. "Better check for swimming trunks. We'll look pretty stupid if he's on a long holiday."

"Two pairs in the bottom drawer," she replied. "My guess is he didn't only plan the murders, but he had a contingency for us working out that he was responsible."

"You're thinking he relocated before the killing started?"

"He could be anywhere. A hotel, a B&B, a rented place..."

"Maybe he's got the room next to yours at the Holiday Inn."

"Not funny."

The team reassembled downstairs.

"This is bloody disastrous," Gillingham said. "Now we have a serious prime suspect, but no real idea where he might strike next and not the remotest idea where he is."

"All we can do is put his picture out on the media asking the public to keep an eye out for him, and issue a general warning to anyone who might have been involved with his separation," Archer said.

"Except it may go even further than that," Baines said. "We don't know how far Morgan's blame for what happened might extend. Dealers who supplied James Baxter, for instance."

"If all he's going to do from now on is take some more drug dealers off the street..." Gillingham spread his palms. "It could be worse."

"But that's my point, sir. We simply don't know."

"Phone Collins," the DCI told him. "See if she's got anything."

* * *

"Not much," Collins said when he asked the question. "Except the judge who awarded custody to Sharon Morgan is dead."

Baines' stomach knotted. "You mean Morgan has already got to him?"

"Nothing like that. A car crash, a couple of years ago. About a month after he made the decision, as a matter of fact."

"Any possibility of foul play?"

"No. A heavy lorry crossed the central reservation on a dual carriageway and ploughed into the judge's car, killing him instantly. The Dutch driver apparently nodded off at the wheel."

"Okay, thanks Joan. Anything else?"

"The nearest CAFCAS office is in Oxford. Jason's given them a call. They'll check their records, identify the officer who was involved in the Morgan case, warn them obviously, and then get back to us."

"Good."

"Has Gillingham said anything about Edwards?"

"Yeah, he wants us to hold him for now." Baines grimaced. "He says not so long ago we were as sure about Edwards as we are now about Morgan. We just might want to question him again. I think Morgan's the one, but it's not my call."

"His brief won't be pleased. We're holding him, but not actually questioning him."

Baines pondered. "Fair point. Grab a senior officer - Steve Ashby if you can find him - and ask him a few questions, for form's sake."

"Such as?"

"I don't know, Joan. Make it up. Ask him about his hobbies

ERS

if you like. Maybe he'll get all animated about his bloody stamp collection."

28

As Archer was walking from her office to a midday team meeting, she met Steve Ashby coming the other way. She had seen little of the man who shared her office in this first week and, from what she had seen, that suited her just fine. But she knew enough already to know that his presence in the building this early was rare, if not unprecedented.

She saw with satisfaction that he was pale and heavy-eyed.

"Couldn't sleep?" she enquired sweetly.

"The boss insisted I make an early start," he grumbled. "He's convinced this missing kid's going to end badly, and wants to pull out all the stops. Like it makes any difference what I do. The little bugger's disappeared into thin air. He'll either go home when he's ready, or he'll turn up dead when somebody's dog goes snouting in the wrong place."

"So compassionate, Steve," she said. She wanted to tell him he was a callous bastard, but what would have been the point?

"I gather Brandon Clark has looked at some pictures and identified the gun as a Bruni Olympic," she said. "The same as used in the petrol station holdup."

"So? Not my problem, as I keep saying. The petrol station's yours, and the Brandon Clark shooting has solved itself. My job's sorting out this bloody mess you and Baines made."

She was in no mood to prolong this discussion. She rolled her eyes and headed off for the incident room.

* * *

In addition to the regular team that had been working on the hammer killings to date, the team now boasted three augmentees, pulled off of other jobs now deemed to be of relatively low priority.

There was also DCI Ian Baker from Norfolk, who had pitched up a little after 11 am. Archer still thought he sounded like a yokel when he spoke, but he looked the complete opposite. Well-cut dark-brown hair, tanned, chiselled features and twinkling blue eyes. A beautifully cut charcoal suit and shoes that gleamed like mirrors. When they'd shaken hands half an hour ago, she could see him taking in the scar on her face, but not dwelling on it, and she'd seen no sign of him taking a furtive second glance the way some people did.

Gillingham was the last to arrive. As the week had progressed, he'd been a sort of Picture of Dorian Gray in reverse. She imagined a portrait in his attic growing ever more youthful and vibrant, whilst the living man degenerated into haggard exhaustion.

The DCI had shown a couple of times that he had a nasty side, but there was one area where Archer had to give him credit. However much pressure he was under, he'd mostly managed to shield the team from it and allow them to get on with their jobs.

"Okay," he opened now, "we all know the score. A warning to anyone who knows Shaun Morgan went out on the news this morning. Last night he murdered the Director of Children's Services. Who knows how many other people he blames for his children's deaths?"

With the judge who had unwittingly sealed Emily and Oliver Morgan's fate already dead, albeit not by Shaun Morgan's hand, everyone involved in the custody battle had been accounted for apart from the still unknown CAFCAS officer. But no one was assuming that would be the end of the killer's hate list.

"What do you think Shaun is planning to do, once he's killed everyone he holds responsible for his kids' deaths?" Archer had wondered. "His children are gone, so is his ex-wife, and his two-year mission for revenge will be over."

"I see where you're going, Lizzie," the DCI had replied. "My guess is that he might well decide he has nothing left to live for and top himself."

He turned to DC Collins. "Collins, you tried to contact the social services earlier, just to check that no one else in their team might be a target for Morgan."

"I spoke to Stephanie Merritt's supervisor," said Collins.

"Elaine Staples?" Archer prompted.

"She rang in, actually. Amazingly, it had occurred to her that maybe we ought to be looking at Morgan, but she hadn't seen fit to mention it until her boss was killed."

"Two violent deaths in the office do so concentrate the mind," Baines murmured. He seemed a little subdued. Archer hoped he wasn't going to be moody today.

"Jesus wept," moaned Gillingham. "She could have tipped us off days ago."

"In all fairness, she only became aware of Stephanie Merritt's involvement in his case last night," Collins said.

"So tell us, Joan," urged Archer.

Collins nodded. "Okay, well, it seems Shaun Morgan walked out on his wife over her drug taking. As soon as he started renting somewhere, he got onto social services, saying she was unfit to look after the kids and he should have them. It was Stephanie Merritt who started the investigation, but local social services backed off when CAFCAS got involved."

"And that was the extent of Stephanie's involvement in the case?"

"Yes, guv. But not social services'."

"No," Archer acknowledged. "Because he got back in touch with them later to say Sharon was using again. Do we know who looked into that, if anyone did?"

"That's where it gets interesting," said Collins. "He got in touch with then saying Sharon was back on drugs and the kids ought to be taken away from her. Believe it or not, it was Brian Hughes who looked into it. Elaine Staples didn't know that until last night."

"Why not?" Gillingham demanded.

"Because she joined the department right at the end of the internal inquiry, and no one was saying anything. It's a cultural thing, apparently."

"What, to sweep things under the carpet?"

"She described it as learning from failures, moving on and never talking of them again. For my money, it also avoids harking back to things that are a bit embarrassing or sensitive. Although in this case it seems they've nothing to be ashamed of. They played it by the book and did nothing wrong."

"So what did they do?" Baines wanted to know.

"Hughes spoke to Sharon Morgan. He spoke to the kids. He spoke to the school. The children were attending school regularly, Sharon seemed okay when he saw her, and the kids seemed happy enough. The inquiry concluded that the children might have been covering for their mum - getting her up in the morning, that sort of thing. But on the face of it, she was making a go of it, and they had no evidence for taking it further."

"So this Hughes is a potential victim?" Gillingham looked bemused. "So why target the Director? Guilt by association?"

"Not quite, sir. The fact is, he might not have known about Hughes' involvement. The department wrote to him saying they had looked into his concerns and wouldn't be taking any action, but Brian Hughes didn't sign the letter."

"So who did?"

"The then Assistant Director for Children."

"Don't tell me. Hannah Hudson."

Collins nodded.

"Why am I not surprised?" The DCI massaged the ridge between his eyes. "Anything else?"

"No, sir."

Gillingham turned to DI Baker, whom he introduced, and then asked if the Morgan case had come up at all in the Norfolk enquiry.

"No, sir," Baker said. "Although, to be honest, I was never sure I entirely bought the idea that Susan Downes and her partner moved simply to fulfil a dream."

"Why?"

"I can't put my finger on it. I just had the feeling that Susan had been glad to get out of family law when it came to it. However, I did phone the partner, Lesley Pope, on my way here this morning, and I asked her about it specifically. She confirmed that everything changed when Susan found out what had happened to those children."

"Changed in what way?"

"She said it was like something inside her died. She felt she'd let the family down - even Sharon Morgan, who killed the kids. It haunted her. She never stopped wondering how she could have represented Mrs Morgan and yet never seen what was coming."

"Ian," Archer chipped in, "did you get the impression that they didn't so much move to King's Lynn as run away?"

"What? To get away from Shaun Morgan?" Baker frowned. "You're asking if Susan felt threatened by him?"

"Did she?"

"I don't think so. I put that very question to Lesley, and she said no. They just felt sorry for him. He'd made no threats, not even got visibly angry when he lost his application for the kids to live with him. And they never saw or heard anything from the family afterwards. They knew about the murders, followed the trial in the papers, but that was that."

"You were bringing a file up?" she reminded him.

"Yes, but it won't help you much, I don't think. I mean, you've got a prime suspect now, and it's all about catching him before he does too much more damage. To be honest, having worked the case at my end, I just wanted to see if I could help bring it to a conclusion, if you don't mind having an outsider for a couple of days. I'll have to be back at my desk on Monday."

"I'll take any pair of hands I can get, for as long as I can have them," Gillingham told him.

He looked around the room. "Bell. What do we know about Shaun Morgan that we didn't know last night?"

Bell flipped through his notebook. "I spoke to his parents. He's 37 years old. He and Sharon were childhood sweethearts, you know. Both went to St Martin's School, here in Aylesbury."

"That was my old school," Baines said. "It closed down a few years ago. Cuts."

"Fascinating," Gillingham said, "and irrelevant, Sergeant. Shall we keep our eye on the ball, please, before Morgan smashes any more heads? Go on, DC Bell."

"It seems she acquired a drug habit in her teens, but Shaun thought she was over it when they married. But it was on, off, on, off, even after the kids came along. As we know, he got fed up with it, filed for a divorce, and applied for sole custody of the kids."

"And, as we also know," Archer said, "it didn't work out that way. Sharon fooled everyone."

"She even fooled Shaun's parents, who were dead set against the divorce at the time. But they said he seemed to resign himself to the situation when the court's decision went against him, and just concentrated on being the best dad he could. Always on time to pick up the kids when he was having them, always sorting out treats that were educational. He was destroyed when the children were killed, became very withdrawn. Chucked his job and lived on his savings."

"Did they suspect he was planning anything like this?"

"No, sir. They still can't believe it. They kept saying they wished someone had listened to Shaun when he tried to warn them about his wife. Social Services. The police -"

"The police?" Archer echoed. "Hang on, Jason, can we rewind?"

"He told the police?" Gillingham echoed. "Who? When?"

"It seems he came to the station urging someone to arrest James Baxter for supplying. They claim he got pretty short shrift. So, all in all, he was pretty bitter -"

"Hang on, Jason." Archer interrupted again, a sick feeling in her stomach. "Back up again, please. You say he warned the police and thought he'd got the brush-off? "

"That's what they said, ma'am."

"Who did he see?"

"They didn't know that."

"Oh, shit," said Joan Collins out of the blue.

Archer looked at her. Everyone looked at her. Her face was a mask of horror.

"Joan?"

"Fuck," she said. "Excuse my French, but -"

"Out with it, Collins," Gillingham growled.

She made frustrated fists. "I knew the name James Baxter rang a bell, but I just couldn't think why. The drugs link seemed to fit, too, but I just couldn't remember."

"Not like you, Joan," remarked Baines.

She held up her hands, palms out. "I know, I know. It kept niggling away at me, but it was like something right on the tip of my tongue. And every time I thought I was close to remembering, something else came up that I had to deal with, and it went out of my mind again. What Jason said just now? That was it."

Gillingham looked bemused.

"What was what?"

29

May 2010.

A wet Friday afternoon. Constable Joanne 'Joan' Collins is enjoying a relatively quiet last day in uniform, and happy to make the most of it. On Monday it will be plain clothes and having to remember to introduce herself as 'Detective Constable Collins'. She is looking forward to it, but suspects that sedate days like this will quickly become a thing of the past.

It's about 3.15 pm when she gets a call from Sergeant Will Robson on the front desk.

"Joan," he wheedles in his endearing Geordie accent, "any chance you can relieve me, so I can relieve myself?"

It's an old joke. Will is a few months off retirement, and his plumbing isn't what it was. At least once during each stint as desk sergeant he has to find someone to hold the fort so he can go and have a wee. He's got used to making Joan his first port of call, either because he trusts her to be efficient, or because he knows she's a soft touch.

Joan cheerfully goes and takes over, reminding him that he'll have to find someone else after today. Sometimes reception looks like A&E on a Saturday night, but this afternoon it seems like crime has taken a holiday. She leans on the desk, hoping Will's wee won't take all afternoon, and that is when the man comes in and scuttles up to the desk.

Everything about him is medium, her observer's eye tells her, and he has as bland a face as she's seen. An eyewitness's nightmare, she reckons. His photofit image will look like everyone and no one.

"How can I help you, sir?"

He looks jumpy, worried. Indecisive.

"Yes, sir?"

"Who do I report a crime to?" he says finally.

"That would be me, first off," she tells him. "After that, we'll see."

"Okay," he says, pacing in front of the desk. "Okay. Look, there's this guy. James Baxter is his name." He pulls a folded slip of paper from his inside pocket, opens it out, and smoothes it on the desk in front of her. "Here's his details."

"And what do you want to tell me about him, sir?"

"Well, he's pushing drugs. All sorts. He's pushing to my ex-wife, and I'm worried about our kids. I mean, living with a junkie. They're only little. It's not right."

"And you are...?"

"Never mind all that. What are you going to do about this man? You need to arrest him straight away. It's her turn to have the kids this weekend, and she'll be off her face again."

"I understand, sir," she says. "But if you think there's a danger to your children, you really ought to speak to the local social services first. I can give you the number..."

"They're fucking useless," he sneers. "They were the ones who helped get me into this mess in the first place. Now they say they've looked into it and they don't think she's using at all. Bloody useless, they are."

Out of the corner of her eye, she sees a familiar, scruffy figure come in out of the rain. He hovers near the desk, earwigging their conversation.

"I see," she tells the man, trying to sound sympathetic. "Well, our first port of call would be social services if we had reason to believe -"

"If?" The man becomes more belligerent. "If you had reason to believe? What - you think I'm lying to you?"

"I'm sure you're not, sir."

"Never mind social bloody services. You need to arrest James Baxter."

"Why are you so sure he's supplying your ex-wife?"

"I've followed her a couple of times. She always gets her gear on a Friday afternoon. It's him she meets."

The man who stands dripping rainwater on the floor and listening in takes a step towards him. "How do you know they're meeting to do a drugs deal?," he says. "How do you know they're not friends? Lovers? I mean, you said she was your ex-wife. So she can meet who she likes, can't she?"

The bland-faced man turns to him, looking even more annoyed. "What business is it of yours, mate?"

He is rewarded with a look of contempt. "That's Detective Inspector to you, sir. And you can't come in here making unsubstantiated accusations and demanding we arrest people without evidence. Now, why don't you help the nice lady to fill in some details in her log book and leave it to us?"

"What's the point?" He spreads his arms wide. "What's the fucking point?"

"Language, sir. There's a lady present. At least," the inspector adds with a creepy smirk in Joan's direction, "I think she's a lady."

"You're all the same. Pushing paper and never actually doing a damn thing. I don't know why we pay our taxes. You're too busy persecuting motorists to go after real criminals, like Baxter."

The inspector shrugs. "Do you have any actual evidence, sir?"

"Well, not as such, obviously. I mean, I can't supply bags of drugs with his fingerprints on. For Christ's sake -"

"Then you have a choice. Either fill in the form, and we'll decide if there's anything worth investigating. Or stop cluttering up our nice police station."

The man snatches up the piece of paper with what purports to be a drug dealer's details scribbled on it. "I'm going. But God help you bastards if anything happens to those kids."

"That sounds like a threat, Mr..."

"Never mind my name. I want yours."

"My name, sir? Certainly. Detective Inspector Ashby."

30

"Ashby?" Gillingham leaned forward in his chair. "You're saying DI Ashby had an altercation with Shaun Morgan? You're sure?"

"I'm really sorry," Collins said. "It was two years ago, and I haven't given it a moment's thought since. I don't even know why the name Baxter stuck in my mind, but when Jason - DC Bell - mentioned Morgan trying to get him arrested for supplying, it suddenly clicked."

"And you're certain it was Morgan?" Archer urged.

Collins frowned. "Like I say, he didn't give his name." She got up and walked over to the picture pinned to the board on what they called the murder wall. The picture that had been passed out to the media together with a contact number and a warning to the public not to approach him. "I honestly don't know, guv. Sorry. I sort of seem to remember he had an instantly forgettable face, like our suspect has, but I couldn't swear it was him."

"I think we must assume it was," said Gillingham. "Someone had better get Ashby on his mobile and warn him to be careful."

"I think he's in the office," Archer said. She resisted the temptation to add 'for a change'. "He was earlier."

"Someone get him in here," said Gillingham.

"I'll go," said Baines.

A silence settled on the room after the door closed behind him. After a few moments, Gillingham said, "Of course, that CAFCAS officer is most likely to be higher up on Morgan's hit list."

"I'll get back on it as soon as this meeting breaks up," Bell said.

"Can anyone think who else might be at risk?"

"Anybody's guess, sir," Archer said. "Apart from any officials he may have dealt with that we're not yet aware of, who knows who else he may have tried to involve in his campaign to keep the kids, and later to get them away from his ex? For all we know, he bears a grudge against some barman who didn't show him enough sympathy when he was in his cups."

"You've issued a general warning," Baker said. "And your statement did urge anyone who feels threatened by Morgan, or has any other information about him, to come forward. Once we've contacted this CAFCAS person, I think that's probably all you can do about putting potential victims on their guard. What we need to do now is concentrate on finding him."

"We've already done a house to house in his neighbourhood," Archer said. "He's not been seen for at least three weeks. Everyone said he was a nice enough chap, kept himself to himself, would always be ready to do someone a favour."

"Broadmoor's packed with nice people who would do anything for anyone," observed Bell.

Baines stepped back into the room. "DI Ashby's been and gone, sir."

Gillingham pulled a face. "Already? I don't suppose we know where?"

"As a matter of fact, we do, sir. He was in chipper mood when he left. Told the desk he might just have a breakthrough in the search for Marcus Clark."

"What sort of breakthrough? He said nothing to me."

"I think he'd just had a call."

"And he went off just like that? On his own?"

Baines shrugged. "You know DI Ashby, sir. No offence to him, but he's never been a team player. Likes to do things his way, using informants and contacts."

Archer thought it sounded typical Ashby. Keep things to himself and claim all the glory if he could bring the boy home. Ashby the hero.

"He gets results," Gillingham declared.

Baines looked sceptical but didn't respond.

"Still, if he's got information about that missing boy, he should have scrambled his team - not just gone off by himself," grumbled Gillingham, but he sounded more like an over-indulgent father than a boss. There was that little note of grudging admiration there. Despite the DCI's words, she sensed that Ashby was going to be cut his usual slack over this.

"Sir, we ought at least to phone him," Collins suggested. "Warn him to keep an eye out for Morgan."

"I agree," Gillingham said. "Although I doubt he's going anywhere that will make him an easy target. If the other victims are anything to go by, Morgan's studied his routine and already worked out where and when to strike."

"Good luck to him with that," Baines remarked. "I've never seen DI Ashby as a routine sort of guy."

"Let's ring him anyway," Gillingham said. "Forewarned is forearmed."

* * *

Steve Ashby supposed he had noticed the disused school on several occasions, but he had paid it little heed.

Back at the turn of the millennium, there had been two schools in this locality, both housed in crumbling buildings, each with failing heating systems, dangerous wiring, and falling rolls. The Local Education Authority had decided that, rather than attempt to maintain both, a better solution would be to move the staff and pupils from the two schools into a new purpose-built site, thereby halving the administrative costs and leaving them with two sites, ripe for development, that could be sold off.

The move had come into effect five years ago, during the summer holidays. What the LEA hadn't bargained for was not then being able to offload both properties. A small housing development now stood on the site of the other school, but St Martin's resolutely failed to attract any interest, perhaps because of its location or the relatively limited grounds that went with it.

Now the site where teenagers had kicked footballs, chatted, fought, and had their first serious romances looked dilapidated and sorry for itself. Where there had presumably been tidy gardens, there was now a fledgling jungle. From outside the wrought iron fence at the front of the school, Ashby could see several broken windows. Maybe former pupils had come back to throw stones at their old alma mater.

For Ashby's part, he had no time to dwell on the sorry state of the place. He'd got into the office at an obscene hour to find the usual wad of telephone messages on his desk. He tended to ignore them. More often than not, if he ignored people long enough, they went away. It was a sort of filtering system. But he usually responded to anything relating to a case he was working on.

And he was certainly going to respond to a call about Marcus Clark.

To be honest, he didn't much care whether young Marcus turned up alive and well, or dead in a ditch. He had little doubt that the little sod was from the same stock as his brother, for whom Ashby foresaw a long career residing in Her Majesty's prisons. He was highly sceptical about this fairy story of the kid shooting his brother by accident, or simply stumbling upon the gun for that matter.

Ashby had a different scenario in mind. In his opinion, it was highly likely that Brandon Clark had wanted to elevate his Barracudas gang into a whole new league, and had obtained the gun for just that purpose. Indeed, he agreed with Archer's conjecture that the weapon had been used in the petrol station holdup, but he suspected the robbers had been members of The Barracudas.

In Ashby's version of events, Brandon and his brother had been fooling around with the gun and it went off. Maybe Marcus had known it had been used by his brother in a robbery, and that was why he had legged it.

Ashby didn't give a toss about that, either.

No. What Detective Inspector Steven Ashby cared about was being the one to bring a little lost boy home to his overjoyed mother. Not out of sentiment, but because he would enjoy the limelight. And it would do his promotion prospects no harm.

He had moaned plenty of times to Paul Gillingham about having been a DI for too long and been fed little more than platitudes. But being on TV, modestly making all the right noises about being glad to have been able to bring the child home and reunite him with his family was something people noticed.

So, when he'd seen a note telling him he'd had a call about Marcus, and that the caller would speak to DI Ashby and no one else, he hadn't hesitated. The man had said he thought he knew where the boy had been hiding, and he could show Ashby. But he was to come alone, or the man wouldn't show.

Ashby assumed the man had been up to no good when he had spotted the boy - or traces of him - but had wanted to do the right thing. He didn't care about that.

"St Martin's school," the caller had said. "You'll find a gap in the fence down the right hand side where the railings are rusted and broken. Squeeze through and meet me round the back."

He'd scribbled a note on a yellow sticky, peeled it off, and set off. Now he found the gap easily enough and got through without difficulty. As he did so, he felt his phone vibrate in his pocket. He had turned it to silent in case it turned out that Marcus was actually here. The last thing he wanted was for the thing to start warbling just as he was creeping up on the boy. Marcus would probably scarper again, and Ashby's forty fags a day meant he was more likely to have a coronary than to catch up with him.

He took the phone out and looked at it. Gillingham again. The second call in five minutes. Well, it could go to voicemail and later he could claim he'd had no signal.

He put the phone away, then threw down the cigarette he had been smoking and ground it beneath his heel. With a buzz of anticipation, he moved towards the school.

* * *

"Still not answering," said Gillingham, tension etched on his face.

"Look, sir," Baines said, "DI Ashby's a big boy. I'm sure he can take care of himself. And we don't even know for sure that Shaun Morgan has him on his hit list."

"Oh, I think we'll find he has a long memory," Archer said. "He's been angry for two years, and you've only got to look at what he does to his victims to see how angry he is. And how irrational."

"But you can't be certain he'll go after Steve."

"Last night he bludgeoned a woman to death for signing a letter. Trust me, Dan. He'll have remembered being given the bum's rush by Ashby, and he'll be including him in his list of people to blame. In his eyes, Ashby should have listened to him and arrested James Baxter immediately. If he'd done that, Baxter would never have supplied the acid that turned Sharon Morgan into a murderess."

"But," Jason Bell held up a hand, "even if he'd been arrested for supplying, even if he'd been charged - well, he'd have been let out on bail, wouldn't he? I mean, he could have gone right on supplying? It mightn't have made any difference."

"And your point is, Jason?"

"Well, ma'am. Just that... thinking DI Ashby could have prevented what happened - it's just insane." He reddened as soon as the words left his mouth. "Oh. But then we're dealing with someone who is insane, aren't we?"

"Thank you, Bell, for the psychological profile," Gillingham said coolly. "I'll ring him again."

"With respect, sir, I think you're wasting your time," Baines said. "He's either out of signal range, or more likely his phone's off. Or he's ignoring it."

Gillingham scowled at him, but didn't contest the point. Archer was surprised at how wound up he was. It added fuel to the sense that the DCI and Ashby must be close friends. She had tried a couple of times to imagine the pair of them having a pint and a laugh together in a pub and had utterly failed. But it took all sorts. Maybe they had some shared interest, like fishing or train spotting.

"Maybe you should put out an all cars alert for him, sir," Baker proposed. "Maybe a patrol car will spot the good inspector."

"I hear what you're saying, Ian," Gillingham replied, "but it seems over the top."

Archer was trying to imagine Ashby taking the original call, anything he might do that could give them a clue to his whereabouts. She re-ran the images in her mind, and then stood up abruptly. "If you'll excuse me, sir, I've got an idea."

"Well, let's hear it."

"I just need to check something."

She walked briskly down the corridor to the office she shared with Ashby. As usual, his desk looked as if it had been hit by a paper tsunami, but she spotted the pad of yellow stickers immediately. She held it under the light and squinted at it. There was an impression on the top sheet where Ashby had pressed down to write something.

She hunted her pockets and the desk for a pencil, cursed when she couldn't find one, and hurried back to the incident room with the pad.

"Anyone got a pencil?" she demanded, interrupting the conversation that was going on.

"What are you playing at, Archer?" snapped Gillingham. "Dashing out, dashing in, demanding pencils..."

"Here." Baker offered her a smart propelling pencil.

She held up the little yellow pad. "Steve Ashby never seems to use a notebook. He scribbles everything on this and then peels off the sheet he's written on. I'm sure he loses half of them, but-"

"But what, Inspector?" Gillingham cut in, impatient.

"But he might just have written down something useful when he got this lead he's gone off on." She began to gently shade the top sheet of the pad with the pencil. The shading missed the indentation, and yellow, sunken lines began to appear against the grey background she was creating. Within seconds, they had resolved themselves into words:

ST MARTIN'S SCHOOL

GAP IN SIDE
ROUND BACK

"That's the school where Shaun and Sharon met," Bell pointed out. "DS Baines' old school."

"You think that's where he is?" Gillingham's question was such a statement of the obvious, that Archer couldn't help thinking the DCI had temporarily lost his grip.

"Sir, why don't just a couple of us go round there and see what's going on?" she suggested. "It's a bit early for an armed response unit to go in with lights and sirens, especially if this tip off's on the level. If Marcus does happen to be hiding out there, he'll bolt again."

"I'll go," Baines offered. "I know the way, after all."

"I'll come with you," Archer said.

"And me," Baker added.

"All right," Gillingham said before anyone else could volunteer. "You three. But keep in close touch. I don't want to finish off with half my officers off the radar."

31

Inside the perimeter of the school fence, there was a profusion of rubbish. Most had been chucked over the fence, Ashby imagined, but he doubted that he or Marcus Clark were the first people to have ventured through that gap. He was reasonably sure somebody had given those weak and rusty railings a helping hand in creating the opening in the first place.

The building might have been imposing at one time, he supposed. Now, close up, it had a creepy, horror film quality about it. If Marcus Clark was hiding here, had been here for a couple of nights, the kid must be of stern stuff.

Ashby moved to the back of the building. There was more litter, but no sign of anyone. Maybe the caller had some sick idea of what constituted a practical joke.

"Over here." The stage whisper came from his right. He could see a man leaning out of a ground floor window, beckoning him.

Ashby went over to him.

"You're the one who called?"

"You're Detective Inspector Ashby?"

"That's me."

"Right. Well, this window's broken, and I managed to get my hand in and open the catch. Can you climb in?"

The man was shabby and looked tired. Ashby looked at him dubiously, wondering who had broken the window. "Can I ask what you were doing breaking into the place in the first place?"

The man blinked. "This was my old school. I often take an early morning walk, and I found myself here today. I spotted the gap in the fence, and then the broken window, and... well, I just fancied having a look round the old place." He shrugged. "But look, we're wasting time here. I saw something in the hall I thought you should take a look at. Are you coming in?"

With a little help from the other man, Ashby managed to clamber in through the open window. Inside, the place had a sour, unpleasant smell. There were a lot of cobwebs and some more litter. They were in what must once have been a classroom. Quite high ceilings. Faded blue carpet quietly rotting away. A whiteboard on one wall, with equations on it. Maths had never been Ashby's strong suit.

He fancied a cigarette. He supposed with the litter it would be a fire hazard, but on the other hand, maybe burning this dump to the ground would do everyone a favour. With a shrug, he fished out a fag, offered the packet to the other man, who refused, and lit up.

"So what's this you've found?"

"I think you'd better see for yourself."

The stranger's almost theatrical attempts to be mysterious grated on Ashby, but he kept his irritation in check. "And you say it was in the hall that you saw this mysterious evidence? What's your name, by the way?"

"I'll keep that to myself, if you don't mind. I don't want to get involved. I just want to help you find Marcus."

That was fine by Ashby, at least for the time being. If there was anything significant, he could oblige the mystery man to make a statement then. "So where's the hall?"

"Follow me."

He followed the other man out into a dingy, smelly corridor, past notice boards with curling papers still pinned to them, past more empty classrooms. He almost imagined he could hear the ghosts of generations of St Martin's children, chattering, laughing and playing. They turned left and followed the corridor, which turned to the right at what Ashby supposed was a corner of the building.

Just after the corner were some stairs and then, halfway to the next corner, his guide halted at some glazed double doors.

"In here."

Whilst they had been walking, Ashby had been puzzling over the likelihood that this person would decide on impulse to sneak into his old school for a peek at the very time Marcus Clark was - or had recently been - using it as a hideout. It seemed a strange coincidence, but then over the years the police had been assisted by more coincidences, accidents and colossal strokes of luck than they tended to admit.

He also had to admit that he didn't care much for his escort. He was dirty and scruffy, and his cargo trousers were almost at half-mast on one side, presumably because of the weight of whatever was in a bulging pocket.

The doors were on self-closing hinges which creaked as they shut behind them, finally coming together with a thud.

The hall was spacious and, if the windows had not been so filthy, would probably have been light and airy. The floor was a light, varnished wood, badly scratched, and with various indoor sports courts painted in it. It was strewn with litter, and there was a metal dustbin in the middle of the floor which looked as if it had been used for bonfires, perhaps so some itinerant could keep warm in the winter. In a corner were some ancient-looking gym mats. There was a strong smell of urine.

"Sorry about the stink," the other man said. "I don't think we're the first ones in here since the place closed." He looked around him, as if suddenly really seeing the hall for the first time. "You know, I met my ex-wife in here. Well, I'd seen her about for a couple of years, but that was the first time I talked to her. I was fifteen and she was fourteen."

Ashby hadn't come in here for childhood reminiscences. "Where's this evidence?"

His companion gestured towards the gym mats. "Have a look behind those. See what you think. It might be nothing, but... well, you'll see."

Ashby looked at the mats, relieved that at least it didn't sound as if he would find a small, still body behind them. He wondered why this joker couldn't simply come out and tell him what he thought he had found, but he was willing to humour him if it meant a real breakthrough in the search.

Out there, coppers who had been allocated to him were searching woods with dogs, preparing to drag the canal, and running out of people to question. There had been any number of reported sightings, but none of them had amounted to anything useful. Even the shopkeeper, who had at first been sure it was Marcus who had robbed him of soft drinks and chocolate, was now changing his tune to the point where the thief could pretty much have been any boy under ten.

In truth, Ashby was holding out less and less hope for whatever lay behind the mats. At best it might show that someone had been in here recently. He wondered if the helpful fellow beside him was one of those sad bastards who just want to be in on anything exciting happening around them. Well, Steve Ashby would do him for wasting police time, if that was all it turned out to be.

With more hope than expectation, he approached the mats and started trying to move them.

"No, behind them," the other man said. "If you get right in there, you can see."

The mats were six inches or less from the wall. He squeezed up to the end and hunkered down, peering into the gap. All he could see was dust and darkness.

"There's nothing here," he said, starting to turn around.

And then the world exploded in pain and bright light.

* * *

Baines stared out of the car window.

"I don't remember it looking half so gloomy when I was here," he said. "But then I haven't come near the place in yonks."

"Let's save your trip down memory lane for after we've found DI Ashby," Archer said, stinging him. He wondered if he'd ever get the measure of her and settle into a working relationship that was entirely comfortable.

"Well, there's his car." Baines indicated a tatty Toyota.

He, Archer and Baker got out of the car and moved to the right of the perimeter fence. Halfway down that side was a gap, just as Ashby's note to himself had anticipated.

Archer started through the fence. "Actually, one of us ought to wait outside. It would be pointless all three of us poking around inside while Ashby, or Morgan, or even Marcus Clark, comes sauntering out."

"As I have no idea what this Ashby looks like, maybe that had better be me," said Baker. "At least you two know who you're looking for."

"Okay," Archer said. "But if Morgan comes out, follow him and call for back up. Don't approach him. An unarmed man against a nut case with a hammer won't be much of a contest."

Baker agreed, relieved Baines of the car keys, and went back to wait beside the vehicle, from where he would have a good view of the school.

Baines followed Archer through the gap.

"We need to find a way in," he said.

"Obviously, Dan. You look this side, and I'll go round the other way. We'll meet around the back."

A couple of minutes later, they were in a litter-strewn playground at the rear of the school. A couple of portakabins stood to the sides, looking long overdue for demolition.

"There's a couple of broken windows on the first floor," Archer said. "One's near a drainpipe..."

"No need for climbing," Baines was glad to inform her. "There's a broken window back there with the catch undone."

"Either someone got in that way ages ago..." Archer began.

"Or much more recently," he finished for her.

"Fuck," she said, measuring the height. "Of all the days to be wearing a skirt."

"I'll give you a boost," he said.

"Fine. But I'd better not catch you looking up my skirt."

He tried not to look, but still caught a glimpse of black underwear as she scrambled over the ledge. He climbed in himself and they moved from the abandoned classroom they were in to the corridor beyond.

The door closed behind them with a gentle thud.

"Keep the noise down," Archer hissed.

"Sorry."

"Never mind," she said. "You know the layout. How are we going to play this?"

Having stated more than once that this was his old school, Baines suddenly felt foolish. It was about twenty years since he'd last stood inside this building, and the memories had dimmed.

"Er," he began underwhelmingly, "I seem to recall this corridor goes all the way round. Stairs are... in the corners, or maybe in the middle. There might be some corridors off the main one..." He spread his hands. "It's been a long time."

She rolled her eyes. "You haven't got a clue, have you?"

He didn't answer her, but stood listening.

"Well?" she demanded.

"I can't hear anything."

"They could be anywhere in this building. If it's a 'they'. If Ashby's here on his own, I don't suppose he's singing to himself. Belting out Westlife's greatest hits, or whatever."

"He detests boy bands," Baines told her, but he knew what they were both thinking. Ashby could be lying round the very next corner with his head and face scrambled. If so, he wouldn't be making any sound at all.

"All right," Archer said, "let's split up. I'll go to the left, you go to the right, and we'll meet up somewhere. Yell if you see anything. Better still, call my mobile."

Baines shook his head. "Not a good idea. The sound will carry in here."

"You're right. Let's set them to vibrate."

"Besides, is it a good idea to separate? That was wise counsel you gave DI Baker about not approaching Morgan. For all we know, either of us could stumble upon him."

"The alternative is to recce the place as a pair and take twice as long over it. If Ashby is here, and he's in trouble, we could be way too late."

"I don't like it," he said.

"Maybe that's because you still have some good looks to lose," she snapped. "I, on the other hand, don't have that problem."

He had no idea where that had come from, but bit down on the riposte that came to his lips. It was as if she deliberately wished to take the less prudent option. He wasn't going to argue the point further.

"All right," he said. "But let's both be careful."

* * *

Ashby came round, his head feeling like it had split in two. He tried to put a hand to the centre of the pain, but found his hands were restrained. So were his feet. He could see that his ankles were secured with duct tape.

He was propped against a wall, with a gym mat behind him, as if his attacker had suffered an attack of remorse and wanted to make him comfortable.

It was coming back to him. The phone call, the school, the scruffy individual, the cock-and-bull story about some evidence relating to Marcus Clark behind the mats. He turned his head left and right, fresh explosions going off in his brain as he did so. His vision kept blurring in and out of focus, and he was terribly afraid he'd been seriously injured.

The man who had lured him here sat just off to his right on a bench seat. He held a hammer in his hand.

"You're awake, then," his captor remarked. "That's good. I just gave you enough of a tap to put you out. I hope your head hurts?"

"Just a bit," he grated.

"Good. It will hurt even more soon, but not for long. The one comfort I have about my kids is that they wouldn't have suffered for long."

"I have no idea what you're talking about," Ashby said.

"No? It's all over the news that you lot are looking for me. How can you not know?"

But Ashby had spoken the truth. Of course he knew that the team investigating the hammer murders wanted to interview a man called Shaun Morgan, and supposed this must be him. But he hadn't been in on any team meetings about the case and didn't know anything of their theories in Morgan's background or motivation. That was being withheld, and Ashby was as ignorant as any member of the public.

"For what it's worth, you're the last of them," Morgan told him. "Ideally, it would have been Baxter, but I had to leave you till last. Everyone else had nice, predictable habits and patterns. But not you."

"I try not to be boring," Ashby said with false bravado, desperate to keep the conversation going. That was what they said, wasn't it? Keep them talking. And this lunatic seemed eager enough to talk.

"Then there you were on the news," said Morgan, "appealing for information about that missing kid. I guessed that might be a way for me to get you alone. I've been studying you for well over a year, and I'd seen enough to know you don't work with colleagues much. I guess you like to grab all the glory, yes?"

Ashby ignored the rhetoric. "I don't understand. Why those victims. Why me?"

He tried not to flinch as Morgan moved closer. Close enough for him to make out his own blood and hair on the hammerhead. There was some darker, crusted matter there too, suggesting dried blood from previous victims. There were tufts of hair that were plainly not his own.

The killer looked at him suspiciously, and then laughed harshly.

"You really have no idea, do you? Two years ago, I came to your apology for a police station, looking for help. But you were more interested in impressing that black girl behind the desk than doing anything about James Baxter."

Ashby squinted at him. Black girl? Did he mean Joan? She had occasionally covered the desk back in her uniform days, and Ashby had to admit that he'd had a bit of a thing for her for a while. But she'd made it abundantly clear, when he'd tried it on at Will Robson's retirement do, that he wasn't her type. It was the glass of wine she'd thrown over him that had finally convinced him.

"I do hope it got you into her knickers," Morgan said, "because your playing the big man got my children killed."

Ashby shook his head in an attempt to clear it. Fireworks went off inside his brain.

"Your children?" he repeated, hearing the slur in his voice. "I don't know anything about your children. Killed, you say?"

"Don't you dare say you're sorry for my loss. That's what all your mates said after it was too late. 'Sorry for your loss'. No one really gave a damn. It was just another domestic to you."

He was getting worked up now, and Ashby didn't think that was a good sign.

"I begged you to arrest Baxter. I told you he was supplying my wife with God knows what. It started when we were engaged. A night out with the girls. She tried it for a laugh, because all her mates were doing it. A few girls' nights out later, she was hooked. When it became obvious, she told me what had happened and I helped her get off it."

He shook his head. "Or so I thought. She stayed clean long enough for us to marry and have the kids, but then she slipped back again. Post natal depression, she said. Another night out with her junkie mates, just to cheer her up, she said. I knew it was a mistake. A moment's weakness, and there she was, hooked again, and trying to hide it from me.

"In the end, it became obvious, even to an idiot like me. I wasn't having it around the kids, and I couldn't trust her, so I filed for divorce. I thought the court would let me take the kids with me, get them away from her. But no. She was very clever. She managed to cut down for a while, and they only saw what they wanted to see. Everyone so desperate to award custody to the mother. As if being female made up for everything."

"She must have hidden it well," Ashby interjected, keeping him talking and trying to see a way out. No one knew he was here, so there was no cavalry coming. And no way he was going to break free of his bonds. Sooner or later, Morgan would run out of words and finish the job.

"Oh, yes," the killer said softly, "she hid it well, all right. The CAFCAS social worker was convinced she'd put the drugs behind her, her solicitor was good and only cared about her fee."

"What about your solicitor?"

"Peter Nish? Fucking useless. He was only interested in his fee. When I picked him up after he'd finished with his whore, he didn't even recognise me. Well, I think he had an idea he'd seen me somewhere before, but he was dead before he worked it out.

"That fat bastard of a judge didn't need much convincing to make the obvious decision. The kids to live with her, visiting rights for me. And I got them every other weekend.

"More than once, I went to pick them up and she was half-shitfaced. The kids mentioned how scary mummy could be when she was 'in one of her moods'. That was what they called it. One of her moods."

"Didn't you go back to social services?"

"Of course. The Assistant Director wrote me a letter. All in the garden was rosy, she said. They promoted the smug cow later, to Director. I promoted her to Heaven last night." He smiled. "Or to Hell."

Before Ashby could reply, he heard, somewhere in the building, a sound a little like a door softly opening and closing. Morgan froze.

"Don't go away."

He went out into the corridor. After a moment or two, he returned.

"Maybe it was the wind from that open window. Where was I?"

"Trying to justify killing - how many is it now?"

"Five. It would have been seven, but the judge and the CAFCAS guy are already dead - a car crash and a heart attack. I feel cheated. As for the rest... they're justified all right.

"Oh, Sharon was an accomplished liar, but everyone took the lazy way. Emily and Oliver never stood a chance. They delivered my kids to a mother who was a ticking bomb. Social services didn't give a toss. They were happy to be conned by her. And you, DI Ashby, simply didn't give a shit."

"I'm sorry," Ashby said. "Really sorry. I don't even remember the incident."

"Which proves my point. You brushed me off and then forgot. Well, days later, Sharon got burned by some bad acid. I saw her afterwards in prison. The stuff gave her hallucinations, paranoia, the lot. Somehow she convinced herself that the kids were devils or something and that she had to defend herself.

She grabbed the handiest weapon - which happened to be one of these-" He held the bloody hammer up for inspection. "- and she..."

He trailed off, covering his eyes with this free hand. Ashby could see his shoulders shaking, hear him stifling sobs. When he took the hand away, his face was wet with tears.

"You should have seen what she did to them," he whispered hoarsely. "Their poor little faces. They didn't look like my kids any more. They didn't look like anyone any more."

"I'm sorry," Ashby said again.

"For my loss," Morgan sneered. "Yes. Well, Sharon couldn't live with what she did. She killed herself. She's probably burning in Hell herself now. She deserves to. But in a way she's as much a victim as our kids were. No one did anything to save her from herself. No one saved her from Baxter.

"I suddenly saw it all. My life stretching out before me, bitterness eating me up, and I knew then I had to give it all some sort of meaning. So I decided to give everyone responsible a taste of what my children went through. I had all the time in the world to observe you all and plan it. Who, when, and where. After today I don't care what happens to me. I don't plan on being taken alive. Call this a dying man's confession. Shame you won't be able to repeat it to anyone."

Ashby knew the killer had run out of words, and dread settled on him like a heavy grey cloud.

"The others," he said, trying to humour him, "they deserved it. But not me. I didn't even know your wife, or your kids. If you let me go, I can help you. I'll speak in mitigation. I'll even admit I was a bit negligent."

Morgan hawked and spat on the floor, as if to rid himself of a nasty taste caused by Ashby's words.

"You were fucking negligent, all right. And now you're trying to save your shitty little skin, you pathetic... No wonder there's so much crime. Poor excuses for law enforcement." He was getting worked up. His knuckles were whitening as he increased his grip on the hammer shaft. "Well, this is one mess you can't weasel your way out of."

His shoulders straightened and he adjusted his grip. "It's time to die," he said.

32

Baines glanced back over his shoulder and saw Archer walk around the corner and out of sight. They had been carefully, quietly, opening classroom doors and closing them again as they went along. Nothing so far.

He too had reached the corner at his end of the corridor, and he made the left turn, still feeling a little strange about being back here after all this time. Shaun Morgan was a year younger than Baines. It struck him that he and the Morgans had to have been pupils here at around the same time, over several years. He might even have seen them holding hands or making moon-eyes at each other. Love's young dream.

A prelude to an awful lot of violent deaths.

He closed his eyes and tried to see the people in the two photos on the major incident room wall as adolescents. It worked with Sharon. Failed with Shaun.

Earlier, during the team meeting, it had been impossible for him not to feel some sympathy with the killer. Despite the horrors he had been perpetrating, he was a man who had lost everything. A man whose children had been taken away from him in horrendous circumstances.

Who, faced with such a situation, would not want to avenge his loved ones? Certainly, Baines had fantasised on occasions about the things he would do if he had the Invisible Man helpless in his power for just twenty minutes.

A flight of stairs ran up to his right, at least vaguely confirming his memories of this place. He and Archer had agreed they would try the next level if they found nothing on this floor, but he had a feeling that, if Morgan was here with Ashby, this was where would do his grisly work. In fact, he had already decided where the killing ground would almost certainly be - it had come to him just as he parted from Archer.

237

The school hall was the most obvious place. Plenty of space. Good acoustics, too, if that was important to him. He wished he had a better recall of the layout of the building.

He realised he was standing at the bottom of the stairs, thinking when he should have been moving. He didn't like Ashby, was sure Archer positively detested him, but that didn't mean he deserved to die like Morgan's other victims. While he stood here, the killer could have dispatched his latest victim, might already have made his escape.

Unless he wanted to talk first. One of the unknown factors in all the previous murders was whether Shaun Morgan would have wanted to talk to each of his victims before really starting to hit. To tell them why he was doing it. There had been precious little evidence to support that in Stephanie Merritt's case; all the signs were that he had started bludgeoning her almost the moment she opened the door. But serial killers often introduced new refinements and embellishments as they progressed.

Right now, such a desire to talk, to savour the moments leading up to the actual killing, were Ashby's best hope of coming out of this alive.

Of course, he and Archer would look stupid if Ashby really did have a genuine lead in the search for Marcus Clark. But he strongly doubted that.

He was about to move away from the stairs when he glimpsed movement on the half-landing above him. He looked up.

A now-familiar figure in blue and white stood there, looking right at him. He felt his heart squeezing its way up into his throat.

"Jack," he croaked.

The boy turned and put a foot on the bottom step of the next flight up. He looked down at Baines, who somehow knew he was meant to follow. He knew it was crazy, knew he was probably crazy, but he had no choice. Thoughts of why he was here slid away as he started up the stairs towards the lad. As soon as he did so, the young man began to climb upwards.

Baines followed, each step leading him further away from Ashby. Further away from Archer.

Further away from a killer.

* * *

"Don't," Ashby whimpered as Shaun Morgan took one slow step at a time towards him. "Please. Please don't do this."

Morgan laughed hollowly. "You're begging. Do you think my kids begged, when their mother was smashing their heads to bits? Do you? I do. I dream about it sometimes, and I can still hear them when I wake up. *Please mummy, don't, don't.* It didn't do them much good, either."

"I can help you. I can."

"You just don't get it, do you? Not even now. No one can help me. Everything I've done, what I'm about to do, I've had to do. No choice. What I did to those people... The act made me feel sick to my stomach, but I feel no remorse. I don't want help. I'm so fucking tired. Once I've finished my work here, then I can sleep forever. Do you think there's a Heaven? Do you think my kids are there? I won't be going to see them, I suppose. Not after all this."

"But I -"

"Shut up!" bellowed Morgan. "Stop whining and die like a man."

He towered over Ashby and raised the hammer high.

And that was when the hall door swung open and a clear, strong voice said, "Police! Put the hammer down."

* * *

The figure in the QPR shirt waited at the top of the stairs until Baines reached the half-landing, and then made a right turn into the corridor above. Baines followed, wanting to call out to him to wait, but somehow terrified that it would break the spell. That the boy would vanish like before.

He supposed he knew by now that the boy probably wasn't real. He still had no idea if this was some waking dream, or even some future ghost of a long-dead son, but he was desperate to know. Desperate to find out this time.

To absorb what knowledge the apparition might be able to impart to him.

The boy moved along the corridor ahead of him and then paused outside a classroom door, two thirds of the way along. As Baines approached, he opened the door and entered.

Baines walked briskly, wondering what was significant about that particular room. What it was Jack wanted to show him. He reached the open door and stepped inside.

The room was empty.

Jack - if it was Jack - had disappeared into thin air again. Maybe it was simply some association of the school and teenagers that had conjured up the phantom this time.

He stood in the doorway, his heart so heavy he felt it was weighing him down. For so long he had tried to bury his feelings. Even in these recent days, when Jack had begun to emerge from his dreams and appear to him in the light of day, he had tried to deal with it. To compartmentalise it while he got on with his job. Now he realised he had no idea how many more times he could do this and still maintain some semblance of whatever sanity he had left.

A part of him wanted to sit on the floor. To lie down maybe, give in to whatever was systematically shredding his mind. But something nagged away at him, urging him to resist the seductive pull of surrender.

Ashby. He had allowed everything except Jack to go out of his head. It could have cost Ashby his life. And what if Archer, unarmed and alone, had run into a hammer-wielding psychopath? Baines couldn't see why she would be a target for Morgan, but if she cornered him...

He turned quickly, anxious to catch up with his boss, wondering what he would tell her when he did. As he reached the open door, he stopped, puzzled.

Whether it had been Jack, or some other kid, he knew for certainty that the door had been closed until he'd seen the teenager open it. So, unless he'd seen a ghost that could open doors, where were they now?

He scanned the room, looking for a place of concealment. Under a desk?

He bent down to look, and saw a movement to his right. Standing up, he saw a small figure bolting for the door and moved quickly to cut it off. The next moment, he was staring down the barrel of a gun, a gun so heavy for the person holding it that his shaking hands could barely keep the barrel upright.

He had found Marcus Clark.

* * *

"Put the hammer down."

The man she knew must be Shaun Morgan stared at Archer. "I don't think so."

"Come on," she coaxed, trying to reason with him. "Let's calm down and talk about this."

Let's calm down. As soon as they had left her lips, Archer recalled a previous time when she had uttered almost the same words. For a moment, she was back in the pub, facing a drunk with a broken bottle. It had ended disastrously for her, and been instrumental in so many changes in her life: her breakup with Rob, her loss of self-esteem and self-confidence, her ill-judged decision to transfer out of the Met.

This time she could go one further. This time, those words could end her life.

Where the hell was Baines?

When she'd insisted they separate to make the search go more quickly, she hadn't really wanted to do so. Every alarm bell inside her, every voice in her head, had urged her not to do it. She had ignored them all, almost recklessly. Whatever else she did today, she was determined to force herself to face up to her fears.

She'd finally reached the hall and seen what was going on through the glazed doors. Now it actually came to it, she hadn't had a plan at all. There were just two of them without backup, and this guy was handy with a hammer. More to the point, there weren't even two of them at this precise moment, because Baines hadn't appeared yet. Since Ashby and Morgan were right before her eyes, she couldn't imagine what was detaining him.

Maybe it was the novelty of being back on his old stomping ground. Maybe he'd chosen this, of all times, to take a trip down memory lane.

All the time Morgan appeared to be talking to Ashby, she thought she could afford to wait for her DS to deign to honour her with his presence. But when the killer started advancing purposefully towards his prey, she knew she couldn't wait any longer. If she didn't act now, she would funk it. And, if she did that, and Ashby died in front of her, she thought that would finally destroy her.

As she threw open the door and announced herself, she had that old familiar feeling of time slowing down.

Shaun Morgan, hammer poised for the blow, turned his head her way, puzzlement in his eyes.

"How did you find us?"

"We're detectives, Mr Morgan. My name's Archer - Detective Inspector Lizzie Archer. Now, why don't you put the hammer down, so we can talk?"

"We're a long way off talking."

"Shaun, we know why you've been doing what you're doing. You need help."

"I needed help two years ago. I begged - " He gestured at Ashby with his hammer. "- begged this bastard for help and he practically laughed at me."

"But I'm not laughing, Shaun. Yes, I'm sure mistakes have been made, but this isn't the way."

"It works for me."

On the way here from the station, she had focused her thoughts on his motivation. Now she tried a different tack.

"It doesn't work for your victims' families, Shaun. Husbands, wives, partners, children. All grieving the way you're still grieving for your children."

"That's right-" Ashby chipped in.

"Shut up, Steve," she said. "You had your chance to do something useful two years ago. Don't be part of the problem now." She turned her attention back to Morgan. "Don't you see, Shaun? In dealing with your own misery, you're just increasing the amount of pain and heartache in the world. Whatever wrongs you think these people have done to you, do you truly believe their families deserve what you've inflicted on them?"

"Shut it," he said, but without any real sense of conviction. "You're messing with my head. I've started this, and I've got to finish it."

"Why?" she protested, wondering again where the fuck Baines had got to. "You've already made your point."

"It's not just about making a point, though, is it? It's about the people who let my children down. Giving them what they got."

"But, Shaun," she said, shifting onto what she knew was very dangerous ground, "you already see the person who really let your family down, every single day, when you look in the mirror."

"What?" Rage flared in his eyes. For a moment, she glimpsed the real madness that prowled just beneath the surface. He raised the hammer a little and took a step towards her. A step away from the helpless Ashby.

She pressed on, knowing what a deadly gamble she was making. "You let Emily and Oliver down, Shaun. Sharon, too. You should have stayed around. Tried to help her with her addiction."

"I did try," he protested. "For so long. In the end, I got so tired of it. Sick and tired"

"So you gave up. Gave up on all of them. Couldn't be arsed to give it one more try and decided to walk away."

He shook his head, trying to deny it. "It wasn't like that. I tried to get full custody."

"Yeah, right," she snorted. "You must have known that would never happen. The powers that be bend over backwards to leave their kids with their mum. So they got it wrong. What happened after that was entirely predictable. And preventable, Shaun. I bet you blame yourself for leaving that hammer lying around as well. Don't you?"

"How was I to know...?"

"How was anyone to know? You seem to think everyone else should have seen the danger to your children, Shaun. Do you honestly think you can exclude yourself, of all people, from that? And, when you knew James Baxter was supplying her again, what did you do? You contacted Children's Services, got the brush-off and gave up. You went to the police station, got little sympathy from DI Ashby here - who, by the way, is an utter disgrace to the service - and gave up again."

She could see that Ashby didn't like that last remark, but sod him. She'd keep him alive by whatever words it took.

"You couldn't even take the time to fill in a form when Constable Collins asked you to," she persisted. She saw surprise in his eyes that she knew so much. "Oh, yes, Shaun. I've spoken to her. She's given me her account of the whole sorry incident. She was ready to take down the details of your concerns and try to get them addressed. But you were so self-righteous. And then you just let this idiot railroad you. And now you're trying to put all the blame on him, instead of taking responsibility for yourself. I bet you didn't even make a complaint about him, did you?"

Morgan's arms hung by his sides now, as if the hammer had become too heavy for him.

"And you also blamed social workers and solicitors who were just doing their jobs the best they could. Even your own lawyer, because he did his best, but didn't have a magic bullet to win you your case. Blamed everyone but yourself, and decided to kill them all."

She knew she was playing with fire. Any moment, he could spin off and attack her. Where was Baines? Yet she thought that maybe she, at least, was safe from him. She had done nothing to wrong him, and she hoped that, in his warped morality, she thus deserved no punishment. With that thought, another realisation dawned on her, and she grabbed at it.

"As for Hannah Hudson, she did nothing at all to deserve what she got. You didn't know that, did you, Shaun?"

He looked at her as if she was an idiot. "Don't be stupid. I went to social services, said Sharon was using again, and she wrote back to say everything was fine."

"She might have signed the letter, but she didn't do the investigation. Someone else concluded all was well. Somebody else who was fooled by Sharon. Hannah Hudson just signed the letter because that's part of her job. You killed the wrong person."

"No," he protested, but she thought the mad certainty in his eyes might just have faded a fraction. "I don't believe you."

"It's true. And you can't take that back, Shaun. How does it feel?"

"She shouldn't have signed the letter."

"And that was enough to kill her for? Get over yourself. You beat an innocent person to death with a hammer, just for signing something. I don't see how you can sleep nights knowing that, I really don't."

He had been standing side on and now he turned to face her. He stood slightly slumped, looking hideously tired. She pitied him. Pitied what had happened to his family, what that had done to him, and what it had driven him to do.

He was mentally ill - probably had been since the deaths of his children. Even if he ever got better, how would he live with the things he had done? What had Baines said? Something about scars beneath the soul?

"What happened to your face?" Morgan said suddenly, as if reading her mind.

Her fingers strayed to the scar. "That was me doing my job. Someone was about to be attacked with a broken bottle, and I tried to save them. Did save them. But this was the result."

"I'm sorry," he said. "You're a nice looking woman. Can't anything be done? You know, to get rid of it?"

"They've done all they can," she said. "This is as good as it gets, I think."

"I'm sorry," he said again. "Sorry about everything."

"I know you are, Shaun." She took a tentative step toward him. "But it's time to stop now. Why don't you put the hammer down?"

He shook his head, and then it all happened so quickly that she had no time to react.

Shaun Morgan gave her a crooked smile and then raised the hammer, swinging it at his own temple.

"No!" she screamed, but the solid crunch of metal on bone was already echoing around the hall and he was swinging at his head again, even as his legs buckled. He collapsed, face down.

Fighting nausea, Archer rushed over to him. There was blood pumping from the wound, and also leaking from Morgan's ears. But there was a thready pulse.

"Jesus!" Ashby squawked. "Is he dead?"

"Not yet," she was pulling out her phone. As she started tapping in a number, Ian Baker burst in.

"You'd been gone so long-" he began, and then he took in the scene. "My God."

"Ambulance," she said when her call was answered. "I need an ambulance now."

From somewhere else in the building, she heard the unmistakeable sound of a shot ringing out.

33

Dan Baines could see that Marcus Clark was a very scared
child. But he was a scared child with a very real gun. He had
his finger on the trigger, and he had already fired one shot by
accident, hitting his own brother. If the gun went off this time,
Baines thought he might not be as lucky as Brandon had been.

So he put up his hands.

"Don't shoot, Marcus," he said. "No one's going to hurt
you."

Marcus's hands were shaking badly. He was very pale, his
mouth a grim line.

"You've come to take me in, haven't you? No way, copper."

He managed not to smile at the tough guy talk. He thought
Marcus might be a fan of the old black and white American
gangster movies they sometimes showed on TV on Sunday
afternoons. He half expected to be denounced as a dirty rat at
any moment.

"Marcus, you have nothing to worry about, I promise. The
only place I want to take you is back to your mum. She's so
worried about you. So is Brandon. We all have been. I
promise you you're not in any trouble."

"You're lying!" The boy was becoming agitated. Not good
when he was the one with the firearm. "Brandon said I'd go to
prison."

"No one's going to prison," he insisted. "We know it was all
a big accident, Brandon getting shot. We know you didn't
mean it. And, Marcus, that gun you found... We think it might
have been used by someone else in a robbery, before you found
it. Have you seen *CSI*?"

The boy nodded warily.

"Then you know all about fingerprints. Well, we're hoping
yours aren't the only prints on that gun. We're hoping to find

DAVE SIVERS

someone else's prints and maybe prove they did the robbery.
All because you found the gun."

Marcus looked at him as though he had just been set a really
difficult maths problem.

"I didn't do no robbery."

"No," he said patiently. "We know that. But if you hand the
gun over to us, we might be able to catch someone who did.
Imagine that. You'd be a hero, Marcus. The boy who found
vital evidence."

In an episode of *CSI*, especially *CSI: Miami*, where Horatio
Caine seemed to make promises to children in every other
episode, the child in question would have trustingly handed the
weapon over. But Marcus Clark was apparently not one for
blind trust.

"It's a trick," he said with trembling voice.

"No trick, Marcus, I swear."

"Brandon promised he'd make it all right after I shot him,
and then you came to arrest me."

"Not to arrest you, son. Just to ask you some questions. We
had no idea you were the one who accidentally shot your
brother when we came round."

The boy still looked suspicious, but perhaps a little less so.

"Why don't you put the gun down? You don't want anyone
else to get hurt, do you?"

Marcus shook his head.

"That's good. Because I'm the one having a real live gun
pointed at him, and I have to tell you, Marcus, I'm frightened. I
don't want you to shoot me by accident. So do you think you
can just put it down on the floor, so we'll both be safe? Then
we can walk out of here together."

"There's another man here," Marcus said.

"Where?" Baines asked carefully.

"Downstairs somewhere. Is he one of you?"

So Morgan, or Ashby, or both, were definitely here.

"Put the gun down," Baines said again, "and then you can
tell me what this man looked like."

He could see the effort of keeping the heavy gun trained on
him was proving an effort. The barrel was shaking quite

violently. At any moment, the boy could inadvertently squeeze the trigger.

"Go on," he urged. "You know you want to."

Then, to his relief, the boy nodded.

"Carefully," he cautioned.

But suddenly the gun seemed to be like a hot potato for the boy. He seemed to be caught in a bizarre muddle of trying to set the gun down carefully on the floor and wanting to get rid of it as quickly as possible. Somewhere along the line, he fumbled it.

The sound of the gunshot filled the room.

* * *

Archer took the stairs two at a time. She had handed the phone to Baker, told him to make sure the ambulance arrived and stay with Ashby and Morgan. Then she had set off to find the source of the gunshot. She had no idea who had fired it, or why, and the correct approach should have been caution, but someone may have been shot, and she didn't know where Baines was.

She had been furious with him for not being there to back her up. Now she was convinced that a bad morning had just turned worse.

The shot had come from upstairs, she was sure of that. She wanted to bellow Baines' name at the top of her voice, but she had no idea what the situation was. She didn't have time for the luxury of a silent approach, but there was no sense in making more noise than necessary.

She hurtled along the corridor, flinging open classroom doors, rounding a corner into another dusty corridor and repeating the process. She turned the next corner just in time to see Baines emerge from one of the rooms. In one hand he held a revolver by his fingertips. The other hand held the paw of a small boy.

Relief flooded through her, its intensity taking her by surprise.

"Jesus," she said, "I heard a shot. Is everything all right?"

"Everything's fine. Remember Marcus Clark?"

She stared at him, dumbfounded. Looked at the boy, mentally comparing his face to the one that was all over the local media.

It was Marcus, all right. Dirty, tired, but definitely Marcus.

"I don't understand. Was Morgan holding him hostage or something?"

"No, nothing like that. I think it was just one of those crazy coincidences. Shaun Morgan isn't the only one who can suss out good places to hide, right, Marcus?"

The boy looked at him, then at Archer. "Who's Shaun Morgan?"

She ignored him. "What made you come up here?"

"I, uh, heard a noise."

She could tell when someone was being evasive, but now was not the time to pursue it.

"So what was the shot?"

"Ah. Well, Marcus had a bit of a mishap putting the gun down. There's a hole in the floor, but no got hurt." He paused. "Any sign of Morgan or Ashby?"

"Oh, yes. They're both in a bad way. Especially Morgan. Baker's with them. I've called an ambulance."

"Christ, what happened?"

"Long story."

"But it's all under control?"

"Morgan's going nowhere. The case is solved. I can't say I feel exactly triumphant, though. It's all a bit late in the day."

"No one could have worked it out any quicker."

"No, but if I'd asked Social Services to delve further back in their files, then maybe-"

"And maybe not. You did as well as anyone could have, Lizzie."

She studied his face to see if there was anything patronising or ironic about his words. She wished she could read him better.

"I'd better get back downstairs."

"And, if it's okay by you, I'd better get this one home," Baines said, nodding at Marcus. "At least something good has come out of today."

"Go. His mother will probably commend you for a medal."

On the way downstairs, Archer agreed that Baines should take the car and she'd get a squad car to pick her and Baker up. Baines and Marcus exited the way they'd come in, as the building was still locked up. She phoned the station and asked them to send someone who could get a door open, then went back into the hall.

Baker was sitting beside Ashby. He was jacketless and shirtless. He had covered Morgan's upper body with his jacket, presumably to help keep him warm. Ashby held the rolled-up shirt to the wound on his head.

"How's Morgan?" she asked

"Not good, but he's still with us." Baker said. He shook his head. "What kind of courage does it take to smash your own skull in with a hammer?"

"Not courage exactly," she said bleakly. "Just the same resolve it takes to smash five faces to pulp. That and utter hopelessness."

"So *was* that a gunshot?"

She told them briefly about Baines' discovery of Marcus Clark and the accidental firing of the gun.

"Two accidental discharges in a week," Baker remarked. "He should steer well clear of guns from now on."

"I think he probably will."

"Ian," Ashby said, speaking for the first time. "Can you give us a moment?"

Baker looked from one to the other of them and then nodded. "Of course. I'm in the corridor if you need me."

The door closed behind him.

Ashby didn't look at her. "I just wanted to thank you for what you did," he said gruffly.

She looked at the unconscious man on the floor. She didn't want this hateful man's gratitude. "I was just doing my job," she said stiffly.

"Still - you handled it brilliantly. First seeming to be on his side with all that stuff about me being a disgrace to the force. And then the way you turned him against himself."

She stiffened and looked at him with contempt. "You are an arse, Steven. All I was trying to do was stop anyone else from getting hurt, including Morgan. I didn't want to turn him against himself, as you put it. I didn't actually want to drive him to suicide."

He mumbled something.

She shook her head wearily. "And as for me seeming to be on his side. Let's get something straight. I meant every word that I said about you being an utter fucking disgrace. You're a lazy, useless sod, as far as I'm concerned. If you'd taken Morgan seriously that day, instead of acting like some sort of cave man, none of this might have happened." She started to walk away. "I'm going to ask Gillingham to find me a different office. I'd rather work in a toilet cubicle than share with you for a moment longer."

He opened his mouth as if to riposte.

"I'd say no more, if I were you," she warned. "The mood I'm in, I might just pick up that hammer and finish Shaun's job for him."

She walked out on him and found Baker, who looked a little cold. She shocked herself by noticing, despite the circumstances, how fit and lean he looked.

"Do you want my jacket?"

"No, you're all right," he said.

"What a bloody mess."

"Look on the bright side. Two cases solved simultaneously. Not too shabby for your first week."

"I just can't help feeling -"

"We do the best we can," he said. "Whatever you think you'd have done differently in hindsight, let it go, Lizzie." He looked down at himself. "I'd offer to buy you a coffee, but..."

She could hear approaching sirens. "I'd like that. When the cavalry arrives, we can send a uniform off to buy you a new shirt. On me."

34

The pub was heaving with Friday night drinkers, but the team had managed to commandeer a corner for their little celebration. All in all, it had not, Archer thought, been such a bad day. Shaun Morgan was in a coma and not expected to live. Keys found in his pocket had been traced through a leather estate agent's fob to a flat he had rented in an assumed name, and there had been found a mountain of notes, books and printouts from the Internet, all part of his meticulous research for his killing campaign.

Amongst the papers, there was a lot of stuff about the human skull and the damage that could be caused by blows to the head and face. When Morgan had set out to initially render Ashby unconscious, with the intention of finishing him off later, he had known exactly what he was doing.

Meanwhile, forensics had moved quickly - for a change - on the gun taken from Marcus Clark, and the results were better than Baines could have hoped. As well as Marcus's, there were some other good prints, and a match was quickly found on the National Fingerprint Database - those of Michael Sturridge and his brother Ryan. Further examination of the CCTV footage from the petrol station had revealed that the robbers appeared to be of a similar size and build to Michael Sturridge and two of his cronies.

All three had been dragged in for questioning.

Since Ryan Sturridge had been inside at the time of the robbery, Michael was firmly in the frame. He had tried to talk tough for a while, and his fat, oily solicitor had tried to dismiss the evidence as weak and circumstantial. But the tune changed rapidly once Baines made it clear to Sturridge that his two best mates were being interviewed separately.

Sturridge was no Brain of Britain himself, but Baines thought he was astute enough to know that the other two made him look like a comparative Einstein. And that they wouldn't hesitate to sell out their own granny if they thought it would get them off the hook for a serious crime.

After that, it hadn't lasted long. Baines spelled out that the maximum penalty for armed robbery was life imprisonment, but that there were deals to be done that might make it go easier for the young thug. Such as telling the police where he got the gun from.

Sturridge had caved. He'd found the gun under the floorboards in his brother's room. Once he'd shown it to his gang, it hadn't taken long to conceive the idea of doing a holdup. But, after the deed was done, the three would-be hard men had suffered a mutual panic attack, and Sturridge had tossed the gun out the car window as they circumnavigated a roundabout, only for Marcus Clark to find it.

Clive Edwards had been released without charge. He had sarcastically thanked Gillingham for his hospitality and, rather more darkly, said he was thinking of a little holiday in France.

As he had sauntered out into the street, Archer had exchanged a glance with her boss.

"Do you think that was a veiled threat against his wife?"

Gillingham had simply given her an exaggerated shrug. "Who knows? We can't save everyone, Lizzie. If he goes after her over there, that's a problem for the French police. God help her," he had added.

Now Baines had gone off to the loo, and Archer had been left momentarily alone, happily watching the rest of the team enjoying themselves. Gillingham was making a fool of himself, trying inoffensively and unsuccessfully to chat up Joan Collins, and Jason Bell was playing darts with two of the augmentees.

They weren't such a bad bunch to be working with.

DI Ian Baker forced his way through the crush and pushed another pint of lager into her hand.

"Cheers," Baker said, raising his glass of cider. He'd decided to stay over, join the celebration, and drive back to Norfolk early tomorrow. He'd been divorced a couple of years and it was his turn to have the kids for the weekend. A similar arrangement to the one the Morgans had had, but hopefully not one that would end so badly.

"Not a bad first week for you," he remarked for the second time that day. "At this rate, you'll have cleared up the entire Aylesbury Vale crime rate in time for the summer holidays, and you'll all spend the rest of the year counting paper clips."

"I wish," she scoffed.

"I bet you thought you were coming to a cushy billet here. The trouble is, wherever you find people, you'll find villains."

She gave him an innocent look. "You're saying Norfolk isn't a cushy billet either? Surely there must be a police station somewhere in the country where a lady DI can put her feet up and read Hello magazine all day long?"

"I thought that was what the Met was really like," Dan Baines said, coming up beside her. "All champagne and cigars."

Before she could retort, Collins detached herself from Gillingham and came over to them.

"The boss wants us to gather round so he can say a few words," she told them.

"On our way," Archer said, rolling her eyes at her companions.

Baines winked at her. "Let's humour him. He so likes to do his Churchill bit."

A couple of minutes later, everyone was assembled in a loose semi-circle around Gillingham. Archer was seeing a whole new side to him. His collar and tie were slightly askew and he was red in the face. He held what looked like at least a triple whisky in his hand.

"I just wanted to congratulate everyone on a job well done," he said. Archer was impressed to note that there wasn't the hint of a slur. "Especially to our newest recruit, DI Archer, on her first result, and to DS Baines for finding young Marcus Clark and, in the process, solving the petrol station holdup. But thanks to all of you. This job's all about teamwork."

He sipped his drink. "Which brings me to absent friends. The latest on DI Ashby is - he's going to be just fine. Another good officer injured in the line of duty."

Or, Archer thought, in this case injured in the line of recklessly seeking glory without backup.

She hadn't spoken to Gillingham yet about a change of office. On reflection, she doubted he was going to listen to any suggestion that Steve Ashby could do wrong. She wondered again what it was between those two.

As the DCI ended with a tear in his eye, proposing a toast to DI Ashby, she decided she'd had enough for one night.

35

Archer woke to the smell of coffee and the clink of cups. She opened her eyes and saw sunshine streaming through half-opened curtains.

"Good morning," Ian Baker said, placing a cup beside her and leaning over to kiss her bare shoulder. He was smiling, and she smiled back.

After she had made her excuses and left the pub, she had dithered outside. She must have had four pints and really shouldn't be driving. But she didn't know this town well enough yet to know where or how to get a taxi to the Holiday Inn.

Then Baker had come out and joined her.

"Thought we might as well go back together," he said, "seeing as we're staying in the same hotel and I don't know the way."

"I was thinking about a taxi," she said. "I'm well over."

"I've only had a couple," he said. "Why don't I drive? I can bring you back to your car in the morning."

It had made perfect sense, and so they had a nightcap in the hotel bar. One nightcap had led to another, and one thing had led to another. Now, with him looking at her in the cold light of day, she prayed he wasn't asking himself what on earth he'd been thinking of.

"Coffee in bed," she said as lightly as she could manage. "This is a real treat."

"So was last night," he said. "It was very special. And so are you."

He looked as if he meant it.

"Maybe I made a mistake," she said. "Maybe I should have transferred to Norfolk, if they're all like you."

"I wish you had," he told her. "Probably not the best career move for you to look for another transfer after just a week, though."

She sat up and sipped her coffee. "I guess so. So this has been a one-off, then? I mean, Aylesbury to King's Lynn is a bit of a trek when we've both got busy jobs."

She was giving him an out, but he simply kissed his fingertip and pressed it to her lips to silence her.

"I'm sure we can work something out," he said. "I don't want it to be a one-off."

She put her cup back on the bedside chest and kissed him on the mouth.

"Let's make the most of things while we can, then."

Pretty soon, the coffee was forgotten.

* * *

Baines had awoken late with a mild hangover. After a shower and breakfast, he had felt a little more human and had decided to make a quick call on the Clark family, just to see how they were. Julie Clark had hugged him while the boys made gagging noises and made finger-down-the-throat gestures, and had thanked him again for finding Marcus. She had waived away his attempts to assure her that, in the end, it had been pure fluke that he had found the boy and been able to return him safe and sound.

She had asked about Ashby, and he had assured her that he would be fine. He had nothing worse than a slight hairline fracture of the skull.

One good thing had come out of the week's activities. With Sturridge and his lieutenants facing custodial sentences, and Brandon Clark promising to disband The Barracudas, it looked as if the gang nuisance on the Northfield estate was as good as over. Baines just hoped that it didn't leave a vacuum that would be filled by something worse.

He went home and made himself a lunch of coffee and bagels. He had the weekend ahead, but no plans. He might go and see his parents.

Family ties. In the end, his feelings about Shaun Morgan had been complicated by his own experience. The destruction of his own family had enabled him to see the world through a killer's eyes, and he privately thought that Morgan's mistake had been to take it all too far. If he'd simply taken out the drug supplier, James Baxter, then Baines might just have been secretly cheering. But Morgan had lost his sense of proportion.

He had rightly seen the death of his children as the consequence of a complex chain of events, but had chosen to see everybody in that chain as equally guilty and equally deserving of a terrible punishment. Baines had briefly wondered how many people might go on his own personal hate list, apart from the Invisible Man, if he started thinking that way. He had hastily locked the thought away, reluctant to go there.

He wondered again about the dreams he had been having about Jack, and the strange sightings that had culminated in his being led to Marcus Clark's hiding place. He wondered if the sightings had all been leading up to him going in search of one lost boy and finding another. And what that might mean.

Was Jack alive or dead? Was he being haunted by the ghost of a dead boy, a ghost which somehow managed to age in real time? Or by a projection of a boy who was very much alive?

There had been no more sightings since the old school, and his feelings on that were torn between the fear of not knowing and a relief that, just maybe, he could once again shut the door on his losses and carry on pretending they had never happened.

Somehow, he suspected that, having opened that door, he would never quite be able to close it again.

He finished his lunch and put the dishes in the dishwasher. He wondered if there was any sport on TV. As he rooted down the side of the sofa for the remote control, he heard the doorbell ring. He abandoned the quest and went to open up.

Just for a moment, he confused Karen with Louise. Maybe it was something to do with all the dwelling he had been doing on Jack in the past few days. He recovered almost instantly, but not in time to conceal the wave of different emotions that washed over his face.

"I'm sorry," Karen said. "I think maybe it's a bad time. I was out this way and I took a detour and saw the car outside, and so I thought..."

"It's fine," he said. "Come in, please."

She stood in his hallway, looking uncertain, looking half as if she wished she was anywhere but here.

"We need to clear the air," she said. "Wherever this relationship's going, I need to keep you in my life. I want that more than anything. As a friend, if that's all you want. As a lover, if you want to give that a try. But if we do try it, and it doesn't work - I think we'll still need each other. We understand one another too damn well to throw it all away, whatever happens."

He wasn't entirely sure what she was saying, but at that moment, he didn't really care. All he knew for certain was that he had missed her, and he needed her as much as she said she needed him. He opened his arms and she stepped into his embrace.

"You're right," he said. "We do need to talk. But not today, if that's okay by you."

She stiffened. "When, then?"

"Soon, I promise. Today, what I'd really like to do is watch TV and drink too much wine. We could do it together. How does that sound?"

After a moment, she relaxed, and her lips brushed against his cheek, a kiss as light as a ghost's.

"It sounds like a plan," she said.

* * *

After they had made love, Archer and Baker had showered together and had a quick breakfast before he'd driven her back to her car. He'd set off promising to be in touch, although she wondered if that resolve would last the journey back to Norfolk.

With his busy career and being a father to two kids to juggle, he had baggage, and she still didn't see how the geographical distance could practically allow a relationship to develop.

Best to treat the night as the pleasant interlude it had been.

Meanwhile, it was Saturday, no fewer than three cases were solved, and she could finally take some time out to see her mother. Archer swung her Renault into the drive of the West London semi. The house hadn't changed much since she had lived there with her parents and her brother. Since her father had died, Adam had taken over the maintenance jobs he used to do - looking after the garden, painting and decorating and other bits and pieces. But, with a demanding job and a home and family of his own, he did no more than keeping things ticking over these days, and Archer sensed that even those few tasks were an occasional source of friction between him and his wife.

The rational side of her told her that it was his choice to devote time to his mother, and that she, Archer, was entitled to make her own choices. She also reminded herself that Adam hadn't put himself out much for his sister when she had been hurt. Somehow, none of that assuaged the guilt she felt as she rang the doorbell.

Adam wasn't there, and Jane Archer herself answered the door. She looked pale and very tired, but was up and dressed and insisted on making tea.

"I'm going to do things for myself for as long as I can," she said as she dropped teabags into a pot. "I'm still waiting for some test results, and then I'll know if they can do anything and, if they can't, how long I've got."

"Don't say that, Mum."

"Just being realistic, love. Whatever's going to happen, not talking about it doesn't help. I have enough of your brother, sitting staring at me like a gloom cloud, as if I'm going to pop my clogs there and then, and never, ever talking about the chance that I might not be around much longer." She added boiling water to the pot. "If the worst comes to the worst, I'm going to have to put my affairs in order - ghastly phrase - and someone's going to have to help me do it without going all sentimental on me."

"I'll do what I can, Mum, you know that - but the job..."

"I haven't forgotten what the job's like. If you can find any time, that would be great. If you've got a murderer to catch, then that's what you have to do."

"Let me know when you're going for your test results, and I'll make the time," she decided. "I seem to have inherited a good team, and I reckon they can get by without me for the odd few hours. It's just that this first week in the new job has been so crazy..."

"I've heard it on the news," she said. "You've certainly been busy. Which case was yours? Those murders or that little boy who was missing?"

"A bit of both, as it turned out."

Jane Archer finished pouring the tea into mugs and passed one to her daughter.

"Come on," she said. "Let's take these in the other room. I want to hear all about it."

Also by Dave Sivers

ARCHER AND BAINES NOVELS
Dead in Deep Water

LOWMAR DASHIEL MYSTERIES
(Crime Fantasy)
A Sorcerer Slain
Inquisitor Royal

SHORT STORY COLLECTION
Dark and Deep: Ten Coffee Break Crime Stories

DAVE SIVERS

Dave Sivers was born in West London and worked for years in the public sector, occasionally moonlighting as a nightclub bouncer, bookmaker's clerk and freelance writer.

Since giving up the day job, he has spent more time on his writing, which includes newspaper and magazine articles. He published *A Sorcerer Slain*, the first of the Lowmar Dashiel series of crime fantasy novels, in 2011. His published work also includes the anthology *Dark and Deep: Ten Coffee Break Crime Stories*.

The Scars Beneath the Soul is the first in the popular Archer and Baines series of contemporary crime novels.

He lives in Buckinghamshire with his wife, Chris.

www.davesivers.co.uk

Printed in Great Britain
by Amazon